Pride & Prejudice & Assassinations

A. Legacy Novel by
Leo Charles Taylor

Pride & Prejudice & Assassinations
Published by Jokat Publishing

This book is dedicated to my wife for whom I strive to be a better man.

Chapter 1

It is a curious fact that the citizenry comprising the Highest Order are perceived to adhere to a stringent code of justice and honour. This is a noble perception, grand in its ideals, if not warranted by its validity.

The Highest Order, not being oblivious to the disparity in ideals and reality, and with the belief these ideals are worthy to uphold, have taken it upon themselves to ensure this frail perception remains intact.

- - -

"Darcy, I would declare by your countenance that we were headed to a funeral. If your appearance were more dire I would further conjecture the funeral might well be your own," Charles Bingley said with a smile.

Not hearing a question or statement which required a response, Mr. Darcy continued his stern examination of the countryside meandering past his carriage window.

"You must admit to some excitement about visiting the countryside and experiencing new social interactions."

"I certainly must not. I should imagine that after all these many years in my company you would know enough of my temperament to realize the foolishness of your previous statement."

With a smile on her face, Miss Caroline Bingley replied that she as much knew the truth of Mr. Darcy's statement.

"I personally eschew such social engagements as those in the country," stated Miss Bingley.

"However, while I find the parties boorish and the general populace to be less well bred, my brother does enjoy attributing the grandest qualities to gentry of this locale. I will enjoy hearing your strictures on the matter, Mr. Darcy."

"Then you also misrepresent me in your esteem. While the details of the misrepresentation vary, the sentiment of my response will not. I should have thought you to know me well enough to realize a simple truth of my character; I do not engage in idle stricture. Unless I am required to divulge them to satisfy a direct question, or to address a manner of import, my opinions of people are kept private."

"Surely you may address the general nature of the country gentry, as well as their choice of lifestyle, without trespassing on your ideals of stricture with regard to any particular individual."

Mr. Darcy paused for a moment and made not to reply, but in an attempt to end the conversation he merely stared out the window and replied that his estate of Pemberley, of which Miss Bingley was fond, was located in the country.

Miss Bingley, not a lady to take quick offense in matters regarding Mr. Darcy, turned the conversation to her sister and her sisters' husband, the unassuming Mr. Hurst.

"I believe our brother and Mr. Darcy have procured a reasonable place to lodge. Netherfield appears to be large enough to accommodate our party, with enough acreage for general amusement such as walking and horse riding. Do you not agree Louisa?"

"I do indeed, and the neighbors seem to be cordial enough. While I have not met any personally I believe Charles has met a few."

"Yes I have," Charles replied with a smile and frivolity akin to a child, "I believe we shall meet several of them at the ball this evening."

"No doubt you shall have your choice of partners for the evening. I imagine that even Mr. Darcy will not be in want of a partner. I only hope you save a dance for myself and Louisa."

Darcy turned to Caroline at this remark.

"It is not my intention of putting myself forward to ladies of which I am unacquainted. If I am to dance, I intend on keeping my choices limited to the ladies of this carriage."

This comment pleased Caroline Bingley. It had been a long while since she had set her sights on the marriage between herself and Mr. Darcy. The attainment of this goal still eluded her; however, being a subtle and conniving woman, she was determined in her aspirations.

Mr. Darcy, not oblivious to Caroline's motives, saw no reason to behave any differently in regards to his current interactions with the Bingleys. He admired Charles and found his innocent exuberance to be a refreshing contrast to the seriousness of his own business dealings. Charles' sisters, Caroline and Louisa, were accomplished and from a well respected family; and even Mr. Hurst, who having married Louisa more for position of society than love, was a respectful and honourable man.

It was partly because of this friendship that Mr. Darcy had journeyed to this part of the country to assist Charles with the let of a house. It had long been the desire of the Bingleys to own an estate, and Netherfield was a promising beginning. The previous month's work, which consisted of touring the surrounding area of Hertfordshire, meeting neighbors, and signing contracts, was to culminate tonight with a ball in Meryton. It would be here that Charles Bingley and his sisters, who had only just arrived from London, would first meet many of the areas inhabitants.

Chapter 2

Entering the ballroom at Meryton, Darcy quickly assessed the local culture, citizenry, architecture and general layout of the room. His friend, the ever joyful Mr. Bingley, was content to enter the room in a friendly flourish and engage immediately in social conventions.

To Mr. Darcy's dismay it was readily apparent that, should not more gentlemen arrive, the ladies attending this evenings event would outnumber the men. This fact would undoubtedly lead to more than one suggestion, from an attendee, for Mr. Darcy to engage in dancing. Mr. Darcy, being a well accomplished dancer, was able to fulfill this social obligation, however, this evening his mind was focused on a more pressing matter, and as he gazed about the room he spied the subject of that focus.

Across the room stood an elderly gentleman of three score and a handful of years. Darcy watched him carefully and recalled in his mind the description of Mr. Shantly. Deciding the description was apt, and that this gentleman was indeed Mr. Shantly, Darcy moved across the room so as to study the man more closely.

Shantly appeared gracious, accommodating, and quite at ease with the ladies and gentleman at the ball. The number of women at the party did not disagree with him in the least. On the contrary, it appeared to fit his social graces and demeanor.

Darcy began to move about the room and watch Mr. Shantly with an observant but unobtrusive eye. This task was made more difficult as he was pulled into introductions of the various attendees.

As the night progressed Mr. Shantly was never without a partner and, being as the men were so few, he could easily have his choice of ladies. If a lady of his liking were not available for a particular dance, then he merely had to wait until the next dance when she would be available.

It was noticeable to Darcy that Mr. Shantly certainly preferred the younger ladies and, on the occasions in which he stood up with a more mature lady, he positioned himself in such a way that changing partners mid-dance would allow him access to a lady more to his liking.

To be sure, most of the attendees perceived Mr. Shantly to be a very agreeable gentleman, and in his manners and speech Darcy could find little fault. A report from Sussex prepared him for this fact and allowed Darcy to look more deeply at the man currently dancing with a girl of but fifteen; Lydia, if Darcy remembered correctly. The couple danced well and Shantly seemed pleased with the liveliness of his partner.

Throughout the evening Darcy attempted to be minimally social and was aware that he failed in this attempt, but his mind was little worried about such matters. Mr. Bingley, as Darcy knew he would, enticed him to dance with a local lady.

``Come, Darcy," said he, ``I must have you dance. I hate to see you standing about by yourself in this stupid manner. You had much better dance."

``I certainly shall not. You know how I detest it, unless I am particularly acquainted with my partner. At such an assembly as this, it would be insupportable. Your sisters are engaged, and there is not another woman in the room whom it would not be a punishment to me to stand up with."

``I would not be so fastidious as you are," cried Bingley, ``for a kingdom! Upon my honour I never met with so many pleasant girls in my life, as I have this evening; and there are several of them, you see, uncommonly pretty."

``*You* are dancing with the only handsome girl in the room," said Mr. Darcy, looking at Miss Jane Bennet, the oldest daughter of five who Darcy and Bingley were introduced to at the outset of the evening.

``Oh! she is the most beautiful creature I ever beheld! But there is one of her sisters sitting down just behind you, who is very pretty, and I dare say very agreeable. Do let me ask my partner to introduce you."

``Which do you mean?" and turning round, he looked for a moment at Elizabeth Bennet, the second eldest daughter of the family. Catching her eye, he withdrew his own and coldly said, ``She is tolerable; but not handsome enough to tempt *me*; and I am in no humour at present to give consequence to young ladies who are slighted by other men. You had better return to your partner and enjoy her smiles, for you are wasting your time with me."

Not meaning to be rude, Darcy was still forced to be firm in his affirmation not to dance. Unfortunately this led to a perceived insult for which Darcy was aware. Miss Elizabeth Bennet, seeming to have overheard the conversation, stood up and crossed the room to join her Mother, Mrs. Bennet, and her sisters. He had little time to consider his unintentional insult as he made his way across the room to sit and collect his thoughts.

Darcy was content to spend several minutes deep in his thoughts, analyzing the evening and the people. His attention still on Mr. Shantly, he noticed an odd nature to the gentleman. It was a flash of emotion across his face that was quickly covered by social graces. The emotion lasted merely a second, but a keen and observing eye knew an underlying emotion of disgust was being hidden.

It was at this moment that the lady sitting next to Darcy chose to ask him a frivolous question.

"How are you finding Netherfield, Mr. Darcy?" asked Mrs. Long.

With an internal sigh Darcy forcefully took his gaze off Mr. Shantly and turned to Mrs. Long.

"I find it as I find most country estates, suitable to my needs of the moment."

With the question answered, Darcy refocused his attention and attempted to ascertain the nature of Mr. Shantly's disgust. This now proved more difficult due to his distraction by Mrs. Long, and Darcy could scarcely hide his displeasure. At the moment Mr. Shantly could be heard in conversation with a gentleman and his wife.

"Yes, my dear, I do have a little estate not far from here. Modest to be sure, but the grounds are quite lovely with plenty of room to run free. As you say, you have a servant in need of a position and I believe I could use her services."

"That would be wonderful if you could," replied the lady, "Brigitte lost her husband a year ago and she has only her daughter Angela for company. Angela is old enough to take care of herself, being a child of 12, but they would require accommodations."

"This would not be a problem in the least. My last servants had to make an abrupt trip to the north of England and their cottage is vacant. Brigitte and her daughter are most welcome to stay. I believe I have even seen Angela around your home while I was touring the countryside. A slight lass with braided hair, is she not?"

"Just as you say!" exclaimed the lady. "Well this may work well indeed and seems to be fortuitous."

Darcy watched and listened to the conversation while continuing to gaze about the room, maintaining a vigilant eye on the evening's events. Mrs. Long, his part time seat partner, had left and Darcy was now able to relax into a world of his own thought. By the end of the evening he was content with the information and insight he had gained, although his friend was not well pleased.

"Darcy I do swear that at times you can be most disagreeable. Did you dance with anyone other than my sisters?"

"I saw no reason to dance with anyone other than your sisters and for that reason I did not," replied Darcy.

Caroline gave a wry smile and commented that perhaps the social graces of the country ladies did not lend themselves well to Mr. Darcy's palate. At this statement her sister laughed slightly and the two ladies fell into conversation regarding each of the ladies from the ball. The both of them admired the eldest Ms. Bennet. They found her handsome and gracious, with a pleasing smile, but as to the others they could find very little to recommend. Darcy noticed this did not deter the Bingley sisters from mentioning qualities of the ladies that were not endearing. Wishing to avoid idle conversation regarding minor foibles, Darcy turned his thoughts to darker character traits which manifest in ways most sinister.

Chapter 3

That evening, while the household slept, Darcy made his way through the house with the intention of taking a horse ride. He made no actions of sneaking quietly, but he also made no deliberate attempts to arouse anyone. He merely played the role of a quiet and private individual who, out of respect for the residents, was taking his nighttime restlessness for a midnight ride.

The evening was quiet and the moon shone down providing light across the vast expanse of Netherfield; the large accommodations which Bingley had just let. Darcy admired the grounds and peacefulness of the countryside at this time of night. There was an aspect of the night's nature that spoke to him: quiet, serene, and a feeling of contented aloneness, while still being connected to nature.

In an efficient manner he made his way to the stables, chose his horse, had him bridled, and was out into the countryside at a reasonable gait. Glancing back he could see Netherfield, with the moon shining above, slowly retreat into the distance. It was very peaceful for him, and the thought of his friends asleep within those walls gave him comfort against the task he was undertaking.

Returning his gaze forward he guided his horse along the way he had memorized from his few trips with Bingley into this part of countryside. It was not long before he reached unfamiliar territory, but with skill and determination he continued on for several miles. Avoiding main roads, and landowner's property that might be cause for trouble, he eventually arrived at the property of his desire.

He stopped several hundred yards away, dismounted, and stood overlooking the quiet unassuming house. Not a soul seemed to be awake and the house was very dark, illuminated only by what light the moon allowed. Near the back, as he expected, was the servants entrance allowing ingress to the main floor. Also, as he expected, it was accessible and concealed from light.

Pulling from his waistcoat a small document, he turned to the light of the moon and read notes written in such a fashion as to appear to be a language of mythical creatures; Elves perhaps, or fairies. Gazing at the house before him, he concurred with the intelligence in his hand and hoped that all of the servants were lodged elsewhere, leaving the home owner as the sole occupant.

Putting his note away, Darcy took a long look at the house and sighed with resignation. His responsibilities in life were many and this particular one he did not relish. However, Gentry will police Gentry, and in a delicate matter such as this, personal attention was preferred.

It was with great ease that he made his way to the house, avoiding light, shrubbery, or ground cover that might alert anyone to his presence. Gone was the intention of respectful quiet and in its place was a determined mindset of stealth. At this point, being noticed was not a consideration for which there were many pleasant outcomes.

Into the house and through the main rooms was made rather easy. The floor was covered in places with rugs which muffled his steps, and when the floor creaked in places he was swift to adjust to the outer walls where structural integrity held the boards in less sway.

It was not long before he was in the master's bedroom standing over a sleeping Mr. Shantly. The rest of the house had proved to be empty, as far as he could ascertain, nevertheless he set about his business quickly.

Fetching a scarf from his coat he balled it up. A quick inspection allayed his fear of any loose strands that might be pulled off and left behind. Once he was satisfied, Darcy made peace with himself and placed the scarf over Mr. Shantly's nose and mouth. His other arm then readied to hold the sleeping man. This would not take long as all reports showed Shantly to be in less than perfect health.

Shanty's eyes opened wide and he made as to struggle, but Darcy held him tight and calmed Shantly with a soothing "shhhh" as if he were quieting a baby. Shantly quickly calmed down at the sound and Darcy moved in close to look him in the eyes. They stared at each other for a second; Darcy holding the scarf, and fear in Shantly's eyes.

"A gentleman, of any stature, should not take such an interest in children. Your latest transgression has torn a family from its home while at the same time scarring an innocent child in a manner most grotesque. You shall not be allowed another opportunity to transgress against society, morality, and God."

Darcy moved closer to Shantly and whispered in his ear. “Noblesse Oblige.”

Upon hearing these words the full import of the situation dawned on Shantly. His eyes, already wide with fear, seemed to take on a new dimension as they stretched the credulity of facial expression. *Noblesse Oblige*, the obligations and responsibilities of the nobility, while often spoken of in jest at social gatherings, was something of which the Highest Order did not take for granted. Shantly realized he had trespassed too far into the realm of the Nobility. Relying heavily on his influence and stature he had avoided any scandal or notice from the local authority, but his actions had not gone unnoticed by the nobility and the gentry.

It was not long before the deed was done and Darcy laid the body in a peaceful manner. With a careful eye he examined the room, the bed, and Shantly for any unusual signs that would draw suspicion. The overall appearance was of a man who had passed peacefully in his sleep.

Once Darcy was convinced of this perception, he bowed his head slightly and confirmed his resolve regarding his actions. His mind wandered to the child that was now recovering from a dreadful experience and to the other individuals involved in this nightmare. The parents that must live with the anger of an injustice due to their stature in life, to the bankers, politicians, and socialites required to conceal this event.

Even now a feeling of disgust swept over him and he could not bring himself to feel any pity for Shantly, nor any remorse for his own actions. He only felt anger that Shantly’s indiscretions were not discovered earlier and thus allowed Mr. Darcy to save one or more children from harm. Turning on his heels he headed out of the room, out of the house, and into the night.

Chapter 4

The next few days progressed in a fairly uneventful manner and little or no news was heard in regards to Mr. Shantly's death. Darcy maintained an interest in the local news, and it happened that once Mr. Shantly was found a doctor was quickly called. A pronouncement of death while sleeping was listed, a few words regarding his poor luck were mentioned, and that was the end of the matter; at least in regards to the local citizenry, as the affairs of Mr. Shantly's estate were then to be handled by attorneys in London. Darcy, familiar with the assigned attorneys, knew full well the estate would be handled properly and dispensed with in a manner befitting a soul requiring penitence.

While this particular countryside held little appeal for Darcy it had served its purpose in many functions. The serendipity of his friends letting a place, so near a location he required, was interesting, and Darcy saw no immediate reason to vacate. While he typically abstained from social engagements, it was not long before Darcy once again found himself embroiled in a gathering; although this evening his ear was more bent to the amusements of the night and towards any mention of Shantly or his demise.

This evening Charles and his sisters had brought Darcy to the home of Sir William and his wife, lady Lucas. The frivolity of the evening consisted mainly of dance and little else. As before, Darcy contented himself with observation while Charles contented himself with conversation, and an apparent affinity to dance with Miss Jane Bennet, of whom he had met at the Merryton ball.

Listening to a conversation between Miss Elizabeth Bennet and Colonel Forster, an officer of a local militia, Darcy found himself drawn into the intelligent responses of the young lady, and for a moment lost the reasons of his initial attentiveness. Of Mr. Shantly there was little word and Darcy conjectured the death of a local gentleman, while noteworthy, was perhaps not polite conversation at an evening of merriment.

As he wandered about the room Darcy further decided that this evening centered more on merriment than actual conversation, which lent more respect to the intelligent conversation he had previously overheard between Col. Forster and Miss Bennet. Engrossed in such thoughts Mr. Darcy was unaware that Sir William had made a round of the room as well, and was now standing beside him.

``What a charming amusement for young people this is, Mr. Darcy! There is nothing like dancing after all. I consider it as one of the first refinements of polished societies."

``Certainly, Sir; and it has the advantage also of being in vogue amongst the less polished societies of the world. Every savage can dance."

Sir William only smiled. ``Your friend performs delightfully;" he continued after a pause, on seeing Bingley join the group; ``and I doubt not that you are an adept in the science yourself, Mr. Darcy."

``You saw me dance at Meryton, I believe, Sir."

``Yes, indeed, and received no inconsiderable pleasure from the sight. Do you often dance at St. James's?"

``Never, sir."

``Do you not think it would be a proper compliment to the place?"

``It is a compliment which I never pay to any place, if I can avoid it."

``You have a house in town, I conclude?"

Mr. Darcy bowed.

``I had once some thoughts of fixing in town myself, for I am fond of superior society; but I did not feel quite certain that the air of London would agree with Lady Lucas."

He paused in hopes of an answer; but his companion was not disposed to make any; and Elizabeth Bennet at that instant moving towards them, he was struck with the notion of doing a very gallant thing, and called out to her,

``My dear Miss Eliza, why are not you dancing? Mr. Darcy, you must allow me to present this young lady to you as a very desirable partner. You cannot refuse to dance, I am sure, when so much beauty is before you." And taking her hand, he would have given it to Mr. Darcy, who, though extremely surprised, was not unwilling to receive it, when she instantly drew back, and said with some discomposure to Sir William,

``Indeed, Sir, I have not the least intention of dancing. I entreat you not to suppose that I moved this way in order to beg for a partner."

Mr. Darcy with grave propriety requested to be allowed the honour of her hand; but in vain.

Elizabeth was determined; nor did Sir William at all shake her purpose by his attempt at persuasion.

``You excel so much in the dance, Miss Eliza, that it is cruel to deny me the happiness of seeing you; and though this gentleman dislikes the amusement in general, he can have no objection, I am sure, to oblige us for one half hour."

``Mr. Darcy is all politeness," said Elizabeth, smiling.

``He is indeed, but considering the inducement, my dear Miss Eliza, we cannot wonder at his complaisance; for who would object to such a partner?"

Elizabeth looked archly, and turned away. Her resistance had not injured her with the gentleman; to the contrary, Mr. Darcy admired the manner in which Elizabeth stood her resolve in the matter of dance. He began to study her and wonder if she had also surmised his dislike for dance, which then led her to politely decline the offer and save him from discomfort. He was thinking of her with some complacency, when thus accosted by Miss Bingley.

``I can guess the subject of your reverie."

``I should imagine not."

``You are considering how insupportable it would be to pass many evenings in this manner -- in such society; and indeed I am quite of your opinion. I was never more annoyed! The insipidity and yet the noise; the nothingness and yet the self-importance of all these people! What would I give to hear your strictures on them!"

Darcy momentarily regarded Caroline and her comments on his strictures of individuals. These past years of acquaintance had given her some understanding of his character, but in many aspects she seemed resolute in her incorrect inferences.

``Your conjecture is totally wrong, I assure you. My mind was more agreeably engaged. I have been meditating on the very great pleasure which a pair of fine eyes in the face of a pretty woman can bestow."

Miss Bingley immediately fixed her eyes on his face, and desired he would tell her what lady had the credit of inspiring such reflections. Mr. Darcy replied with great intrepidity,

``Miss Elizabeth Bennet."

``Miss Elizabeth Bennet!" repeated Miss Bingley. ``I am all astonishment. How long has she been such a favourite? And pray, when am I to wish you joy?"

``That is exactly the question which I expected you to ask. A lady's imagination is very rapid; it jumps from admiration to love, from love to matrimony, in a moment. I knew you would be wishing me joy."

``Nay, if you are so serious about it, I shall consider the matter as absolutely settled. You will have a charming mother-in-law, indeed, and of course she will be always at Pemberley with you."

Caroline amused herself chiding Mrs. Bennet, the very opinionated and apparently silly Mother of the Bennet household, who even now could be heard loudly regaling some poor gentleman on the wonderful nature of her fine daughters. While Darcy shared this opinion with Caroline he did not share in her interest to discuss the matter, so he resolved to listen to Caroline with perfect indifference while she chose to entertain herself in this manner.

Chapter 5

Another fortuitous event of Charles Bingley choosing this part of the country was the arrival of the militia regiment to Meryton, of which there contained an individual of Darcy's acquaintance. Being pleased with this turn of events he happily agreed to an invitation for him and Charles to dine with the officers in Meryton.

"Mr. Charles Bingley and the ever stoic Mr. Fitzwilliam Darcy, it is good to see you," stated Major Park as the two gentlemen arrived for dinner one evening. "Mr. Darcy, I believe it has been some time since you and I have been in each other's company. I wish we had been able to meet at Sir Williams, but I was unable to attend, however, I am to understand that you did meet a few officers at that event. I trust you are well and have maintained some semblance of the training which precipitated our first meeting?"

"Indeed I have Major," replied Darcy, "and might I add, the last time we met, you were a lieutenant. Time and fortune have been good to you."

"If war may be called good, then I would agree with your observation. Napoleon does not like opposition and the damage to our ranks while fighting him led to several avenues of advancement. I can see the civilian life has treated you well."

"It has indeed. While the matters of a private citizen may not have the national import of a soldiers, they can be rather heady, but here we may dine and discuss matters of a less stressful nature. I believe you are somewhat familiar with Charles Bingley. He is an amiable sort, and a perfect guest for a dinner of any magnitude."

Major Park confirmed his familiarity with Bingley and proceeded to engage Charles in conversation. It was not long before the two were talking, not of wars and business, but of ladies and society.

"My sisters, Caroline and Louisa, are taking this opportunity to entertain Miss Jane Bennet. Are you familiar with Jane?" asked an inquisitive Bingley.

"I must admit that I am not. I have met many a wonderful lady during our brief time in Meryton. I am to understand that the Bennets are well regarded in the area and have a household of five daughters. Surely that fact may lead many a man to take a close look at one or more of the ladies. Is Miss Bennet a handsome lady?"

"Oh indeed she is. I believe her to be very handsome and accomplished. She smiles in a gracious manner and has a demeanor that is kind and gentle." Bingley could not refrain from smiling and animating while he spoke.

"I believe she has struck a fancy with this young man," cried the Major to Darcy.

"I had not taken a great deal of notice; I suppose you must be right," Darcy replied with an air of social interest not normally befitting him.

"Either way, the ladies will entertain themselves tonight and the most I will conjecture is that Caroline and Louisa enjoy Miss Bennet's company."

Conversations continued around the room as officers mingled. Topics ranged from battle tactics, to specific battles against Napoleon. The discussions spread into more social topics such as the town of Meryton, where the regiment was to winter, and to the ladies of the local community.

Dinner allowed a more focused discussion and as the officers ate the topic came around to military issues; as it must in a setting of this type.

"I find that the respect of the officers on a battlefield is the most important requirement for success. I have my commission, bought and paid for, and my soldiers respect me and follow my orders without question. I know this will allow me to defeat my enemies when I engage them."

"That would be well and good if your training allowed you to lead them in a manner congruent for success; but in the heat of battle, if you do not remember your basics, your orders, should they be forth coming, may be of little practical use. Any man following those orders without question would surely die," Darcy stated dryly in response to this young lieutenant's comments.

"Are you suggesting mutiny Mr. Darcy?" asked the lieutenant.

"Not at all, I merely bring up a fact in regards to blind obedience. In a battle the soldiers will look to the officers for sound advice and solid orders. An officer that perceives those orders to be quality orders merely due to his purchased commission may see many men buried. I have met many a *chosen man* I would follow into battle over a lieutenant with a paid commission and little training or field experience."

"That may be well and good, but the opinions of a mere country gentleman and farmer have little bearing on actual practice."

"Lt. Denny!" exclaimed Major Park in a stern voice addressing the heretofore unnamed officer.

"I will have you know the man you are addressing is wealthy enough to purchase a hundred commissions and no mere farmer. Not only could he afford the commission but he has undergone more rigorous training than I daresay you have. When I first met Mr. Darcy he was engaged in a personal training schedule implemented by many of the type of men he holds in regard. While his rank in society allowed him an air of superiority, it was not a right he chose to exercise. Darcy was a determined and excellent soldier; if not one in actuality, then definitely in spirit. I have seen him shoot competitively with the best *chosen men* and win. His battle skills are superb and I daresay you could blindfold him, take him to the countryside, and leave him; upon returning to your command tent you would find him sitting at your table and drinking your favorite sherry. You would do well to respect him and his opinions in light of such information as I possess. I personally would wager on his military skills against yours if needs be."

Upon the completion of these statements Mr. Bingley leaned excitedly towards his friend. "Darcy, you never let on you were interested in the military. My, you do surprise me."

"It was a passing interest in my youth and one which pleased my family. As an obligation to my family and their responsibilities I undertook certain training so that I may better fulfill my role as head of the household when the time arose."

The chatter around the table separated into several smaller groups and then quickly centered on the topic of a wager. It was not long before several of the officers agreed that a shooting contest must be held between Lt. Denny and Mr. Darcy. After more debate and an attempt by Darcy to defer, the entire group found themselves outside in a suitable area for shooting.

"I do hope you are as good as the Major has stated. I would find it boorish to beat you so readily. I will inform you of the fact that I am one of the best shots in the regiment. Although beating a gentleman will not gain me much esteem in the eyes of the local ladies, it may add to my general reputation."

Darcy eyed Lt. Denny with amusement as the two examined the muskets they were assigned. He found the man to be sincere in his speech and confident in his abilities, if a little taxing in social graces. The Lieutenant's physique and manner in which he held his weapon revealed an underlying skill set not to be underestimated; Darcy made sure to not make an error of estimation.

"It is a shame we have only muskets and not rifles. While muskets will suffice, I find the weight and accuracy of a rifle to be much preferred." This comment, by Darcy, unsettled Lt. Denny slightly, as it was proof of experience.

In a few minutes a target was selected and Lt. Denny was allowed to shoot first. He was efficient, loaded his weapon rapidly, took aim and hit his target knocking it about. The officers cheered at his good shot and slapped the young man on the shoulder as he made his way amongst them.

Darcy moved to position, made his weapon ready, took deliberate aim and when ready, fired. At first the crowd stood in silence as it looked to be that Darcy missed his target, but it quickly became apparent that he had hit the target dead center in such a manner that it stood firm in place; had this been a man, the shot would have been directly through the heart.

The remainder of the evening continued with a return to the table and the serving of more food, followed by dessert. The officers, while still engaging in conversation with each other, refrained from conversing with Mr. Darcy. All except Colonel Forster and Major Park, who enjoyed reminiscing with his old friend and thanking him for subduing the pride of the younger officers.

Chapter 6

That evening Mr. Bingley and Mr. Darcy returned to Netherfield only to find the ladies of the house in a most egregious state. It seemed that the eldest Miss Bennet, having accepted their invitation for dinner, had been obliged to arrive on horseback, as the Bennet carriage and carriage horses were otherwise engaged.

Caroline Bingley remarked that the gentleman must have undoubtedly noticed the rain earlier in the evening. As it transpired, poor Miss Bennet had been caught in a downpour and arrived at Netherfield in a very wet state.

Neither Bingley nor Darcy commented on the rain. They were well aware of the inclement weather; however, it had not affected their dinner nor the shooting match.

"The poor dear. She arrived here in a manner befitting that of a kitten caught in a downpour. Louisa and I took immediate pity upon her and rushed her inside for warmth and dry clothes."

Bingley became noticeably upset and immediately inquired as to her well being.

"Alas, I must admit she is quite unwell. I made her a cup of tea to warm her, but this did little to aid her situation. It was not long before she was overcome with a headache."

"Is she here? May I see her?"

"She is here but resting. The poor thing seemed to progressively take ill. Both Louisa and I were required to help her into a bed. I trust she will be well by morning."

While Darcy took the news in stride, Bingley seemed nearly beside himself. He hopped about from foot to foot as if deciding whether he should visit Miss Bennet. His sisters politely and quickly assured him that nothing could be done, Miss Bennet was resting, and they should all wait for the morning.

As the couples separated throughout the house, Caroline addressed Darcy and inquired as to his evening.

"It was a dinner and conversation befitting the gentleman and soldiers of the evening. I found the food agreeable and conversation interesting."

"That is good to hear."

As they turned to part Caroline suddenly stopped and re-addressed Darcy.

"Oh, I did mean to tell you that I inadvertently used your tea. I do hope you will forgive my accidental trespass. I was in a hurry to attend to Miss Bennet and did not notice which tea I brewed until I returned to the kitchen."

"My tea?" Darcy asked, as much as stated, while his eyebrows arched and his face became grave.

"Yes. The tea you made as a special gift for your aunt. I know you had been gathering the plants and drying them. I personally found your thoughtful act endearing. You must please your aunt with your spontaneous acts of kindness." Caroline said this last with an air of flattery.

"I do apologize for the error and will assure you it was only enough to brew a single cup for Miss Bennet. I am sure there will still be enough for your gift."

"Thank you for informing me. I am sure you are correct and that I shall have more than enough."

The two then parted ways and Darcy, who initially intended to retreat to the parlor, made a quick change of direction and headed to the kitchen. Upon arrival he quickly found his tea and examined it. To his dismay he could confirm his tea must have been served to Miss Bennet.

This was a carelessness for which he admonished himself with rigidity. As he held the tea he thought about the ingredients and the primary flower, Lords-and-Ladies, that the tea consisted of. In a small dose little harm would befall anyone, but in a large amount death could ensue.

Lords-and-Ladies, also known as Arum Maculatum, was a personal favorite of Darcy. The common name conveyed a sense of honour, and the plants effects conveyed an immobility that he sometimes found useful. This particular brew was not meant to kill, merely inconvenience an individual. Darcy pondered on the situation of Miss Bennet and conjectured she would most likely recover, but in the meantime she would need a careful eye upon her.

Making his way upstairs he discreetly checked into the room of the sick young lady. Miss Bennet was asleep and Darcy, leaving the door open to counter any possible perceptions of impropriety, quickly and efficiently checked the lady for serious symptoms. He determined she was suffering mildly from the tea and, convincing himself that she would be fine for the moment, left her to rest.

Heading down to the parlor he thanked the weather and appearance of a common sickness for covering this unfortunate event.

Chapter 7

The next morning, Jane Bennet was well enough to dispatch a letter to her family at Longbourn, her family estate, informing them of her condition and that Mr. Jones, a local apothecary, would be examining her on the insistence of Caroline and Louisa. The visitation of an apothecary concerned Darcy, but he could hardly refuse the idea. He did take solace in the fact that the effects of the tea were meant to mimic a cold, and it was all but the most astute individual that would diagnose anything but.

While the household awaited Mr. Jones they saw fit to engage in normal activities. It was a bit of a stir when a servant announced Miss Elizabeth Bennet; who, upon receiving her elder sister's note, had walked across the rain soaked countryside to Netherfield.

She was shown into the breakfast-parlour, where all but Jane were assembled, and where her appearance created a great deal of surprise. That she should have walked three miles so early in the day, in such dirty weather, and by herself, was almost incredible to Mrs. Hurst and Miss Bingley; and Elizabeth was convinced that they held her in contempt for it. She was received, however, very politely by them; and in their brother's manners there was something better than politeness; there was good humour and kindness. Mr. Darcy said very little, and Mr. Hurst nothing at all. The former was divided between admiration of the brilliancy which exercise had given to her complexion, and doubt as to whether the occasion justified her coming so far alone; the latter was thinking only of his breakfast.

Her enquiries after her sister were not very favourably answered. Miss Bennet had slept ill, and though up, was very feverish and not well enough to leave her room. Elizabeth was glad to be taken to her immediately, and Jane, who had only been withheld by the fear of giving alarm or inconvenience, from expressing in her note how much she longed for such a visit, was delighted at her entrance. She was not equal, however, to much conversation, and when Miss Bingley left them together, could attempt little beside expressions of gratitude for the extraordinary kindness she was treated with. Elizabeth silently attended her.

When breakfast was over, they were joined by the sisters, and Elizabeth began to like them herself, when she saw how much affection and solicitude they showed for Jane. The apothecary came, and having examined his patient, said, as might be supposed, that she had caught a violent cold, and that they must endeavor to get the better of it. He advised her to return to bed, and promised to return with some draughts if she did not speedily recover. The advice was followed readily, for the feverish symptoms increased, and her head ached acutely. Elizabeth did not quit her room for a moment, nor were the other ladies often absent; the gentlemen being out, they had in fact nothing to do elsewhere.

When the clock struck three, Elizabeth felt that she must go; and very unwillingly said so. Miss Bingley offered her the carriage, and she only wanted a little pressing to accept it, when Jane testified such concern in parting with her that Miss Bingley was obliged to convert the offer of the chaise into an invitation to remain at Netherfield for the present. Elizabeth most thankfully consented, and a servant was dispatched to Longbourn to acquaint the family with her stay, and bring back a supply of clothes.

Chapter 8

Evening found the household gathered in the drawing room engaged in a game of cards. Elizabeth, who had spent most of the evening with Jane, entered the room much later in the night and was invited to join.

She turned to Caroline at the invitation and after a moment of thought politely declined remarking she would defer from a game in order to engage in reading. Mr. Hurst looked at her with astonishment.

``Do you prefer reading to cards?" said he; ``that is rather singular."

``Miss Eliza Bennet," said Miss Bingley, ``despises cards. She is a great reader and has no pleasure in anything else."

``I deserve neither such praise nor such censure," cried Elizabeth; ``I am not a great reader, and I have pleasure in many things."

Darcy, sitting at the table, watched the interaction between Caroline and Elizabeth with interest. Caroline was gracious and polite with a hint of insincerity. This was a habit of Carolines he had learned to live with over the years and, while he could not condone the habit, he admired Caroline's skill at implementing it. Miss Bennet appeared to sense the insincerity and in a skillful manner deflected the subtle social impropriety.

Darcy was impressed with this skill and admired Elizabeth's ability to not only recognize an insincere comment but to quickly assess the situation and implement a suitable response.

``In nursing your sister I am sure you have pleasure," said Bingley; ``and I hope it will soon be increased by seeing her quite well."

Elizabeth thanked him from her heart, and then walked towards a table where a few books were lying. He immediately offered to fetch her others; all that his library afforded.

Darcy observed an odd reaction of contemplation to this offer. After a moment Elizabeth assured Charles the books in this room would suffice. She proceeded to the table of her original intent and thereupon seized one of the books. Appearing content in her selection she chose a seat and opened the book to a page already marked.

Conversation in the room continued on the subject of the Bingley Library and a comparison to Darcy's own. Darcy admitted his library was quite old and vast. He himself had taken a consider amount of time adding to the collection and took great pleasure indulging in the material.

Shortly the conversation turned to the quality of ladies and their ability and opportunity to become accomplished. Elizabeth, who had monitored the conversation, and who was now content with the material she had read, engaged in the topic with Mr. Darcy.

The main premise centered on what the gentleman believed a woman required so she may be counted as accomplished. Mr. Darcy spoke of many admirable traits he found necessary for ladies. At the near conclusion of his list he added yet another requirement.

``All this she must possess," added Darcy, ``and to all this she must yet add something more substantial, in the improvement of her mind by extensive reading."

Miss Bennet, hardly to be agreeable on the matter, commented that Mr. Darcy's list of requirements were so stringent it was a surprise he should know even six ladies of accomplishment.

Caroline and Louisa made such a hue and cry as to Elizabeth's remarks that Mr. Hurst was forced to bring them back to the game at hand. In the midst of the ladies objections Darcy kept an eye on Elizabeth who in turn kept an eye on him.

The two stared at each other, one with a calm look of interest and respect, the other with a raised eye of defiance and a slight smile of the mischievous. As the ladies returned to the game Elizabeth broke her gaze from Darcy and returned to her book. Darcy found Elizabeth's return to reading, so soon after his comment regarding a woman's need to read, to be a subtle jab at his previous argument.

Gazing at her for a moment, he concluded Elizabeth Bennet was either more intelligent and artful than the average lady or that he was misrepresenting her in his estimation. Returning himself to the game at hand he dismissed the thought for the moment.

Shortly, Elizabeth finished her reading and headed up to check on Jane. Upon her absence the ladies of the room took the opportunity to ridicule Elizabeth. Darcy and Bingley engaged in the banter in a minimal manner and the former only to the extent of discussing general human traits while avoiding the application of those traits to any individual, especially that of Miss Elizabeth.

Near the end of the game Elizabeth returned to the drawing room and informed the household that Jane was still quite unwell.

"We must send for Mr. Jones immediately!" cried Mr. Bingley.

"Indeed not Charles, if the eldest Miss Bennet is this ill we must dispatch to London for a Doctor of repute. I do not trust to the skill of a local man."

Darcy sat upright at Caroline's suggestion of a doctor from London, but his fears were put to rest as Elizabeth continued into the room with her book in hand. Darcy once again noted Miss Bennet's tendency to read and decided that she must she must have taken it upstairs to read to Jane. Elizabeth placed the book upon the table and objected to a doctor from London.

"I believe Jane to be most ill but do not believe it to be so grave as to require the expense and inconvenience of a man from London."

"But she must be cared for in any manner that we find available!" Charles exclaimed.

"I know my sister well, and, while she has an appearance of gentleness, her constitution is strong. I will watch her closely this evening and through the night. If she is not better in the morning then we can certainly dispatch for Mr. Jones."

Darcy was well pleased with this idea and commented to Charles that in regards to Jane Bennet the care should be deferred to Elizabeth's experience and familiarity of familial constitution. Charles grudgingly agreed and the matter was settled.

As the time was late, the party broke up and the individuals went their separate ways. Darcy, being pleased with the outcome, only as much as a local apothecary was preferable to a reputable doctor, was slightly more pleased as he watched Elizabeth engage Charles' sisters in cordial conversation.

"I do appreciate the care for my sister you two have shown her this last day. I imagine she must have been gravely sick upon arriving at your home."

"Indeed she was not so ill as we see her now. I wish we could have attended her better…"

The conversation trailed off as the ladies continued through the house, and Darcy made his way to his room. He would have preferred to check on Jane Bennet once more, but the activity of the household prevented this action. Instead, he settled his mind with a reminder of his initial assessment of her situation and his conviction she would weather this illness with positive results.

Chapter 9

The next morning, Jane Bennet once more received the attention of Mr. Jones, the local apothecary. As fate would have it, Mr. Jones arrived shortly before Mrs. Bennet, who was summoned to Netherfield by a note Miss Elizabeth dispatched early in the morning.

Deciding not to arrive alone, Mrs. Bennet entered the establishment accompanied by her two youngest daughters. This flourish of activity allowed for Darcy to spend a few minutes time with the apothecary and the ill Miss Bennet. Even this was difficult as Elizabeth was in little mood to be separated from her sister, but in the end she relented as everyone could hear the raucous caused by the arrival of the members of her family.

Trusting to the attentiveness of Mr. Jones, Elizabeth left the room and headed to greet her mother. Darcy took this time to watch Mr. Jones; the gentleman seemed fairly competent. He felt her forehead, asked Miss Bennet some simple questions, and begged her to drink from a draught.

Darcy kept his distance and observed from outside the room. Arum Macalatum could easily be mistaken by many a trained physician, however, it did have a few peculiarities, such as a numbness of the mouth. An astute eye could detect this and perhaps cause Darcy more trouble than he wished.

However, in regards to this particular situation, he need not have worried. Mr. Jones, while a competent man in many regards, was content to attribute Jane's illness to the cold and wet she encountered two days prior. His eyes were perhaps keen in some matters but not as keen as Mr. Darcy's, who assessed the apothecary as competent but not overly concerned to the point of searching for nefarious reasons for a young girl's mild illness.

Noise from lower in the house caused Darcy to withdraw and take himself deeper into the manor. Having met Mrs. Bennet on two previous occasions, he would have normally felt pity for what Mr. Jones was about to encounter, but in this case perhaps the flamboyance of her character would add to the confusion of his diagnoses.

Time progressed and soon the household, minus Jane, was gathered in the breakfast parlour. Darcy's insight into the abilities of Mr. Jones proved correct, and Mrs. Bennet herself confirmed what was suspected of Jane's condition; she was very ill and should not be moved, but she would recover.

Bingley made such a cry on the thought of her being moved from the house that Darcy was forced to take more notice of the his friends attachment. While he himself found Jane pleasant enough, the inferiority of her family lineage left much to be desired. Thinking on this, he cast his eyes over to Elizabeth, who he found was at this very moment studying him.

The reverie of contemplation was broken as Mrs. Bennet commented loudly on Jane's health and then suddenly changed topics to the let of Netherfield by Charles. It was her strong desire that he should remain at Netherfield for quite some time and not consider immediately vacating.

``Whatever I do is done in a hurry," replied he; ``and therefore if I should resolve to quit Netherfield, I should probably be off in five minutes. At present, however, I consider myself as quite fixed here."

``That is exactly what I should have supposed of you," said Elizabeth.

``You begin to comprehend me, do you?" cried he, turning towards her.

``Oh yes! I understand you perfectly."

``I wish I might take this for a compliment; but to be so easily seen through I am afraid is pitiful."

``That is as it happens. It does not necessarily follow that a deep, intricate character is more or less estimable than such a one as yours."

"Lizzy," cried her mother, ``remember where you are, and do not run on in the wild manner that you are suffered to do at home."

``I did not know before," continued Bingley immediately, ``that you were a studier of character. It must be an amusing study."

``Yes; but intricate characters are the most amusing. They have at least that advantage."

``The country," said Darcy, ``can in general supply but few subjects for such a study. In a country neighbourhood you move in a very confined and unvarying society."

``But people themselves alter so much, that there is something new to be observed in them for ever."

``Yes, indeed," cried Mrs. Bennet, offended by his manner of mentioning a country neighbourhood. ``I assure you there is quite as much of that going on in the country as in town."

Everybody was surprised; and Darcy, after looking at her for a moment, turned silently away. Mrs. Bennet, who fancied she had gained a complete victory over him, continued her triumph.

``I cannot see that London has any great advantage over the country for my part, except the shops and public places. The country is a vast deal pleasanter, is it not, Mr. Bingley?"

``When I am in the country," he replied, ``I never wish to leave it; and when I am in town it is pretty much the same. They have each their advantages, and I can be equally happy in either."

``Aye, that is because you have the right disposition. But that gentleman," looking at Darcy, ``seemed to think the country was nothing at all."

``Indeed, Mama, you are mistaken," said Elizabeth, blushing for her mother. ``You quite mistook Mr. Darcy. He only meant that there were not such a variety of people to be met with in the country as in town, which you must acknowledge to be true."

Mrs. Bennet saw fit to continue her conversation and Darcy with a shrewd eye examined Elizabeth. 'Who is this woman that sits before me?' he asked himself.

It was not often that Darcy encountered an individual with such an interesting assemblage of character traits. Miss Elizabeth simultaneously confused, worried, and intrigued Darcy.

``Oh Yes!I understand you perfectly."

This is the comment she made of Charles, and by Darcy's estimation she was correct in her assessment of his friends character. Elizabeth then understood Darcy's position regarding the country citizenry and applied that knowledge in a correction of her mother's opinion. Not two weeks prior Darcy had corrected both Charles and Caroline in a matter of misrepresentation of his character. Here, and now, sat a precocious woman who, in the span of a few weeks, had made an adept observation of him.

Conversation turned to the local society and the youngest Bennets soon convinced Charles to hold a ball at Netherfield. Charles, of course, excitedly agreed and stipulated only that Miss Bennet be healthy before such an event was to take place. The young Bennets agreed wholeheartedly, and with enthusiasm showing more an excitement for the ball than the health of a sister.

Mrs. Bennet soon departed with her two youngest daughters and Elizabeth immediately returned to Jane's bedside. Darcy watched Elizabeth leave and admired her loyalty.

"I find Mrs. Bennet to be a most loud and opinionated woman. Her daughter Elizabeth seems determined to follow her lead; if not in volume, then in irritating inclinations."

Darcy refrained from commenting on Caroline's witticism; however Louisa saw no such occasion to refrain.

"Indeed. Mrs. Bennet appears to be overly opinionated on many topics and overly fond of praising her daughter, Jane. I will forgive her the second annoyance as Jane is a pleasant lady."

"My word you ladies are overly judgmental!" cried Charles. "I found the whole family to be lively and entertaining."

"Entertaining may be a strong description of interacting with them. I daresay, Mr. Darcy, Miss Elizabeth seems to take particular pleasure in vexing you. Perhaps those 'fine eyes' will eventually grow tiresome to you."

Darcy chose not to engage Caroline in this line of conversation. Years of exposure had taught him that responding in any manner would only lead to a longer conversation; although years of exposure to Darcy had not taught Caroline of his distaste for individual censure.

Continuing as if Darcy were actively engaged in the conversation, Caroline commented on the color of Miss Elizabeth's eyes, comparing them to the brightness of the local flowers. The cynicism of her comments did not escape Darcy. Unknown to Caroline, the intended insults had the opposite affect; as Darcy engaged his mind in the pleasant contemplation of Elizabeth's eyes and the local flora.

Chapter 10

Day turned into evening and, as with the day before, the primary occupants of the house found themselves in the drawing room. Elizabeth contented herself with needlework, while Charles and Mr. Hurst played cards. The Bingley sisters amused themselves by watching the other occupants and commenting on their activities. Caroline became increasingly annoying to Darcy who at this moment was fastidious in letter writing.

My Dearest Aunt,

As you have already been informed, my business dealings in this part of the country were concluded in a most satisfactory manner. Please inform the ladies of Sussex how much I appreciate their insights. I found their assessment of the local culture and countryside to be as described.

Business in general proceeded efficiently and I trust the lawyers in London will properly address the matters of fund dispersal as well as restitution required for the parties involved.

The follow up assessment to our dealings is most pleasing. I find no further need for involvement or any untoward sign of distress. I should regard all dealings closed and the entire matter to be at rest. This will conclude my personal involvement with regards to this endeavor.

Fitzwilliam Darcy

“You write with such a beautiful hand Mr. Darcy,” Caroline commented. “I often wish my writing were as graceful.”

After addressing the letter and setting it aside Darcy proceeded to read a letter from a stack of business papers; all the while ignoring Caroline’s attempt to flatter. Her notice of his handwriting in the letter was of no concern to Darcy. He correctly surmised Caroline had not read the letter in its entirety or any significant part. If she had made the actual attempt she would have found little useful information for someone of her intellect.

Placing his reading aside Darcy drew a fresh sheet of paper; and with careful deliberation set his mind to more pleasant thoughts as he began to write.

Dearest Georgiana

The countryside at the moment is pleasant, and I can admit for wanting little except the gaiety of your presence. Business proceeds in an efficient manner and you may rest assured my mental constitution is strong.

…………

Caroline found need to interrupt Darcy again as he wrote.

``Pray tell your sister that I long to see her."

‘`I have already told her so once, by your desire."

``I am afraid you do not like your pen. Let me mend it for you. I mend pens remarkably well."

``Thank you, but I always mend my own."

``How can you contrive to write so even?"

He was silent. This time his silence did not serve as an end to the conversation and Caroline continued in a mundane fashion. It was not until Elizabeth conjectured an opinion on the humility of Charles Bingley that Darcy was able to take a serious interest in conversing.

``Nothing is more deceitful," said Darcy, ``than the appearance of humility. It is often only carelessness of opinion, and sometimes an indirect boast."

This statement set in motion another pleasant argument between Elizabeth and Darcy. Elizabeth commented on the loyalty and character of friendship while Darcy conjectured on the quality. Poor Charles found himself in the middle and while the two combatants seemed pleased with their actions Charles was left to attend to himself.

In the end Charles was left with exasperation and stated an unintentional censure of Darcy. Elizabeth made to laugh, but upon seeing the comments affect as a criticism rather than a jest, stifled her visceral reply. Darcy took the criticism in kind and gave Elizabeth a slight nod as a token of appreciation for her social wherewithal to restrain her reaction.

It was decided to end the argument for the sake of Charles; and upon Elizabeth's general suggestion, Darcy returned to his letter. This task was now more pleasing; being that it could be completed without Caroline's previous interruptions.

Within a few minutes the room stood quiet and Darcy finished his letter quickly. Content with his work he entreated Louisa and Caroline to perform musically. Taking the opportunity of the music Darcy moved to Elizabeth and uncharacteristically asked her to dance. At first she was silent, and upon a re-iteration of the request smiled coyly and politely declined.

Elizabeth, having rather expected to affront him, was amazed at his gallantry; but there was a mixture of sweetness and archness in her manner which made it difficult for her to affront anybody; and Darcy had never been so bewitched by any woman as he was by her. He really believed, that were it not for the inferiority of her connections, he should be in some danger.

"Is there some manner in which I currently amuse you Miss Bennet?" Darcy asked as he had noticed her eyes widen in their previous conversation.

"Amuse? Not at the moment Mr. Darcy. I am currently analyzing your character and find it more intricate than that of Mr. Bingley."

"You are attempting to reach a conclusion regarding my character?"

"As you say. I am not amused by you in any particular manner, but I do amuse myself by classifying individuals into their proper categories."

"This could be a dangerous pastime. Many people are not so easily categorized and a single error in judgment could lead to catastrophic results."

"Catastrophic you say! In regards to balls and social etiquette? I would use the word injurious. You seem to delight in espousing the most dire attributes to the human race."

"In matters of social graces you may be found to be correct in a majority of cases; but within even the most hallowed social circles a disease of malice may appear. I only suggest that categorizing people may lead to missing a serious character flaw."

"While I understand your comments, and their underlying beliefs, I will allay your concerns. I notice a great many things and believe the underlying character of an individual is readily apparent. In this assessment I am rarely surprised."

Caroline watched from across the room as Darcy and Elizabeth conversed. She saw enough of the interactions between the two to become jealous. Within her logical mind, she told herself there was little about which to worry. Miss Elizabeth's familial connections were too scant to entice Mr. Darcy; quite the contrary, the connections would be reason enough to quite any thought of marriage.

These logical thoughts from premise to conclusion were within the intellectual grasp of Caroline, but her emotional state did not allow for their full understanding. Thus she continued her teasing well into the evening and the next day, commenting on how well Darcy would enjoy his new mother-in-law or how lovely a family portrait would look hanging on a wall at Pemberley.

Darcy spent that next day avoiding Caroline when he could. While he found her initial teasing annoying, the increasing volume of comments began to show an aspect of meanness; and, while Darcy did not agree with the motivation behind the comments, he was forced to agree with the logical conclusion regarding the low status of the Bennet household.

Chapter 11

From a second floor window Darcy watched the carriage remove Jane Bennet and Elizabeth from Netherfield. In many regards he was happy to see the sisters leave. Jane had recovered and he deemed the consequences of his stupidity in regards to the tea were well and over.

As to the matter of Elizabeth, he found her too alluring and enchanting for his logical mind. Caroline's incessant teasing, which had become annoying, would now end, and indeed her manners towards Elizabeth increased with rapidity as the carriage prepared to take them away.

Darcy's mind cast back to the previous night in which he and Elizabeth arrived at a darker impasse in argumentation. Caroline, as usual, attempted to precipitate a conversation revealing another perceived flaw in Elizabeth. Aware of Elizabeth's interest in people she asked for the assessment of Mr. Darcy.

``Your examination of Mr. Darcy is over, I presume," said Miss Bingley; ``and pray what is the result?"

``I am perfectly convinced by it that Mr. Darcy has no defect. He owns it himself without disguise."

Darcy suspected this answer to be an attempt in distracting Caroline from her intended task. He nodded politely but with a sincere interest in Elizabeth's observations he responded boldly.

``No" -said Darcy, ``I have made no such pretension. I have faults enough, but they are not, I hope, of understanding. My temper I dare not vouch for. It is I believe too little yielding, certainly too little for the convenience of the world. I cannot forget the follies and vices of others so soon as I ought, nor their offences against myself. My feelings are not puffed about with every attempt to move them. My temper would perhaps be called resentful. -- My good opinion once lost is lost for ever."

``*That* is a failing indeed!" cried Elizabeth. ``Implacable resentment *is* a shade in a character. But you have chosen your fault well. I really cannot *laugh* at it; you are safe from me."

``There is, I believe, in every disposition a tendency to some particular evil, a natural defect, which not even the best education can overcome."

``And *your* defect is a propensity to hate every body."

``And yours," he replied with a smile, ``is willfully to misunderstand them."

Realizing she had lost control of the conversation, Miss Bingley cried for music. Louisa soon joined and the evening ended more joyfully.

Now, as Darcy watched the carriage depart Netherfield, he thought about Elizabeth and her beliefs. Leaning forward he placed his hand on the glass as if it would grant him the touch of her face.

``There is, I believe, in every disposition a tendency to some particular evil, a natural defect, which not even the best education can overcome.''

“Perhaps one day you may encounter that evil. I pray you are prepared for it.”

Darcy turned to leave, took a few steps, and then turned back to the window; the carriage was now out of sight. He gazed for a minute with an expressionless face. Caught between peaceful contemplation, and disbelief of the last few days, he came back to his senses and quickly left the room.

Chapter 12

Within a few days time Charles set it upon himself to visit Longbourn and inquire as to the health of Miss Bennet. The suggestion of sending a letter requiring a response was not to be entertained by Charles; and, in a mood of solemn acceptance, Darcy agreed to ride with Charles.

The thought of seeing Elizabeth peaked Darcy's interest, but the passage of a few days time had lessened her appeal in Darcy's mind. He was not disposed to reverse the effect.

The ride into town was pleasant enough, and Bingley and Darcy fell into easy conversation. The former conversed mainly about Miss Bennet and the latter tolerated the topic. The sway of Miss Bennet on Bingley was becoming apparent to Darcy, and concern arose in regards to the Bennet lineage.

The logical detractors Darcy held for Elizabeth held just as firmly for Jane Bennet. This fact, coupled with Darcy's inobservance of a particular affinity by Miss Jane Bennet, were reason for Darcy to worry on Bingley.

"Charles, you seem presupposed to ascribe feelings to a lady for which you are not well acquainted. I wish you would tread more carefully in matters of the heart."

"Would you have me sit home all day and read letters or dispatch orders as you do? I say, Darcy, I want to live a little and enjoy the pleasantries of life; and I find Miss Bennet to be one of the most pleasant things in my life at the moment."

"You are making that fact clear to many an individual; however, I do not see her offering a reciprocal reaction. I merely wish to caution you on putting forth emotions which may not be met with equal regard."

"Shall I forego all society and restrict myself to business matters such as yours?"

Darcy's horse whinnied and bolted for a second. Quickly reigning the beast, Darcy replied to his friend.

"If I were to choose between the present social situation and business of my nature then I would wish you all the fanciful girls you could desire," Darcy said with a smile.

Bingley, knowing full well that Darcy's business dealings were much more intricate than his, let the matter drop. Darcy on the other hand, looked at his friend and truly wished him a happy life, free from some of the horrors familiar to Darcy House.

On the way to Longbourn the two rode, as they must, through Meryton. Engrossed as they were in conversation, they came across Miss Elizabeth Bennet and a few of her sisters. The small group was gathered near the center of the road engaged in conversation with two gentlemen.

Charles took the opportunity to approach without caution and partake in immediate conversation; revealing his intent to visit with Jane. Darcy nodded politely to Elizabeth who in turn gave a non-committal reply.

The gentleman, of whom the ladies were conversing, turned their attention to the men arriving on horseback; it was a simultaneous realization of the acquaintance. Before Mr. Darcy stood Lt. Denny whom he had met just a week prior. That fact was overshadowed by the recognition of the second gentleman.

Darcy's face turned red as George Wickham's paled. This reaction did not go as unnoticed by Elizabeth as it did by other members of the party. The fear attacking Mr. Wickham's mind recoiled him mentally, but he soon gained composure and was able to maintain a semblance of normality.

Wickham, having grown up in the same household as Darcy, was well aware of the darker side of the family. Charles Bingley enjoyed the company of Mr. Darcy but remained pleasantly ignorant regarding some of the more objectionable business the family attended; not so for George Wickham.

The late Mr. Darcy, Fitzwilliam Darcy's father, was Godfather to George Wickham. It was his intention for George to work closely with the family and assist in many business dealings. With the passing of Mr. Darcy, George Wickham turned to more pleasurable pursuits, relying on his childhood friend, the current Mr. Darcy, for financial support.

This tactic did not play as well as Wickham supposed it would. One troubling matter after another ensued; until Wickham found himself in a predicament that Darcy found unforgivable. Wickham's saving grace was Darcy's sense of honour and pride. *Nobless oblige*.

George Wickham was familiar with the term and its obligations. He was also familiar where the obligations of the Darcy family began and ended.

While his youthful follies were an annoyance, and an embarrassment to Darcy, they were not within the realm of serious trespass; and for this reason Darcy would not employ the powers at his disposal.

This knowledge allowed Wickham freedom within society to the extent that his good manners and pleasant personality allowed. In many ways he was a counterpointe to Darcy. Where Darcy showed conservation and restraint, Wickham showed disregard; moving with ease and recommending himself to ladies and gentlemen of any rank. The ease and grace of his smile, his flair for flattering remarks, and a seemingly pleasant personality, worked well within society.

Had Wickham attempted these schemes years before, he would have met with more challenging obstacles. As it happened, recent wars and rapid changes in nobility across Europe allowed for a larger crack in society, whereby the odd serpent could slither. Wickham used this weakness in upper society for his personal gain and personal pleasure.

It was not until evening and the return to Netherfield that Darcy allowed himself to seriously contemplate the arrival of Wickham. Sitting in the drawing room, he wrote several letters to be dispatched immediately. To the ladies of Sussex he inquired as to Wickham's most recent exploits. The emissaries in London, as well as the attorneys, were prevailed upon for similar reports and to his dear friend Colonel Fitzwilliam a request for information regarding Wickham's possibilities of a commission in the ranks.

Darcy did not relish the idea of Wickham purchasing a commission. Although he could scarcely believe the man possessed the required funds, he did believe Wickham possessed the needed charm to obtain the funds.

Darker thoughts came to mind as Darcy brooded in the drawing room. The site of Miss Elizabeth with Wickham provoked unsettling emotions. Darcy trusted the motivation of Miss Bennet to analyze character, but he questioned her skills to arrive at correct conclusions.

Wickham was artful with his craft and should he prevail upon any of the Bennets they might be the worse for it. Knowing Wickham as he did, Darcy hoped the man would realize the limited means of the local families and choose to locate himself elsewhere.

Chapter 13

Netherfield was lighted with gaiety and a good many candles on the evening the Bingleys chose to hold their ball. In attendance were many of the local families as well as a good portion of the officers from the local militia.

The music was lively and conversation was abundant as preparations were made to begin the dancing portion of the evening. The arrival of the Bennets stirred Charles to pry himself from conversation and attend to Jane. He inquired as to her health and, learning she was well, stated he was overjoyed to hear the good news.

Miss Elizabeth and her sisters immediately took to conversing with the officers and upon the conclusion of one such conversation Mr. Darcy approached Miss Elizabeth.

"Pleasant evening for a ball I should imagine. I trust you are doing well Miss Bennet?"

"I am well, as you say; and I too find the evening adequate for a ball."

The coldness of her reply did not escape Darcy's attention.

"It is pleasing to see your sister is well. Has she fully recovered from her tortuous ordeal?"

"My sister's health is a private matter for which she is better suited to answer than I; she is now, as you see her."

Elizabeth nodded towards Jane, demonstrating that the health of her sister was available for anyone who chose to gaze upon her. Darcy bowed in a polite manner and without a word departed Elizabeth's company.

Retreating to social circles that he was more comfortable with, Darcy watched Elizabeth periodically. Her cold demeanor appeared to remain for several minutes and darkened as she took to the floor for the first of the dances.

She did not stand up with any gentleman of Darcy's acquaintance. This gentleman appeared unsophisticated in mannerism and less than adept at dance. Rather than confidence with his motions he substituted an apologetic air and a tendency to perform incorrect maneuvers. Darcy could well understand Elizabeth's cold demeanor if she were obligated to dance with this individual.

Elizabeth's mood increased greatly with the completion of the first two dances and with her obligation to her partner fulfilled. The officers whom she then danced with lightened her spirit, and her conversation with the ladies appeared intense and motivated.

Deeming this to be a more apt time for conversation, Darcy crossed the room again and enticed Miss Elizabeth for a dance upon the resumption of the activity. Elizabeth appeared off guard and agreed to the dance, more out of habit and graciousness than of any reflective thought.

Returning to his former position in the room, Darcy contemplated once again on the cold attitude of Miss Bennet. His thoughts were assisted in reasoning as Charles approached him.

"Darcy, I have just had the most unusual conversation with Miss Jane Bennet, followed by another with my sister. Miss Bennet questioned me regarding the relationship between you and George Wickham. She was of the opinion that Wickham is an amiable chap and well liked among the community. I could not support the opinion and remarked as much, mentioning only that he is not a respectable gentleman to my understanding."

"Oh."

"Yes. Shortly after this conversation, Caroline approached me with news of Miss Elizabeth's inquiries as to Wickham's location tonight. She is not well pleased as regards his absence; young Lt. Denny took it upon himself to inform various parties that the absence of Mr. Wickham is in deference to your strictures."

Casting about the room, Darcy found the Lieutenant engaged in an animated conversation with several ladies and fellow officers. He held little malice towards the young man whom he had beaten readily at arms; however, malice aside, Darcy could find little about the lieutenant to recommend. His manners seemed overly forward and he displayed a propensity to boast. This, thought Darcy, will lend his character well suited to Wickham's.

A bell sounded announcing the beginning of the next dance and Darcy returned to claim his partner; albeit in a much sterner mood. The dance began and Darcy refrained from a more pleasant tone of conversation. To her credit Miss Bennet made an attempt at civil conversation to which Darcy was kind but short in reply. After a pause of some minutes, she addressed him a second time.

``It is *your* turn to say something now, Mr. Darcy. *I* talked about the dance, and *you* ought to make some kind of remark on the size of the room, or the number of couples."

He smiled, and assured her that whatever she wished him to say should be said.

``Very well. That reply will do for the present. Perhaps by and by I may observe that private balls are much pleasanter than public ones, but *now* we may be silent."

``Do you talk by rule then, while you are dancing?"

``Sometimes. One must speak a little, you know. It would look odd to be entirely silent for half an hour together, and yet for the advantage of *some*, conversation ought to be so arranged as that they may have the trouble of saying as little as possible."

``Are you consulting your own feelings in the present case, or do you imagine that you are gratifying mine?"

``Both," replied Elizabeth archly; ``for I have always seen a great similarity in the turn of our minds. We are each of an unsocial, taciturn disposition, unwilling to speak, unless we expect to say something that will amaze the whole room, and be handed down to posterity with all the eclat of a proverb."

``This is no very striking resemblance of your own character, I am sure," said he. ``How near it may be to *mine*, I cannot pretend to say. *You* think it a faithful portrait undoubtedly."

``I must not decide on my own performance."

He made no answer, and they were again silent till they had gone down the dance, when he asked her if she and her sisters did not very often walk to Meryton. She answered in the affirmative, and, unable to resist the temptation, added, ``When you met us there the other day, we had just been forming a new acquaintance."

The effect was immediate. A deeper shade of hauteur overspread his features, but he said not a word, and Elizabeth, though blaming herself for her own weakness, could not go on. At length Darcy spoke, and in a constrained manner said,

``Mr. Wickham is blessed with such happy manners as may ensure his *making* friends, whether he may be equally capable of *retaining* them, is less certain."

``He has been so unlucky as to lose *your* friendship," replied Elizabeth with emphasis, ``and in a manner which he is likely to suffer from all his life."

Darcy made no answer, and seemed desirous of changing the subject. At that moment Sir William Lucas appeared close to them, meaning to pass through the set to the other side of the room; but on perceiving Mr. Darcy he stopped with a bow of superior courtesy, to compliment him on his dancing and his partner.

``I have been most highly gratified indeed, my dear Sir. Such very superior dancing is not often seen. It is evident that you belong to the first circles. Allow me to say, however, that your fair partner does not disgrace you, and that I must hope to have this pleasure often repeated, especially when a certain desirable event, my dear Miss Eliza (glancing at her sister and Bingley), shall take place. What congratulations will then flow in! I appeal to Mr. Darcy: -- but let me not interrupt you, Sir. -- You will not thank me for detaining you from the bewitching converse of that young lady, whose bright eyes are also upbraiding me."

The latter part of this address was scarcely, heard by Darcy; but Sir William's allusion to his friend seemed to strike him forcibly, and his eyes were directed with a very serious expression towards Bingley and Jane, who were dancing together. Recovering himself, however, shortly, he turned to his partner, and said,

``Sir William's interruption has made me forget what we were talking of."

``I do not think we were speaking at all. Sir William could not have interrupted any two people in the room who had less to say for themselves. -- We have tried two or three subjects already without success, and what we are to talk of next I cannot imagine."

``What think you of books?" said he, smiling.

``Books? Oh! no. I am sure we never read the same, or not with the same feelings."

``I am sorry you think so; but if that be the case, there can at least be no want of subject. -- We may compare our different opinions."

``No, I cannot talk of books in a ball-room; my head is always full of something else."

``The *present* always occupies you in such scenes does it?" said he, with a look of doubt.

``Yes, always," she replied, without knowing what she said, for her thoughts had wandered far from the subject, as soon afterwards appeared by her suddenly exclaiming,

``I remember hearing you once say, Mr. Darcy, that you hardly ever forgave, that your resentment once created was unappeasable. You are very cautious, I suppose, as to its *being created*."

``I am," said he, with a firm voice.

"And never allow yourself to be blinded by prejudice?"

``I hope not."

``It is particularly incumbent on those who never change their opinion, to be secure of judging properly at first."

``May I ask to what these questions tend?"

``Merely to the illustration of *your* character," said she, endeavoring to shake off her gravity. ``I am trying to make it out."

``And what is your success?"

She shook her head. ``I do not get on at all. I hear such different accounts of you as puzzle me exceedingly."

``I can readily believe," answered he gravely, ``that report may vary greatly with respect to me; and I could wish, Miss Bennet, that you were not to sketch my character at the present moment, as there is reason to fear that the performance would reflect no credit on either."

``But if I do not take your likeness now, I may never have another opportunity."

``I would by no means suspend any pleasure of yours," he coldly replied. She said no more, and they went down the other dance and parted in silence; on each side dissatisfied, though not to an equal degree, for in Darcy's breast there was a tolerable powerful feeling towards her, which soon procured her pardon, and directed all his anger against another.

It was not often Darcy would feel a rage such as he felt this moment. Were Wickham in attendance this evening he might well be receptive to a boxed ear. Calming himself as he knew he must, Darcy engaged in conversation with Louisa and Mr. Hurst.

Shortly Darcy was accosted by the odd gentlemen who previously stood up with Elizabeth at the outset of the ball.

"You are Mr. Darcy I believe. Please accept my apology for being forward with introductions. I am Mr. Collins."

Darcy scrutinized the odd gentlemen with an interested and confused eye. Mr. Collins appeared to be of little breeding, poor stature, and poorer manners. The forward and unannounced introduction accosting Darcy could only be responded to with a curt nod of acknowledgment; not to the receptiveness of the introduction, but to the understanding of the information provided.

"I have recently taken residence at Hunsford as the Reverend for Rosings Park and your aunt, the ever gracious Lady Catherine de Bourgh."

Mr. Collins lowly demeanor became pronounced as he continued to converse in matters of flattery regarding Darcy's family. Darcy, for his part, stood in wonder of the little man and searched his memory for reports of this appointment.

The previous appointment was held by a respectable man of the clergy, and one in which great trust could be bestowed. For all the secrets his aunt could claim access too, Darcy wondered as to her clarity of mind in assigning the post to this individual. Perhaps he would pull the intelligence reports regarding local post assignments.

Mr. Collins continued to display his lack of breeding and manners, allowing only a brief interlude for Mr. Darcy to comment. Being in a state of wonder, the latter could only reply in a polite, curt manner.

Vexation seized Darcy and he determined to discuss the matter of Mr. Collins with his aunt. He could only conjecture that her desire to inject herself in matters well beyond her responsibility had overshadowed good sense.

At the conclusion of the conversation the following information was clear to Darcy. Mr. Collins was recently released from rectory and found a favorable patroness in Lady Catherine de Bourgh, Darcy's aunt. As the fates ordained, Mr. Collins was cousin and heir apparent to the Bennet family and estate of Longbourn, respectively. It was his intent, at this juncture of his life, to seek a wife and repair with rapidity the social ills between the Collinses and the Bennets; the source of which were matters of inheritance and family squabbles which Mr. Collins repeatedly assured belonged to a prior generation.

After much repetitive banter and apologies, Mr. Collins withdrew from Mr. Darcy. Darcy watched the man leave and noted that Mr. Collins was well pleased with himself.

An interesting gentleman to be sure, surmised Darcy; perhaps fine for a minister position in many a small village, but Mr. Collins effeminate demeanor and propensity to talk did not suit a position so close to Rosings Park. Darcy spent the rest of the evening in contemplation of the events that had recently transpired, eventually deciding he could endure little more in the way of surprises.

Chapter 14

The arrival of early morning letters sent the household of Netherfield into a series of activities. Shortly after breakfast, both Mr. Darcy and Mr. Bingley received letters of import. Retiring to the drawing room, the men sat in quiet contemplation of their materials.

Mr. Bingley's letter was dispatched from his solicitor and regarded London holdings which were in the midst of financial change. While the matter could be settled by correspondence, and within the legal authority appointed to the solicitor, Mr. Bingley's input was sorely needed. The letter then attached the needed documentation and requests for an immediate decision.

Darcy's letter was graver and required little contemplation on his part. The letter itself was short and, to any prying eyes, fairly meaningless. Addressed to Mr. Fitzwilliam Darcy, the letter mentioned a matter of serious business dealings requiring his immediate presence in London. The sensitivity of the dealings required no mention of them in writing and begged for Mr. Darcy's indulgence on the matter. As a matter of apology, the author offered a relaxing evening at White's; the letter was signed simply and non-descript.

The mention of White's in a letter of this style informed Mr. Darcy of the seriousness of the matter; no mention of details were required.

"And what evil preys upon us, those that claim the superiority of breeding and intellect?" He mused to himself.

Glancing up, Darcy watched Charles pouring over his paperwork as he flipped from one page to another. He scratched his head in irritation and then resumed to flip pages. Darcy had set his mind to vacate immediately, but Charles actions gave him pause.

"You seem distressed Charles."

"It's these damned papers. I cannot make any understanding of them. I read the words and understand they are written in English, but for all my intellect I would swear they are in French. I cannot fathom the meaning of them. Would you be so kind as to educate me on the meaning of their content?"

"I wish I could, but time will not allow. My letter contains matters which much be addressed immediately in London. I must apologize and make my departure. "

"Splendid! My letter deals with matters in London as well. While I am not required to present myself I could make the journey with you, study the material, and deliver my decision; all more efficiently than remaining here. I could also trespass upon your knowledge of business during the journey; if you would be so kind as to allow it."

Darcy agreed the idea had merit and the next hour witnessed the men of the manor in a flurry of activity packing and calling for the carriage. The ladies were consoled and Mr. Hurst, who found little of interest in the activities, spent time in his usual manner, relaxing.

As the bags were stowed, farewells were made, and Bingley took time to remember his senses. He begged Caroline to take a minute and dispatch a letter to Miss Bennet informing her of his business in London; which would hopefully conclude in three or four days. Caroline readily agreed to her brother's wishes.

Finding a moment of privacy amongst the individuals and their activities, Caroline approached Mr. Darcy.

"And should we expect your return to coincide with my brothers?" Caroline asked with a coy smile.

Mr. Darcy fastened his case to the carriage and tightened a strap with determined force.

"I should not expect an immediate return if I were you. My business will most assuredly require personal attention for an unspecified amount of time."

The elongated absence of Mr. Darcy was a dreadful thought for Caroline and interfered with her predetermined goal of finding the two of them in a more intimate relationship. It was then she decided that more cunning methods would need to be employed to secure her desired end.

"Perhaps it is best that Charles stay with you in London. We can certainly manage here for the moment, and should Charles' business prove unprogressive we may join you in London. I would venture the culture of the city will alleviate our senses of the ill effects this countryside seems to have inflicted."

Darcy answered nothing to this comment; being focused on his packing and little on conversation. Caroline, however, was more intent on Mr. Darcy and relieving his romantic thoughts on the beguiling Miss Elizabeth. She wondered to herself; perhaps there was opportunity in this turn of events. It was at this point that she determined to follow the men and insure they remained in London.

The hours wound and the wheels turned, propelling the two gentlemen toward London and business dealings for which they could only guess the outcome. As Darcy could do nothing in regards to his business, the men were engaged in the act of financial interpretation. The documents strewn about the carriage may appear a foreign tongue to Charles Bingley, but Darcy found them straightforward. He was happy for the mental exercise of standard business dealings, as it secured his mind from the darker contemplations that his letter conjured. With the settling of Mr. Bingley's matters came the settling of his mind as well.

"I shall miss the countryside," Bingley said as he gazed longingly out the window.

"I would conjecture you are pining over the absence of Miss Bennet more than the absence of trees."

"And what of it? I find Miss Bennet to be an enthralling lady."

Darcy could not deny the fact that Miss Bennet had indeed enthralled Mr. Bingley and commented as much. To which he added the following line of questioning.

"Can you specify a particular line of conversation that you may declare Miss Bennet to possess a particular affinity for you?"

"Of course I can. Just the other night, while dancing, she commented on my attire and believed I wore it most flatteringly."

To this, Darcy raised a stern eye.

"I should say the comment says as much about your clothes as it does about you."

"Darcy you must be the most obstinate man. How do you progress with such an indelicate opinion of circumstances?"

"I merely see life as it is and read no more, no more less, than the situation warrants. My concern regarding you and Miss Bennet is not in the sincerity of your emotions but in the sincerity of hers. I will readily agree she is a charming lady, but, in this regard, she is charming to everyone. Her mood is pleasant, her features pleasing, and a smile is ever present upon her face. When pressed for an example of personal affinity you offer a comment regarding clothing. By that token, I must imagine Miss Bennet to possess a personal affinity for many individuals."

"You do not think she cares for me?" asked Charles with a subdued sense of character, as of one contemplating an idea not before considered.

"Again, I cannot attest to facts I do not have. I can only state I have not personally seen any particular affinity towards you; nor can you, from what I deduce."

Charles slunk into the back of the carriage seat and his posture took a more solemn composure. Darcy did not envy his friend the emotional state that he now found himself in. To Darcy's credit he believed wholly in his assessment of Miss Bennet. She was indeed a pleasant and charming lady, complete with kindness of character; wanting only for a better familial lineage and conviction of emotion to Charles.

Typically Darcy would prefer to ride in silence; a journey of twenty four miles such as this could be pleasantly passed with the consideration of many fine thoughts. However, today he found the current state of affairs to be less than positive, and the silence of his friend, in painful contemplation, to be harrying.

Chapter 15

Shortly after the arrival in London, Bingley and Darcy separated to their respective accommodations. Bingley to his London Town home, and Darcy to his family's long time residence; Darcy House.

Dinner at Darcy House consisted of bread, meat, and little else. Darcy ate his meal in an offhanded manner as he was most engaged by the documents upon his desk; of which he had spent the last several hours analyzing. His mood grew grim as he scribbled notes and consulted texts.

Post dinner witnessed a solemn Darcy in deep thought. The fire upon the hearth was warm, and the glass of port to his right remained untouched. Searching about, his eyes darted from one parchment of information to another which he had tacked in strategic places about the room. In a flash of insight, he stood up, reached his desk, and began to dispatch letters. Each letter was carefully crafted, polite, and to the point. After each was finished, he called to his attendant for immediate dispatch.

Late into the night the dispatches were sent, and his family's faithful attendants took each letter in turn, aware the master of the house was fulfilling a duty the House Darcy was honoured to hold. Between writings, Darcy would consult the copious amount of reports, make notes of his own, and then proceed to his next dispatch. By midnight he was very tired and his eyes strained. Sleep was a minor thought and not to be had as the household attendants returned with answers to some of Darcy's dispatches.

The rapidity of the responses pleased and alarmed Darcy. He was happy with the quick replies but realized the serious nature of the current situation called for nothing else. His realization seemed to be shared with other individuals involved.

It was not until after the hour of three in the morning that Darcy was able to rest his head. The solitude of his house was comforting, and the staff so accommodating, that Darcy was not aware of his bed being turned down, the fire of his room being stoked, and the lamps adjusted properly.

Morning arrived and Darcy was up, bathed, dressed and returned to his papers. More dispatches had arrived while he had slept and he devoured the information, all the while adding pertinent information to his notes. More letters were dispatched, and when Darcy took a moment to relax his mind, it remained on matters at hand. He stood by the window at midday and looked out upon the street. Across from the street could be witnessed children at play and many citizens engaged in business as usual.

As he looked out upon the slightly dreary day, the front door of his house opened and an attendant appeared. Darcy could just make out the figure standing below his window. With precision, one of the boys in the street, who had all the appearance of being thoroughly engaged in a game, ran to the house, took the message, and was off at a pace that pleased Darcy. It was not long before another lad entered the street at a similar pace, made a call upon the door of the house, delivered his letter, and joined in the games of the street.

Efficient, thought Darcy as he returned to his desk to await the letter his attendant would be delivering momentarily.

Chapter 16

"Good evening, Mr. Darcy, it is most pleasing to see you return to White's. May a gentleman relieve you of your coat?"

"Thank you Gottfried, but I shall keep my coat if it is all the same."

"As you wish. Please..."

Gottfried's 'please' was accompanied by his directing Darcy farther into the establishment and away from the entryway. On many occasions Darcy would enjoy the culture and relaxation of White's, but on this occasion he was to be denied that pleasure.

Making his way through the establishment he passed two gentlemen determined to best each other in an arm wrestling match and two more which appeared to be racing cockroaches. Ignoring both events, Darcy continued on and was forced to step aside as three men ran into the room, each with another gentleman perched upon his shoulders in what appeared to be a human horse race. Not to be simplistic in design, and in an attempt to honour White's tradition of surrealism, the upper men carried a spoon in each hand with eggs balancing in the bowls.

"Coming through, my good man! Make way. Make way," one of them could be heard declaring.

Passing into a back hallway, Darcy turned to the scene he was leaving. Viewing the camaraderie and fanciful fun, he placed his hand on the wall as if to caress the structure. White's was an establishment older than some of the families who now were privileged to be members. Rules were simple and gentlemanly; only aristocrats were allowed entry, and then only to the gentlemen. Beyond this, and a few more simplistic rules, lay a rule of sterner regulation. No business was allowed to transpire.

Watching the scene in the former room, Darcy seemed almost in a trance. Glancing at his hand upon the wall he muttered almost to himself but with no intention of addressing himself.

"Forgive me and those that enter tonight; for we must trespass upon your good nature and fine tradition."

Anyone overhearing might conjecture the phrase to be a prayer offered to God, but Darcy's intent was to appease his mind at committing a possible offense to the tradition of this great establishment.

Within minutes Darcy reached his intended room. Removing a key from his waistcoat he unlocked the door and entered. The room was already lit and occupied. Locking the door behind him, he took a position near the hearth, nodding to individuals as he passed. He could count emissaries, solicitors, two lords, a duke, an admiral, and other officers of varying rank; both from the army and the navy. Each officer could also be identified by some title or other, but Darcy wished to not confuse his mind with by remembering.

In the corner, at the outer edge of the light, sat two figures. Darcy noted them and their importance but decided not to acknowledge them in any fashion. If they chose to attend this meeting in such a fashion as to remain unobtrusive, then he would respect their wishes. It was a mark of honour and respect for an English gentleman to ignore such details.

A few minutes of silence, and a basic headcount, assured Darcy that the room consisted of the gentlemen he expected. The admiral spoke first.

"Mr. Darcy. We appreciate your presence. I will dispense with pleasantries as we may all assume that we are each of us well. I trust you have read your letters and at moment have a grasp of the situation."

"I believe I do, but let me reiterate in an attempt to clarify the situation in my mind and to allow you confirmation of my understanding."

The admiral nodded stoically.

"Lord Ackerby is now a concern within the ranks of the gentry, the military, and the nobility. Born a baronet, he decided to purchase a commission after completing his schooling from Oxford at a remarkably young age. His intelligence, along with his physical prowess, allowed him, these last several years, to engage in many successful military campaigns against Napolean. The details of those engagements are not within the reports I received. I can surmise the engagements were dangerous; and of a covert nature, as the war with Napolean has been primarily naval."

"You are correct," replied one of the naval officers. "While the missions themselves were kept secret I can attest to landing Ackerby more than once. He is a very capable man and in his time aboard naval vessels became adept at many matters of the sea. I am convinced, had he entered the navy, he would have commanded his own ship."

Darcy nodded. "I can surmise the actions employed the ruthless tactics learned from the war with the colonies, as well as the use of spies, sharp shooters, survival skills, and a propensity to achieve a mission with limited resources."

"Again you are correct. While he was too young for the war with the colonies, Ackerby is a very quick study and spent much time practicing many of those tactics."

"Making a name for himself," continued Darcy, "he advanced within the ranks by merit until he reached his current rank of Colonel. All told, he is an intelligent and very worthy military man."

"As you have said, not all of the details were in the letters. Allow me to clarify. Colonel Ackerby was also one of the men leading the idea for rifleman and light infantry. It was many of his tactics and ideas that led to our current use of that division in an effective manner. He is skilled in hand to hand combat, naval maneuvers, cavalry, artillery, and many other military aspects; perhaps not adept in each one, but manageable enough to command respect."

Another officer took a solemn turn to speak.

"Combining his skills with a commanding personality gave him respect among the soldiers. I fear this is part of our challenge."

"A challenge that would not exist if soldiers commanded a greater sense of honour," replied another.

"Enough!" said the Admiral. "The last decade has seen the British military increase in size by tenfold. The war with Napoleon has forced our position and required enlistment on a level never before implemented. This of course has led to recruitment of the less desirable. Let us not look to causes. Let us focus on the current situation and a means to solve it. Mr. Darcy, please continue."

Darcy nodded and did as requested.

"The current challenge consists of Colonel Ackerby's return to England. Skilled in the covert, and possessed with a military mindset, he is engaged in political and financial gains through the use of assassins, bribery, blackmail, and many other avenues which I am sure we are ignorant. His loyalty amongst his men, and ready access to discharged soldiers, has allowed him to build a network of intelligence and might. Over the past year the growth of that network has allowed it to come to our attention. Now we must deal with it."

Silence prevailed for a minute as the room seemed to take a minute for collective thought. Finally one of the Lords spoke.

"Mr. Darcy I believe this may fall into your particular venue and will require your personal touch."

"How do you mean?"

"I mean for you to meet with Ackerby and end his life."

"That would not be wise I believe," answered Darcy.

"Do you fear him that much?" asked the Lord with a bit of a derisive tone.

"Mr. Darcy fears very little," replied an Earl.

"That may, or may not be, but it is obvious that Ackerby must be killed, although I do not relish the idea of killing a Baron."

"As this occurs on British soil, and involving many of the commoners, I would suggest we involve London's sheriffs. The day and night forces could put an end to this ordeal once they are made aware." This last comment was suggested by an officer from across the room.

Darcy stepped forward to put a stop to the speculation before it digressed further.

"Gentlemen, we shall do none of this if it can be helped. I will address the situation and require only your loyalty and adherence to my orders in the process."

"Do not forget yourself Mr. Darcy. You are a gentlemen by wealth, but all of us our titled by birth. Take care how you address us."

Darcy turned to the speaker, a man for whom he had not met; although he was aware, by report, of the particular identity of everyone in the room. Addressing him by name and title, Darcy drew the man's full attention and spoke to the matter of titles and fealty.

"Beyond these walls we may address each other in accordance to our rank. That is a duty and an honour granted to those of similar nature. Btu, in this room your personal titles mean little to me other than the representation of the ideals for which they stand. In this room it is I who will command. It is my right, my duty, and by royal permission, my obligation. I should not need to inform you as to why these duties fall upon House Darcy."

“Darcy,” The Admiral said quietly and calmly, “your father served his families obligations well, as did his father. The family of Darcy was chosen wisely for these tasks and I believe you will surpass even their great deeds. You are a young man and more gifted than any of your lineage. I think on the dangers of Ackerby and take comfort in thinking he will confront a man of greater ability, with the backing of England’s Nobility, and with command of their resources. Please, tell us how you plan to proceed.”

Darcy nodded and moved to the opposite side of the hearth as he collected his thoughts. He knew he needed more intelligence, but the seeds of a plan were in his grasp. He must now show his command of the situation and move forward confidently. All of this was something for which he was eminently qualified to do.

“Ackerby cannot be killed in any direct manner. His military training and experience has allowed him to become paranoid, and he is currently protected by levels of men. Even in public he is careful, requiring any direct attempt on his life to involve a rifleman; but the prominent assassination of a gentleman of his stature would draw more attention than needed. Furthermore, the analysis of his organization demonstrates it is large enough to survive his death. The organization will assume a new leader. With the limited information we have, the leadership assumption by an unknown individual is an unpredictable scenario I do not wish to explore.” Darcy paused for reflective thought before continuing.

"As it stands we have no need to kill Ackerby at this moment. I will attack him and his organization with methods for which he possesses little experience. English nobility is familiar with the subtle, however, Ackerby is not; at least not to this extent. I shall steal his organization, remove Ackerby from the head, assimilate the parts that we can use, and then disband the remainder. When it is done, Ackerby will be subdued and his members will either be our members or quietly and efficiently released back to the society from which they came."

The room was silent as Darcy's bold plan took time to fully understand. Half of the gentleman were speechless at the idea and could see no reasonable method to implement such a plan. Eventually two figures arose from the corner of the room and headed for the door. The meeting thus concluded very simply, and the matter of planning was resolved.

Chapter 17

It was the beginning of December and Darcy had spent the last few weeks gathering information. The many channels at his disposal were strained with tasks of an enormity never before experienced. Darcy managed them all very well and as information arrived he masterfully developed his plan.

Subtlety was the key to Darcy's plan, which caused his dispatches to appear to be of the most unusual nature. One dispatch simply asked a messenger to inquire regarding a particular gentleman. Another regarded a newspaper notice of an untimely death in a family, and still another was a request to find an individual's mother; slowly across London the small ripples Darcy created eventually became waves to the powerful, but still fledgling Ackerby organization.

"Sgt Stills?"

"eh, what? Wo es it?" The smell of beer from the sot could almost make a man drunk.

Standing over Stills was a man in uniform. "You are Sergeant Stills and a chosen man are you not?"

"Piss off govrnr… I ain't chosen no more. Less you mean chosen to drink this beer," Stills laughed.

"Sgt. Stills. You are being recalled to active duty immediately. We are in need of your specific skills and your record shows you are one of the best men qualified. You are hereby promoted to Lieutenant and ordered to the Defiant which leaves port on the morrow."

“eh. Now you canna do that. I did my bit, I am outta his majesties army.”

“True, Lieutenant. But I am ordered to retrieve you if I can, and if so lieutenant, you are ordered to the Defiant.” The uniformed soldier looked at Stills and wondered what this man could possibly provide the army.

As Darcy predicted he would, Stills came to his senses for a moment and thought about the offer before him. A sense of pride rose in him regarding the offer and shame regarding his current life.

Subtlety was now about to cost Ackerby one of his best assassins and afford the British army the opportunity to reclaim a man who had shown remarkable promise during his military career.

Up until Christmas this scene played in one form or another. One man inherited a small piece of land in Scotland, another was somehow located by an angered husband and met an fitting end. Darcy played his pieces slowly but knew he would not be able to continually remove his opponent’s pieces from the game without eventual notice.

While Ackerby’s methods were messy, Darcy employed art. He used this art where he could and indirect exposure where he could not. London already possessed a criminal element that the nobility allowed the local authorities to keep in check. Darcy used that element as a front for his own ends, and whenever a direct encounter was unavoidable it was always a local thief or gang that took credit.

Upon discovering the blackmail of a local magistrate, Darcy used his connections to mislead the London dailies. Malicious stories were reported regarding the magistrate only to be retracted with evidence of their falseness. This happened to coincide with a trial the magistrate was presiding over; being in no mood to look the fool, the magistrate quickly found the defendant guilty. The defendant, and Ackerby, were surely surprised by this turn, but any attempt to further blackmail the judge would be ineffective, and any new rumours, true or not, would not be believed.

Finances were not left untouched, and it was in this arena Darcy flourished. Ackerby was born a baronet, and with family money he had purchased his commission where his military mind excelled, but finance proved to be the strong suit of Darcy.

Ackerby was wealthy and added to his wealth with his nefarious actions but often in inefficient ways. Where Darcy would have profited 100 pounds Ackerby would garner only 50. The real tragedy for Ackerby was his inability to perceive the conceptual loss.

Darcy watched the financials with interest and was amazed at how poor some of the decisions were. If it were not for the continual flow of ill gotten gains, Ackerby would certainly be in financial trouble.

Spread before Darcy were bank reports, all of which contained confidential information, but attainable to the individuals holding sway over the banks; and thus attainable to Darcy.

Piece by piece Darcy attacked the finances; a short sale here and an inflated price there. Darcy was well educated in the South Seas Trading crash of a century before. England had been brought to her knees from a buying craze of extreme speculation. The desire to suddenly become rich caused the entire nation to over purchase the stock of the South Seas Trading company, leading to almost certain ruin for the entire country.

Watching Ackerby's purchases of buildings and merchandise allowed Darcy to create a buying scenario specifically for Ackerby. An inflated piece of art, followed by overpriced property. The manipulation was rather easy for Darcy. Ackerby was of the belief that any illegally obtained government document must be of value and consist of the truth. Breaking into an office, or murdering a man for his satchel, would produce papers claiming this land or that building was of value. Darcy could easily manipulate that to his own ends.

Around this time Darcy was overjoyed with the visitation of his younger sister Georgiana. Business dealings of late were focused and well under way, allowing Darcy a moment to spend time with his beloved sibling.

The two of them spent the day talking and informing each other of recent events in their lives. Darcy's account of events was edited to an extreme degree and referenced business dealings that Georgiana would certainly find droll. Georgiana was held under no such restraint and was happy to talk about the past several months. Sitting quietly, Darcy reclined, smiled, and enjoyed the respite from the sinister nature of his dealings. Evening brought a visit from Charles and Caroline, who had been successful in her attempts to see Charles remain in London.

"My Dear Georgiana, how wonderful it is to see you again. You are becoming lovelier each time I see you. Do you not think so Charles?"

"Oh indeed, you are lovely Miss Darcy, and that dress is very handsome on you."

"Thank you," replied Georgiana with a smile and a look of pure joy.

"My darling brother purchased it for me since our last encounter. How he has time to think of me with all of his business I shall never know. He must be the most thoughtful brother."

"He is most generous," Caroline stated as she eyed Darcy. "He is also wickedly handsome. I imagine with those attributes he will have a wife and you shall have a sister soon enough."

Darcy ignored Caroline's reference to his becoming married and instead rolled his eyes and took a seat. Caroline, not content to end the matter, continued conversing with Georgiana on the subject of Darcy attending balls and endless ladies enticed by his status.

Conversation eventually turned to their time at Netherfield. In response to inquiries by young Miss Darcy, Caroline happily reported the culture of the land. This was done with appreciation of the countryside but an annoyance of the society.

"Miss Bennet was kind enough I would say; but as to the rest, I found them simple and not of the quality one encounters in the city. Your brother took an abnormal likening to the countenance of one of the ladies, but her manners and opinions soon dissuaded his affections."

“My dear brother, is this true? I should so like to hear about it.”

“Miss Bingley overestimates the bearing of the matter on my mental abilities. The lady in question I can assume is Miss Bennet’s younger sister Elizabeth. I found her to be most intelligent, well read, and with opinions of some merit.”

“But no great family connections!” cried Miss Bingley, “and for that she must be faulted greatly.”

Georgiana wished for more information and Caroline indulged the wish by relating stories of Miss Elizabeth walking to Netherfield and the constant bickering with Darcy.

To Darcy’s relief an attendant entered and announced the arrival of a letter. Darcy opened it while the ladies continued to talk. Finishing the letter he looked about the room at the ladies still in conversation and Charles looking on, with contented fascination. The letter itself was of some import in topic but more important in its arrival, in that it provided Darcy a possible reprieve from the current conversation.

“A matter has arisen for which I must personally attend. I will leave the three of you to dinner and shall return as soon as possible. Please enjoy yourselves.”

The ladies protested about his leaving in such a manner, but Darcy assured them he would return within a few hours; thus sated, the ladies fell back into conversation.

Chapter 18

The letter Darcy received contained intelligence regarding the possible coercion of a lord of parliament. Implications were that the lord would be led into an untenable situation. The public revelation would then be cause for embarrassment. Ackerby had used this tactic in previous encounters, usually with the aid of prostitutes.

Darcy found the letter afforded him the ability to leave a conversation he found irritating, while at the same time allowing him the ability to witness first hand an operation of Ackerby's. The details were vague, but the letter did state the plan would take place this evening.

The night air was chilled and the lamps of the streets cast their glow upon the pedestrians and carriages that past. Darcy himself leaned against a building with his garments held tight about his body and head. He scanned the area and found it an unusual place for prostitutes. Buildings on both sides of the street consisted mainly of business institutions with few residences in sight.

As each carriage and individual passed, Darcy studied them and allocated them to some portion of his analytical mind. Wives, husbands, and children were recognized and deemed harmless.

Eventually a man walked down the street in a drunken fashion. Darcy took a close look at him and judged him to be of particular interest. The gait appeared planned and not in character for someone truly intoxicated.

As he was playing the role of a witness tonight, with no intention of interfering, Darcy decided to investigate closer. He crossed the street and passed the potential drunkard in a slow fashion, all the time glancing at a letter he had pulled from his pocket. He made as to read it in the poor light, which was cause for him to slow and turn this way and that. The drunkard took some note but ignored him, belched, and trudged onward. Darcy took minimal visual notice as they passed, but his nose was keen and the close proximity allowed him to be certain there was no smell of alcohol.

A light on the building nearest them gave the appearance of serendipity to Darcy's false actions; Darcy then moved close to the light to examine his prop letter. The timing of the pass, and his move to this wall and vantage point, was by no means accidental. Appearing tired, the drunk himself stooped to the ground and appeared to rest as he leaned over in a ball against a wall.

It was not long before an opening door a few buildings down revived the drunkard. Darcy watched with interest as two gentlemen exited the building.

If one of those men is the lord in question then this timing is most odd, thought Darcy as he regarded the drunk's arrival and placement within minutes of this gentleman appearing on the scene. The two men began walking down the street towards Darcy and the drunk, until one of the men excused himself to return to the building. Not wanting to wait, the first man continued his journey.

The situation was clear to Darcy as a setup, and as the lord approached, Darcy recognized the man. Not being completely ignorant of politics, he recalled a major issue up for vote and the importance of this lord as to the outcome of that vote; with rapidity Darcy concluded this was not an attempt at coercion but one of assassination.

With little time to think Darcy moved forward. He gauged his approach and judged he would just make it. If he were to increase speed he might alert the assassin which would lead to a response of an unknown outcome; the worst being a rushed assassination with no time to prevent it.

The three men met almost simultaneous. The right hand of the drunk had been concealed in a fold of his jacket while he had been using his left hand as a pretense of needed balance. This led to a predictably of movement for which training could prepare.

As the right hand came free and the glint of steel shone in the light, Darcy approached from behind, grabbed the hand, and folded it back on the wrist, causing the knife to drop. The only individual not startled was Darcy, and he used his presence of mind to force the wrist further and put the man off balance. Not to waste the moment of surprise Darcy retrieved the knife while bringing the assassin to the ground. A quick motion, and the blade of the knife was now buried in the center of the chest.

The Lord standing nearby had stood agape at the situation and appeared unable to move. Darcy looked at him sternly and gave a slight nod.

"My Lord, perhaps you better accompany me to a more secure location."

Darcy did not wait for much of an answer as he guided the Lord through the street and eventually to a cabriolet he was able to flag down.

Assuring the Lord of his good intentions, Darcy directed the driver to the Lords house. Upon arrival, letters were quickly dispatched and, shortly thereafter, men of trust arrived to see to the lord's security.

The intense actions of the nights did not delay Darcy's return to his house, and he arrived home within his estimated few hours where he found the ladies and Charles now well dined. He considered retiring for the night, but his guests all begged for the company of their returned friend. Darcy, just happy to be home, conceded to their wishes. Within a few minutes he was pleased to learn the conversation had turned to matters he found more agreeable than the ones being discussed upon his departure.

Chapter 19

Holiday festivities led to a ball for which the Darcys and Bingleys were invited. Held at the London home of a member of the nobility, the party proved to be a grand and lively event. Caroline enjoyed her time and bounced between interactions, while Georgiana and Charles enjoyed a dance together.

"Mr. Darcy, It is well to see you again."

Darcy turned to the gentleman addressing him. "Yes, Lord Dache as I recall. I trust you are enjoying yourself."

"I am indeed. Please, allow me the honour of introducing my daughter, Marianne."

The woman Lord Dache motioned to was pleasing in appearance, mid- twenties, with dark reddish-brown hair and a polite but stern demeanor.

"Miss Dache," said Darcy with a slight bow to which she responded in kind.

"I wonder, Mr. Darcy, if you would be so kind as to entreat my daughter to a dance. I had promised her the next round, but my back has taken a sudden ache. I do not wish to deprive her of the expected frivolity."

Lord Dache was an individual for which Darcy held respect, and as the evening was festive he complied with the request.

The dance floor allowed for pleasant conversation to which Darcy would have preferred, rather than the more serious tone it eventually took. The entire conversation was treated by Miss Dache more as a business transaction than that of a dance.

"Do enjoy this time of year Mr. Darcy?"

Darcy noted her calm and quiet expression and responded in kind.

"It is enjoyable in its own right."

"I appreciate the time you are taking to attend to my feminine needs for minor enjoyments."

Darcy eyed his partner as they moved about the floor and could not decide if the opposition of her countenance and words were a comment on a hypocritical nature or if there might be a more subtle meaning. There was only one detail to which he could lay positive claim; she was not on the dance floor for enjoyment.

"I respect your father, and, while I usually decline from dancing, I saw fit to indulge him."

"I appreciate the honesty. I believe he respects you to a great extent as well. If he were to have his way he would see me installed in your household as Lady Darcy."

"An appointment that you do not seem thrilled to accept."

"I had my doubts at first, but recent events have allowed me to reconsider, should a proposal be offered," she paused before continuing. "You and I very nearly met a few nights back."

"Did we? I am unaware of the incident."

"You were engaged at the time with a Lord. I was in the vicinity conducting an errand. I noticed your involvement with the Lord, but you were both so rushed I was left to merely note the occasion and continue with my errand."

"Errands this time of year can be very harrowing. What kind of errand were you performing?"

"A delicate errand with regards to the Lord you were meeting. I was to meet with his assistant and sway his opinion on a matter."

The dance ended and the two left the floor still in conversation.

"Were you successful?"

"Circumstances were misjudged and the matter has been solved by other means. I will say; I did admire your attention to the Lord." Miss Dache bowed slightly and left.

The small amount of festive mood Darcy possessed was now gone and as the evening progressed he was little inclined to deal with the other dancers or merry makers. Lord Dache eventually made his way around the room and found himself within Darcy's vicinity.

"Lord Dache," said Darcy with a curt bow.

"Mr. Darcy, I would apologize for my daughter's abruptness in conversation. She can be forward in certain matters."

"I did not find her to be forward in any offensive manner. Although the prospect of marriage is not something I am currently considering."

This last statement brought the lord in closer as he dropped his voice.

"See here, Mr. Darcy. You and I are well aware of each other's positions in life. Your household will need a wife and heir. Your father, bless his soul, took care of those obligations at an early age. You would do well to consider marriage sooner rather than later and Marianne is a fine lady, well educated, and familiar with your particular role in society. I suggest you begin considering the idea of marriage." The lord gave Darcy a cross look and continued on his way around the room.

Surely the Lord meant for Darcy to consider marriage to his daughter; but his last statement allowed Darcy the leeway of considering marriage in general. At the moment his life was too harried to give it much thought, but he did think on the women in his life.

He had a fondness for Caroline, but he found her teasing and strictures of others to be a fault. His aunt, Lady Catherine de Bourgh, would happily see him married to her daughter; and now this Lord wished to see the same for his daughter. He found it slightly amusing that the only lady for which he felt any attraction was the only one he could not claim wished for marriage.

Watching the dances before him he remembered the last dance shared with Miss Elizabeth. It had not gone well; but the thought of her brought to mind other memories. He smiled as he recalled her pleasant mischievous nature as they sparred during conversation; he remembered her quick insight into his nature and the concern it caused him; he then worried over the influence of Wickham which led to their last disagreement.

For the moment the last matter would have to be left to its own devices, as more serious problems required his attention. Thinking on all of this, he did his best to engage with Charles and the rest of his party as the evening progressed and eventually concluded.

Chapter 20

Christmas came and went and into the New Year the Darcys and Bingleys spent much time together. Concern over his involvement in the failed assassination led Darcy to convince Charles to spend much time at Darcy House. Miss Dache's knowledge of his involvement made him realize how dangerous this game was becoming, and Georgiana's presence could be a matter for concern.

Darcy at first attempted to remove his sister from the equation; however, the holidays and her affinity for her brother would not allow such an action. Turning instead to Charles, Darcy was able to convince his friend to visit quite often and even attend to the household staff. It was not long before Charles became a common fixture of the house.

The arrangement was favorable as Darcy was often required elsewhere in the city. He could have certainly hired more staff, but the company of the Bingleys allowed for a more respectable appearance of normality; while also amusing Georgiana and consoling her as to the loss of her brothers immediate presence.

The considerable amount of time Charles spent in the house also meant more visits from his sister Caroline. Darcy tolerated these visits as a necessary requirement for the appearance of society and as an added distraction to his sister. One such occasion proved to be interesting when Darcy was approached by Caroline.

"You do work terribly hard, Mr. Darcy. I believe you even worked through Christmas."

Darcy looked up from his desk and to the open door where Miss Bingley stood. Deep in thought, and contemplating some coded intelligence reports, Darcy took a moment to acclimate to Caroline's presence. Caroline, not wanting to wait for an answer, entered the room and looked about.

"I do not mean to intrude upon your concentration, but I often see an open door as an open invitation for conversation."

"Some might regard it as an invitation for air."

Caroline smile coyly.

"I always enjoy your counterpointes to my statements. You seem to perceive them as arguments to which you must supply a counter argument; however, if you are engaged I will leave you quietly. I did wish to discuss a matter which has recently arisen. It is of a social nature and I am sure a trivial matter for you, but I would welcome your counsel."

Darcy was slightly intrigued and, while his mind was engaged in a focused manner, he was not averse to hearing a challenge of less national import than he was currently embroiled. Directing Miss Bingley to a chair he encouraged her to continue.

"I was called upon recently by Miss Jane Bennet. It appears she is visiting her aunt and uncle in London. During one of their day trips she arrived upon our door step. She is lovely indeed, but I cannot admit to being overjoyed at her arrival."

"It seems odd that Miss Bennet should arrive with no formal invitation or notice."

"I believe she mentioned the dispatch of a letter informing us of her visit, but I daresay the letter must have been lost."

Darcy eyed Caroline inquisitively. Her mannerisms appeared insincere and he could not quite believe the account of the lost letter. Deciding to let it be, he listened as Caroline continued.

"Louisa and I were to be on our way to lunch, so the time with Miss Bennet was short. I believe Miss Bennet had wished for a longer encounter and perhaps to visit with Charles. Your monopoly of my brother's time had thwarted that possibility."

"I trust you have a point at which counsel is needed, but at the moment I cannot fathom what it is," Darcy said this as he lazily removed a piece of lint from his pants.

"Miss Bennet's arrival in town may be a bit distracting. My brother seems to be spending a great deal of time at your house and within the company of your sister. I should think that Miss Bennet's arrival could put a damper on any social interactions of your interest. I believe you have objections to the Bennet family as well and do not wish Charles to be emotionally enthralled."

Darcy had been so involved with London matters, and his protection of Georgiana, that he was unaware of all the social ramifications of Charles' visits. In Caroline's mind the only reason for Charles' visits and time with Georgiana was the probability of romantic entanglements. He realized this line of thought sat well with her constant schemes of marriage.

Problem solving was forefront on his mind at the moment. Just this morning he had impeded two of Ackerby's plans and was about to implement tactics to prevent several more. His current frame of mind allowed him to quickly ascertain the situation presented before him.

Firstly, Caroline was misconstruing the current social relationship between Charles and Georgiana. Furthermore, Caroline wished for the perceived relationship to be encouraged, as she believed Darcy wished for it as well. The arrival of Miss Bennet was cause for concern as the unwanted distraction of a lady to whom Charles had shown previous affection could be problematic.

Darcy agreed with the last conclusion, although for entirely different premises than Caroline. At the moment, Charles was needed as a friend during these stressful times and as a gentleman guardian while Darcy was absent from the house. He quickly devised a plan and decided to enlist Caroline as to its implementation; although he was loathe to manipulate Caroline in such a way.

"I do have objections to the family and more to the point with regards to Miss Bennet's feelings towards Charles. Those feelings, in my opinion, are of a friendly unattached nature. Your brother is a dear friend, but I must admit he is prone to distraction with regards to ladies of pleasurable disposition. I spent a month of time convincing him Miss Bennet was indeed a lovely lady but not within his social status and not to be considered for marriage. If she had shown a genuine interest in Charles I would have, perhaps, seriously considered his fancy; although the family connections were still heavily weighted against. I do not wish to repeat that month's activities should Charles inadvertently come across Miss Bennet. Certainly he would perceive Miss Bennet's wish to visit with you and Louisa as an overture to meet with him. This would fill his mind with fanciful notions of romance and an unsuitable marriage."

"Do you have any suggestions as to dealing with Miss Bennet?"

"If you enjoy Miss Bennet's company I would suggest you entertain her as you would normally. If, however, you can do without her company, I would suggest a polite dismissal of her visits and requests. Charles is engaged here much of the time and I see no reason to inform him of Miss Bennet's arrival. I find that I enjoy his company; as does my sister."

Darcy well knew Caroline's affection for Jane Bennet, but Caroline's partiality to Darcy, along with her desire to see the two families merged, would override the affection. She would undoubtedly see a marriage between Charles and Georgiana as tantamount to one between herself and Mr. Darcy. These ideas allowed Darcy to offer Caroline a polite choice of socializing with Jane without the concern it would actually occur.

Caroline agreed with the reasoning and resolved to be polite to Miss Bennet. She further stated she wished to spend more time with her brother, and this would undoubtedly be in conflict with Jane's visit. Appearing content with herself, Caroline then attempted to turn the conversation to more personal matters; but Darcy begged her leave as he had to resume his business dealings.

The departure of Caroline set Darcy to his next task in regards to the affair with Miss Bennet. Drawing a sheet of parchment he drafted a letter.

Colonel Fitzwilliam,

My dear cousin,

I trust this letter finds you well and in good spirits. The holidays for the Darcy household were pleasant, although business as of late has been stressful. You will be pleased to learn that your ward Georgina is staying with me in London. She has mentioned you in passing and I believe she will welcome a visit. If you could make an effort, we would be pleased with your company. I myself would welcome your conversation and counsel in regards to the young lady for which we both share guardianship.

Fitzwilliam Darcy

Finishing the letter, Darcy sealed it and set it aside for dispatch. He knew his cousin would interpret the letter correctly, and shortly Darcy would have an additional gentleman to aid him. If Charles should learn of Miss Bennet's visitation to London, and if that information should drive Charles to distraction, then the arrival of Georgiana's co-guardian would be needed.

Chapter 21

Caroline took her mission seriously, and it was not long before she could report the situation, as regards to Miss Bennet, well in hand. The former had been kind to the latter and visitations between the two were limited. Caroline did not believe Miss Bennet would be of any distraction to Charles, and while Darcy was unhappy with the methodology used, he was happy with the results; Charles remained ever present and a needed respite from anxieties.

Darcy had just finished a most remarkable financial coup involving a land acquisition of Ackerbys and was enjoying a quiet evening with his sister and the Bingleys. Intruding upon the evening a servant announced the arrival of Miss Marianne Dache on a matter of business. Upon approval, Miss Dache was shown into the room where the household was seated.

"Miss Dache," Darcy acknowledged, standing as she entered the room.

Charles also stood and was happy to meet with the young lady. Darcy gave quick introductions and Charles took the opportunity to welcome her with a cheerful attitude.

"Would you care for some tea Miss Dache or perhaps some pastries? Mr. Darcy's chef is excellent, and I can personally attest to all the delicacies."

"Thank you, No," she replied.

Although she smiled and was polite in her refusal, she portrayed an air of amusement with regard to Charles' boyish good nature. Darcy thought his friend was found to be quite amusing by Miss Dache.

"I understand you are here for business Miss Dache," stated Caroline, "personally I find business matters of all sorts rather boring. I am very happy to have Charles attend to them; of course Mr. Darcy is keen on them and very adept in several industries."

"I understand that to be the case," Miss Dache responded, eyeing Mr. Darcy with a wry smile. "I, however, find the engagement of the mind on matters of finance and politics to be invigorating. I believe Mr. Darcy may share the pursuit for similar reasons."

Sensing a possible challenger for Mr. Darcy's affection, Caroline quickly adjusted and attempted her all too familiar attack on social graces and stature.

"Mr. Darcy may enjoy business, and I do believe he prefers women to be accomplished. His dear sister Georgiana here is well accomplished in language and history. She is even becoming accomplished with the piano forte and the harp; however, I am not sure Mr. Darcy would care for a young lady of her standing to engage in business."

"The harp, Miss Darcy? Are you quite accomplished?"

Georgiana quickly blushed and turned away slightly. She was much like her brother and comfortable only with people to which she was well acquainted. Miss Dache, not hearing an answer, politely repeated her request; Georgiana eventually replied.

"I should not say so. I do love the instrument and my brother is content to listen to my practice, but I have no degree of professionalism," Georgiana said in an innocent and humble manner.

"Well then I should get you a copy of '*en paix'*. It is a piece my father, Lord Dache, commissioned for me to play."

'*en paix'* replied Georgiana. "French, for *At Peace*"

To which Miss Dache affirmed in French. This sent both Georgina and Miss Dache into a minute of civil French pleasantries. Caroline listened with contempt and little understanding as she had failed miserably in her French lessons.

"Miss Dache your accent is very well learned; I wish mine was as smooth. I am also pleased to hear you play the harp. Do you play often?"

"When I can; my father has political connections throughout Europe and recently was able to acquire an original Naderman Harp, made for the French royal courts. It is an exquisite instrument. I do enjoy playing the instrument; but I prefer the new upright piano or violin."

"You play all those instruments?" cried Charles, "and you speak French and are conducting business. You must be a most accomplished lady."

Caroline did not enjoy hearing this and attempted to detract from the newcomer's presence.

"Please forgive my brothers enthusiasm. He finds the accomplishments of many ladies to be grand. I do try to remind him that the proper upbringing of ladies will teach them many subjects. My sister and I were educated by private instructors in many of the social graces. Mr. Darcy can attest to how well we dance, as he rarely chooses another partner."

"I can be sure to believe his opinion. I have had the pleasure of a dance with Mr. Darcy and found him to be competent enough to judge his partners abilities."

This statement seemed to upset Caroline for a moment. Miss Dache witnessed Caroline's discomfort and continued.

"However, I do not share your limited outlook on the social education of ladies; but perhaps that is because my father had the means and determination to educate me in matters of science, math, and business. While I do not partake in the intricate dealing of business, as per social norms, I do assist my father from time to time."

Turning to Darcy she addressed him directly. "I am here to deliver news from my father and receive a reply. Is it possible to attend to this?"

Darcy nodded in agreement and then showed Miss Dache out of the room and up to his formal office. Caroline watched the two of them leave through slightly compressed eyes. She did not care for this new interloper and hoped business would be concluded quickly so that she may bend Mr. Darcy's ears over perceived slights.

In the office, Mr. Darcy and Miss Dache took seats after assuring themselves of privacy. Darcy offered a drink and Miss Dache efficiently declined. Asking the nature of the business which brought her to his house, Miss Dache replied directly.

"Your financial dealings of late are to be commended and I am here to deliver payment."

Startled, Darcy replied to Miss Dache's statement.

"I am unaware of any payment to which you could refer."

"A week ago you surreptitiously enlisted the aid of members of the local criminal element. The intent being to interfere with Ackerby's flow of money before it could be removed from the street and deposited into banks."

"I recall the event. It took several days and many reports for me to determine how Ackerby was moving money. It was a comment from my Cousin about the methods spies used to move money across Europe that gave me insight. I saw a connection and decided to interfere."

"My father's resources were used to assist with your endeavor and I saw an opportunity for benefit. I allowed the criminal element to interfere in the matter and then had them disbanded by men loyal to my father. We were able to retrieve the monies and I am here to offer you a share."

Darcy eyed her coldly.

"It is not my intention to conduct business in such a mode as this. My family is wealthy enough with land and business holdings that I do not need to profit from the actions of criminals."

"Of course you do not; but the situation in which we find ourselves was created by Ackerby. He has overstepped the bounds of the gentry and is now drawing our attention. His ignorance of our existence will be his undoing, and it is not a sin for the victor to take the spoils. As I have been informed, you intend to keep parts of Ackerby's organization. I would think that would include his business dealings as well."

Darcy angered slightly with Miss Dache's presumptions.

"His business dealings I assure you will be disbanded. We are the Gentry, and I will not see us engage in blatant criminal activity. As to his business holdings, I will certainly take possession and have them returned to their suitable owners. When a suitable owner is not determinable they will be handed over to others within our organization who will then decide their fate."

Miss Dache stared at Darcy and attempted to size up the man sitting before her. She was not usually tempted by men of any stature, but the one now in her presence intrigued her. Most of her life was spent attempting to measure up to men in one form or another; a task for which she was well suited and which taught her disrespect for many undeserving men. She was hard pressed to name any man she could fully respect; but Mr. Darcy showed promise, even if he seemed timid in some matters. Still undecided, she smiled coyly and changed the topic.

"Pray tell me, Mr. Darcy, your thoughts the night we almost met. I was ensconced across the street having missed my opportunity to stop the lord's assistant from baiting his employer. Too far to intervene, I was pleased to witness you dispatch the would-be assassin. I admit I am not easily impressed, but I watched you that night with admiration. You quickly disarmed the assailant, took his life, and before the lord was fully aware, you were leading him out of danger. The light from the lamps cut across your face as you secured the Lord, and I must say you were quite the dashing figure. My blood warmed with the exhilaration of it all."

"Miss Dache I can assure you I thought only of the safety of the Lord."

"I find that difficult to believe. I myself am trained in similar fashion and have encountered more than one individual wishing to do me harm. The speed of the action and threat of injury is exhilarating."

"I believe you enjoy your pursuits too much."

"And you not enough," she responded.

Elizabeth Bennet sat before Darcy for a moment; the vision of an intelligent woman engaged in a sparring match was pleasing. The vision and pleasant feelings quickly faded and Darcy could not help but compare the true identity of the lady before him with the one his mind had conjured.

Miss Bennet and Miss Dache both taxed Darcy in regards to verbal argument; however, Darcy had to admit he preferred the more generous nature of Miss Bennet's arguments. Miss Dache seemed to lack this generosity of spirit; Darcy saw fit to test his belief and continued the conversation.

"I came across a report in regards to the formerly mentioned assistant. It seems he was robbed and left murdered; an unfortunate incident."

"I would disagree with your conclusion, Mr. Darcy. The assistant foolishly accepted money to lead a notable member of parliament into a trap. His dispatch was well warranted; but I see your thoughts. Rest assured I did not perform the act personally. I merely precipitated it. He had caused me embarrassment in regards to the Lord and I rectified the situation."

"He did accept money, and all reports led to the conclusion that he did so out of an honest belief the Lord would merely be accosted by individuals with arguments to sway his vote. He did not make himself willingly accomplice to an attempted murder. For this I see punishment and dismissal, but not a death sentence."

"His actions led to a direct attack on a member of parliament, and I am not as wont to forgive the transgression. You seem at odds with the thought of killing, Mr. Darcy. On one hand you dispatched an assassin with skill and precision, and on the other you take great pains to save life."

"It is often easier to take a life than to save it. When time is short we must be prepared for action; but with time to contemplate, I find it more ruthless to choose death over alternatives which allow for life."

"This is why you seem odd within my mind. I am not fully unaware of some of your deeds; highly secret as they may be. I believe you have recently taken great pains to plan and implement the removal of a gentleman from society."

Darcy thought back several months to his encounter with Shantly. He would have been happy to count it the only situation of that nature, but for as rare as it was, it was not unique.

"Each of us, Miss Dache, must confront our own demons and come to terms with our beliefs. We each draw a line in the sand and justify our actions whether they are good or bad. When we transgress that line we will either come to terms or we shall go mad. I assure you I do not take those situations lightly. Each one is carefully considered and only dealt with personally by me when I feel the burden of guilt must be mine to bear."

"Do you perceive yourself a martyr then?"

Darcy turned cold at this remark. He stared at the woman across from him and replied in a tone befitting his mood.

"I see myself as obligated and honourable. When the two conflict in any manner I will fulfill my obligations to the extent that will allow the ideas and codes of honour to be fulfilled; even if that should mean sacrificing my own."

Miss Dache remained silent for a moment. She realized the extent to which she had pushed Mr. Darcy and was not displeased by his reactions. Regarding him as a whole, she coolly tallied the information she had learned about him. This handsome man that sat before her had wealth, family, a genius mind, and a conscience the she did not quite understand. She was sure of one absolute truth as she rose to leave the room.

"Whatever your internal demons are, Mr. Darcy, do not let them convince you that you are without honour. You are more honourable than any man I may claim as an acquaintance."

Mr. Darcy stood, nodded, and the two silently headed out of the office. Miss Dache preceded Darcy through the house with a smile of unmistakable pleasure; all the while thinking she would have this man as her husband.

Chapter 22

Swords clashed and rang out through the room as Darcy and his cousin, Colonel Fitzwilliam, sparred. Mr. Darcy's house did not have a formal fencing room, but the two gentlemen were content to make do with the large drawing room. Initially starting with wood practice swords the two gentlemen had worked up a sweat and now faced each other, bare-chested and with more conventional weaponry.

"This is foolish, Fitzy," the Colonel said with a smile as the two men circled each other.

"You know well enough I do not like that name any more than you do," replied Darcy as he brought his sword down upon the Colonel.

A loud clang was heard and Colonel Fitzwilliam dropped to one knee to better support the force of the downward strike and forward attack. Kneeling there, with Darcy still full force upon him, he laughed and cocked his head.

"Sharing the same name may be an annoyance for us, but I imagine my good nature allows me to tolerate the teasing more than your dour nature does." Drawing in close, and putting more weight on the sword, Darcy searched for an advantage.

"Your good nature is why I tolerate you, however, your sense of attire leaves something to be desired; perhaps a better sense of attire."

The Colonel laughed loudly.

"Fitzy, was that a joke? Dear me, you do need work; I should offer my assistance, but at the moment your closeness concerns me. I cannot determine if you mean to kill me or to kiss me."

"You are not handsome enough for me to kiss you."

Colonel Fitzwilliam then performed a maneuver which Darcy had expected and prepared. The close proximity had allowed Darcy to shift his feet and position his grip. When the Colonel intentionally buckled, Darcy allowed his weight to carry him forward. Tucking his weapon and rolling across his shoulders he was repositioned and back on his feet to the surprise of his cousin. The two were now to far apart to provide a killing blow, but the Colonel was still on the ground as his maneuver took longer to recover. It was a valid and skillful move. Many a swordsman would have been off balance from the sudden buckling, thus allowing the lower man time and positioning to kill his attacker as he sprawled to the ground. Darcy took two rapid steps and did not raise his sword. It was not necessary as the Colonel knew he was beat.

With Darcy lording over him, the Colonel laughed and propped himself up on one elbow. Tossing his sword to the ground he continued to laugh.

"Well that was certainly entertaining. I should imagine you would have made quite the knight if circumstances were different; although the armor might clash with your pedigreed sense of style."

Darcy grabbed their shirts and tossed one over to his cousin.

"Please get off my rug. You may sweat on it and then I shall have to have it cleaned. A more difficult task than cleaning you I should imagine, although I would not care to take odds."

"Oh, leave me here to sweat on the rug. Perhaps the Bingleys will return with Georgiana while I rest. Caroline might get a look at a man lying on the floor, bare-chested, and freshly defeated in battle; perhaps she will take pity and turn her attentions from you to me."

"If that were to be, then I will let you keep the rug and do as you please; but I fear Miss Bingley to be not so easily tempted."

Darcy stretched his muscles and rubbed them where they ached. Looking down he examined a small scar just below his left ribs. The wound was a year old and stupidly occurred during training. It was vanishing nicely and blending in with his otherwise smooth skin. Content, he pulled his shirt on, and then assisted the Colonel to his feet.

The two gentlemen then repaired to the dining room and supped upon cheeses and breads. Sitting across from each other Mr. Darcy proceeded to inform the Colonel of many recent events but leaving out those of a personal nature. The two men shared an affinity for one another, and with this in mind Colonel Fitzwilliam did not inquire into matters which Mr. Darcy obviously omitted. If the situations were reversed, and the Colonel was unable to disclose sensitive military information, then Mr. Darcy would reciprocate by not asking what should not be asked.

"I see the crux of the issue my dear cousin, and I fear for Georgiana as well. I have lodgings in London I will be using. Now that I am here I might as well make myself useful to you with your problems regarding Colonel Ackerby. If Charles were to be unavailable for some reason, then I will come straight away and lodge within the house."

"I appreciate the help in this matter, but as regards to Ackerby, I am afraid you cannot and will not be of any help."

"Oh, do you question my courage now, or perhaps my abilities?" The Colonel did seem to enjoy teasing his cousin.

"You know full well why you are not allowed to help. Now leave me to it. If you wish to be of assistance you could help with any information you may have on Colonel Ackerby. Did you ever encounter him?"

"Not to my knowledge, but the army has grown so large and so rapidly these last years it would be hard to meet even a small percentage of the officers. I believe we shall need the large numbers if the trouble in Europe continues. Perhaps even your role will be changed, should the French ideas of monarchy and nobility cross the channel."

"My role exists, as do many others, to insure the nobility do not allow the situation to arise which precipitated the revolution in France. If the French had held their nobility in check and maintained their sense of Nobless Oblige, then they might not have lost their heads."

Colonel Fitzwilliam nodded at this comment and then attempted to look out the window; he was unsuccessful as it had been covered for privacy. Nodding to the window as if addressing it he commented.

"I wonder how much of the nobility and gentry know of your existence and the role you play."

Darcy followed his gaze.

"Very few, truth be told. We are a myth and a legend. Hidden behind tales of secret societies and attributed to fanciful whims of the English monarchy. Typically we work independently from each other. Solicitors working on their projects, emissaries on theirs, and we only meet when a challenge is brought to our attention. It is then that it is decided by someone higher than me, who should deal with it."

"I should imagine you have a range of spies about, keeping you constantly informed." joked the Colonel. The joke fell flat as Darcy eyed his cousin.

"I should imagine you deal with spies in your career much more than I with mine. We are the guardians, and we are the Gentry. I am here to deal with serious transgressions of nobility, not to ferret out minor idiosyncrasies of the aristocracy."

The two gentlemen continued their meal and turned the conversation to more general matters. The rest of the afternoon was spent in witty banter and light conversation. The Colonel teased Darcy about marriage and potential prospects, hinting at the possibility of Caroline Bingley. Darcy, not to be outdone by his cousin, suggested the personality of Miss Bingley would be better suited to the Colonel.

Chapter 23

The next few months were more enjoyable for Darcy even though his dealings with Colonel Ackerby proved to be slow in developing. The first month of Mr. Darcy's attacks had shown much promise, but Colonel Ackerby proved to be cunning. Reports arrived describing changes within the Colonels operations, and as Darcy read them he understood the tactic.

Colonel Ackerby was not certain he was under attack; the subtleties of Darcy's advances were not something for which the Colonel had experience. He did, however, have experience with losses and was now regrouping and reformulating.

Darcy could see the slight maneuvers and understood the situation. The Colonel had attempted to make his mark on London finances and politics with a frontal attack. Initially finding no resistance, he saw no reason to change. Darcy's manipulations were now creating resistance which ultimately led to the current and more quiet climate.

Meetings throughout London with solicitors, emissaries, military men, and even spies were intermixed with lunches at the Bingleys and dinners on the town. Darcy took advantage of the lull and enjoyed his time with Georgiana and the Bingleys. The danger and interplay of the various schemes proved to keep his mind focused; and when not engaged in immediate planning, he prided himself on detaching from the extremes of intrigue and enjoyed his sister's practice on the piano forte or her insight on a new book.

Business invariably kept him in contact with Lord Dache and his Daughter who Darcy still kept at a distance. Lord Dache himself called upon Darcy more than once and attempted to cajole him into an engagement with his daughter. The Lord believed the alliance of the two houses would be beneficial to both families; Darcy could hardly argue the logic. Both families were wealthy, well connected, and well bred. If Darcy were to choose a bride out of pure logic and concern for political or financial aspirations then Miss Dache was certainly a fine choice. However, Darcy could not bring himself to an emotional state of affection for the lady, and his mind weighed heavily on the matter. His logic argued for the sense of the arrangement, but his heart cried against it.

Standing in front of a mirror one day, recovering from a visit by Lord Dache and his daughter, Darcy scrutinized himself. Must he take a wife? He admitted that he did care for female companionship, but the ladies of his acquaintance were found to be wanting.

Caroline possessed some of the requirements he found needed in a good wife. He considered her for a few minutes and arrived at the same conclusion he always did. The arrangement would be acceptable, she did possess adequate breeding and connections, but he could not see her as head of his household. Her personality would not blend well with his duties. This would leave him with the only option of hiding the family's duties from her; a task which was not impossible since other households and job positions functioned in this manner. But for Mr. Darcy, this was not an option which he considered to be stress free and unproblematic.

Miss Dache certainly had the required breeding and culture, but a coldness Darcy did not care for. He was also aware of her keen desire for him as a husband. When in a private settings she made little attempt to hide her growing affection. Coy smiles, astute observations, and an admiration for his abilities were obvious. Lord Dache himself appeared pleased with Darcy to an extreme amount; this admiration was rising daily as plans against Ackerby unfolded and were adjusted.

Darcy's father had been a well respected man in all walks of life; kind to his tenants, honourable in business, giving to charity, and competent in his sworn duties to the Crown and the Gentry. His son, and heir, Mr. Fitzwilliam Darcy, carried on with the tradition. He lacked some of his father's more personable natures, but in lieu of the social qualities, the son possessed a keenness of mind and strength of physical condition. The last few months' campaigns were demonstrating to the Highest Order Mr. Darcy's talents. Now, Darcy stood before his mirror, thinking about matters, and he realized that while his wealth had brought him unwanted attention, the revelation of his skill would bring even more. If it is not Miss Dache, then it would be another. Perhaps he would meet a more suited lady among the families now watching him; this thought filled him more with dread than hope.

His reflection seemed blurred and turning his head side to side did not correct the visualization.

Staring at the image he gazed into his own eyes and sighed a deep heavy sigh.

"Who are you that stands before me?"

Pausing a moment, and then with more thoughtful composure.

"Is it to be the head or the heart?"

Thinking on his heart brought to mind Miss Elizabeth Bennet, as she was the last lady to touch him emotionally. If not for her connections she might make a more suitable wife. The thought of her as his wife pleased him more than he imagined.

It had been more than a fortnight since he last thought of Miss Elizabeth; and the length of time was growing between each thought of her. Initially she preyed upon his mind daily, but as time passed and her memory faded he found it easier to dismiss the idea as an innocent infatuation; one for which his logical mind, with consideration to his being well married, could easily overcome.

Leaving the mirror, he headed to his desk and prepared his upcoming itinerary. Georgiana was to return to private studies and would be less available. This precipitated a conflict in her schedule of education which did not afford her the ability to spend Easter with her brother. Unfortunately his aunt, Lady Catherine De Bourgh, was made privy to this information and was most strenuously requesting his presence at Rosings Park. Darcy's mind had raced with reasons not to accede to his aunt's wishes, but in the end he decided to visit; he could work his current pace with daily dispatches if needed, and the time would allow him to address issues with his aunt and her estate. He realized this did open him to attack in the form of his aunts continued suggestions to marry her daughter; he sighed and resigned his mind to the fact that he could do little at the moment. He then pulled a sheet of paper and wrote a letter of acceptance to his aunt.

Chapter 24

The journey to Rosings was agreeable to Mr. Darcy and Colonel Fitzwilliam; the latter had also been invited by their mutual aunt, and the gentlemen saw fit to make the journey together. They spent the time engaged in conversation of trivial natures as well as the serious; and of course enjoyed the odd jest and tease.

"I hope your social life is in order Darcy. From hearing your stories of intrigue and schemes I should imagine you have little time for frivolity."

"On the contrary, I have enjoyed much time with friends and acquaintances since our last meeting."

"That is good to hear. I imagine you to be content in your business dealings as well; although I understand the need for secrecy in those regards."

"Business is indeed good and I pride myself on the eventual successful conclusion. Socially I wish for less attention from unwarranted affection."

Laughing the Colonel jested with Darcy.

"A man of your intellect is impressive as he contemplates moves of political or military nature; can you not bring that intellect to bear on the simple matter of a woman's affection."

"It has been my experience that matters of women's affection tend not to be simple. However, I can be effective in their regards, and have recently saved a friend from a most undesirable union."

"Oh! Your friends are to be spared the social injustice but you cannot save yourself. Please tell me of this courageous action of yours."

The Colonel's good nature and welcoming smile allowed Darcy to relax a bit and enjoy himself.

“It was not courage but intellect which allowed me to solve the dilemma. My friend found himself to be infatuated with a young lady of a lower caste. I objected to the lady strongly on her lot in life as well as her inability to show a particular affinity. It was skill and determinism that allowed me to separate my friend from the ladies acquaintance and his personal feelings. I only wish it were as easy to solve my own challenges.”

“Cheer up Fitzy, I am sure a good friend will undoubtedly do you a favour in turn. Who is this gentleman which owes you the favour indebted by your timely interference?”

Darcy chose not to respond to requests of particular details or to the address of ‘Fitzy’.

“Fear not, I believe I can guess the identity of the acquaintance.”

“I would prefer you not; my involvement in the situation was necessary do to events of the time, but I do not wish the information relayed back to the family of the lady. While my objections are valid, I do not wish to cause any harm or embarrassment.”

“Always in the shadows do you lurk. Do you feel nothing for the lives in which you interact?”

This question caught Darcy off guard and the reaction was immediately apparent to the Colonel who, realizing he may have ventured too far into the realm of personal emotions, assured Darcy he was only jesting. Darcy understood the nature of the jest and did admit to his cousin a penchant for maintaining a calm emotional state.

The Colonel smiled, laughed, and continued to entertain his cousin with many anecdotes and jests. In his mind, Darcy was to be admired and respected, and the Colonel held his cousin's abilities in such high regard, one may say it was almost awe. With an understanding of Darcy's role within the Gentry, Colonel Fitzwilliam could think of no one better suited; but flashes of anger and pure emotion could strike across Darcy's face like lighting across a field. Those worried the Colonel as he wondered what his cousin should resemble should he lose that wonderful composure. To many people's opinions, Mr. Darcy was very unemotional, and those individuals attributed it to the nature of his character. Those who knew him best came to realize the unemotional appearance was merely that; an appearance.

How did you maintain your composure all those months ago, upon seeing a snake of a man slithering toward our ward? he thought to himself. The colonel had asked Darcy this question only once and the answer he received was short. "Honour."

The carriage arrived at Rosings in the afternoon and upon turning into the park Mr. Darcy caught sight of an odd man spying at their arrival. He knew this individual, and it took only a moment for the memory to find its way to his conscious. He could not recall directly the man's name but did recollect him from the Netherfield ball; it was the new reverend his aunt had installed. Darcy sighed for a moment and added this gentleman to the list of business matters his cousin and he would need to attend to.

The carriage arrived and the gentlemen wasted little time alighting and moving luggage into the manor. In short order their aunt made an appearance befitting the majesty himself and was most pleased with their arrival; however, she immediately berated them on many accounts from the mode of their travel to the attire they chose to wear. The Colonel and Mr. Darcy exchanged knowing glances, rolled their eyes, and politely responded to their aunt's inquiries. Yes, they were both well. The trip had gone splendidly. No, they did not find the day to be cold.

These comments continued as the gentlemen settled in and Lady Catherine, who possessed more arrogance than intelligence, continued to appeal for updates on family matters. It was a long afternoon as Mr. Darcy and the Colonel were pressed to sit in the drawing room and socialize with their aunt and her daughter.

Miss De Bourgh had not improved much in Darcy's opinion. She was always a sickly child, and her adult life was beginning with the same aspect. She sat quietly on a sofa and participated very little in conversation. Even then her only response was to timidly answer direct questions posed by her overbearing mother.

The evening ended with dinner and dessert followed by assertions by both men of the need for an early night. The claim of a long journey was fronted as a reason for rest, but both men found the previous few hours more taxing than then entire journey from London.

Chapter 25

The next morning Lady Catherine continued her incessant chatter as if the previous evenings sleep had never interrupted it. Breakfast was an affair of considerable talk by the lady of the house and little by any other individuals. On the few occasions Darcy and the Colonel chose to converse, their aunt invariably interrupted to interject her opinion, no matter how ignorant it may be.

Shortly after breakfast Rosings was visited by the local reverend, who took the moment to remind Mr. Darcy of his name; Mr. Collins. He was immediately shown into the drawing room and Lady Catherine insisted they should all be social. Darcy found the man to be exactly as he remembered; weak of spirit and weak of body. His propensity to apologize and placate seemed to fit his aunts overbearing personality, and he understood greatly why she selected this individual for his current position. In just a few minutes Darcy counted no less than four apologies from the man and two were made just in regards to his arrival.

One apology caught Mr. Darcy's immediate attention. This one concerned a visitation to the Hunsford parsonage.

"I do personally and humbly extend an open invitation to my rectory; be it day or night," he said to the nephews with wide hand gestures, "I must apologize that my hospitality may be temporarily diminished upon your arrival as I am newly married, and my wife has a friend visiting, Miss

Elizabeth Bennet. I can assure you that whatever the ladies could be engaged with at the time of your arrival, will be promptly suspended so as to accommodate any visit."

The mention of Miss Elizabeth caught Darcy's ears and he sat forward a bit, finally taking an interest in the words of Mr. Collins.

"Impertinent girl!" stated Lady Catherine with an air of contempt.

"I most vehemently apologize for any slight my cousin, Miss Bennet, might have placed upon you."

Now he is apologizing for other peoples slights, thought Darcy as he wondered if this man possessed any self respect. His interest continued as Lady Catherine proceeded to relay conversations between her and Miss Elizabeth.

Darcy quickly learned Elizabeth had been at Rosings these past few weeks, and on several occasions visited his aunt, much to her continued frustration. One such conversation found Miss Elizabeth bold enough to suggest it was socially acceptable for her family to have all five daughters 'out' in society before the eldest was married. To compound her error in knowledge of etiquette, Miss Elizabeth took it upon herself to defend the position.

"That child's impertinence is indeed troublesome. I should blame it on parenting and breeding."

"Again, I apologize your ladyship; I realize my cousin can be most vexing."

Darcy stifled a laugh at this and was forced to grab his tea to hide his smile. Laughing into his cup he turned away from prying eyes and prayed to the heavens the image of his contorting body would appear to be of a man choking. He collected himself as quickly as he could, and in response to concern for his welfare, assured everyone he was quite all right and needed only a moment to clear his throat.

The entire time he spent laughing he considered the comment of Mr. Collins and concluded the vexation of Miss Bennet upon others was as enjoyable as when she attempted it with him. He could imagine her in this drawing room engaged in conversation similar in nature to the ones shared at Netherfield. Her intelligence, charm, and wit would not be welcomed by the likes of his aunt, who preferred to be surrounded by those individuals with less fortitude of character.

After composing himself, Darcy took a more active approach to the conversation. Guiding the topic around to annual inspections Darcy suggested he and Colonel Fitzwilliam return with Mr. Collins. The rector could then introduce his new wife and the two nephews could settle themselves to a cursory view of the parsonage. Mr. Collins eagerly agreed to the suggestion.

The walk to the Hunsford was short, but each step oddly soured Mr. Darcy's mood. He found himself thinking of Miss Elizabeth and wondered what he was to accomplish with this visit. His normal analytical mind was being intruded upon by feelings of giddiness, and this troubled him. As the rectory grew closer he found himself nervous and unsure how to act. This he believed to be very troublesome and, as he always did in uncertain situations, he fixed a stoic expression and decided to attend to the interactions. It had been several months since his experience with this young lady and he believed he would find her charms less commanding.

Mr. Darcy's belief regarding Miss Elizabeth's charms was short lived. Within a few minutes of being seated, Colonel Fitzwilliam engaged Miss Elizabeth and Mrs. Collins in conversation. The three of them spoke quite easily and with a rapport Darcy could only envy. To his discredit Darcy could only sit and observe for much of the time. After several minutes passed he began to relax and was rewarded by his minds ability to actually engage in conversation. He inquired as to Miss Bennet's family and health; to which she smiled and responded all was well.

``My eldest sister has been in town these three months. Have you never happened to see her there?"

Darcy was thrown off guard by this question and searched for a suitable answer. He found it troublesome that his mind should be thus far out of focus. Replaying the question in his head he realized he need only answer the question honestly.

"I cannot say I have been fortunate enough to see her."

Elizabeth seemed pleased with this reply as she stared at Mr. Darcy. He returned the stare and his mind tickled him with a minor bit of annoyance; he could not put his thoughts to ease why her stare bothered him. Miss Elizabeth smiled politely and turned her attention to the Colonel.

Shortly the gentlemen took their leave and headed back to Rosings. The colonel was in a good mood and conversed with Darcy about the lovely nature of both the ladies. He did find Miss Elizabeth to be charming and asked for Darcy's input, to which Darcy replied.

"I find any Lady that vexes our aunt so amusingly to be most admirable."

Chapter 26

Returning to Rosings after visiting the parsonage proved stressful for both Darcy and Colonel Fitzwilliam. The former was immediately pressed into the service by answering letters from London, while the latter was left to contend to an aunt who insisted on the details of their visit to the Hunsford rectory.

Letters in hand, Darcy made his way to a back office, sealed himself inside, and made use of the privacy to analyze the newest data. Operations were proceeding well, but Ackerby appeared to be on the move again. It was some hours before Darcy could make sense of the communications and only then did he realize he needed more intelligence reports. Resigning himself to the task at hand, he sat and began to send off dispatches requesting specific information. Once the dispatches were completed, he set about arranging the office to his liking in preparation for the arrival of the expected information.

A knocking of the door distracted him from his task, and the opening of it revealed his aunt; not wishing to be granted permission to enter any room in her house, she walked in and immediately engaged Darcy in conversation.

"Business I see is what keeps you from attending to me. I would enjoy a few minutes of your time and have you inform me of your concerns."

"Aunt Catherine I would not wish to burden you with the boorishness of my dealings. The letters of London are of no great import but must be dealt with. I will require a few days to attend to the details."

"Do not attempt to deceive me young nephew. I am well aware of some of your duties, and your locking yourself in this particular office reveals to me you are to deal with matters suited to your father or my brother. If you so choose to follow in their stead then I will welcome it, but I will not be disappointed in regards to the facts."

"Yes, you will," replied Darcy coldly and sternly.

Lady Catherine caught herself for a moment and stood stunned at her nephew's matter of fact response.

"My dear aunt, well you know the role your brother and my father played in English society. Your brother upheld his role as an Earl and passed his legacy to his children. My father and your brother-in-law did similar with his land and duties. While you may be privy to some of the arrangements, you cannot be privy to the details. Your part my dear aunt, is to enjoy your life and protect the family honour. Now please allow me to complete my business."

"Very well young Mr. Darcy, but I will expect you to uphold your obligations to be sociable. I must be attended to in that regard and have my news of London and society. My daughter Anne, also wishes to converse with you, and I expect any nephew of mine to be courteous to his female cousins."

"In this, I will indulge your wishes, and you may hear many stories about the city and recent gossip."

Seeming to be placated, Darcy escorted his aunt out of the office. Turning back to his intelligence he began shuffling documents again. He expected it would be several days before he would be free. By this estimation he soon learned he was incorrect, as it was a full week before he finished his plans satisfactorily.

It was Easter Sunday and the day started with church and then an evening of frivolity. The members of the parsonage were to visit, and Darcy admitted to himself that he was happy for the diversion. His recent work taxed his mental capabilities and more than once he considered returning to London. Determined to remain and solve his challenges he instead used dispatches to begin construction of a more stable system which would allow him better access to information without personal involvement. He was now happy for the acquaintance of Miss Dache; he found her to be quite capable in handling affairs he would normally complete himself.

With the work completed to his satisfaction Darcy now relaxed and concentrated on more pleasant distractions. The arrival of Mr. and Mrs. Collins along with Elizabeth Bennet proved to be a distraction he enjoyed.

Colonel Fitzwilliam and Miss Elizabeth fell into ready conversation. The past week had not affected Colonel Fitzwilliam's ability for society and he had, on more than one occasion, visited the parsonage. Tonight, his amiable personality and growing familiarity enticed all participants, save for Darcy, to engage in conversation.

Mr. Darcy found the evening conversation relaxing and spent much time listening to Miss Elizabeth. He found her banter appealing and her deft conversations with his aunt amusing. The Colonel and Miss Elizabeth spoke on many topics to which Miss Elizabeth lively gave her opinion and logical reasoning for the position. To Anne, she was kind, and made several attempts to include her in conversation.

Lady Catherine continually interrupted conversations and insisted on having a say on any topic. The only pleasing topic of conversation that Darcy partook with his aunt was in regards to his sister Georgiana. He praised her readily in her beauty, education, and musical talents for which constant practice was making her adept.

The topic of music proved too much for the Colonel and he insisted Miss Elizabeth play on the piano forte. The two of them left to the other side of the room and Darcy sat back to enjoy the music. The music was light and lively, but not so lively as to call for dance; this was music to lighten a spirit on a rainy day. It was only a few minutes into the piece before Lady Catherine attempted to bend his ear on an inane topic. Mr. Darcy, for all his faculties, did not hear the drone of his aunt; instead he stood up and walked to the piano forte and stared at Miss Elizabeth. She appeared content and happy. From furtive glances he could tell she was aware of his presence before her, but her concentration was on the music. He took a deep breath and thought on nothing but the moment, the music, and the lady before him. When the music lulled she turned to him and arched a smile.

``You mean to frighten me, Mr. Darcy, by coming in all this state to hear me? But I will not be alarmed though your sister *does* play so well. There is a stubbornness about me that never can bear to be frightened at the will of others. My courage always rises with every attempt to intimidate me."

``I shall not say that you are mistaken," he replied, ``because you could not really believe me to entertain any design of alarming you; and I have had the pleasure of your acquaintance long enough to know, that you find great enjoyment in occasionally professing opinions which in fact are not your own."

Elizabeth laughed heartily at this picture of herself, and said to Colonel Fitzwilliam, ``Your cousin will give you a very pretty notion of me, and teach you not to believe a word I say. I am particularly unlucky in meeting with a person so well able to expose my real character, in a part of the world where I had hoped to pass myself off with some degree of credit. Indeed, Mr. Darcy, it is very ungenerous in you to mention all that you knew to my disadvantage in Hertfordshire and, give me leave to say, very impolitic too, for it is provoking me to retaliate, and such things may come out, as will shock your relations to hear."

``I am not afraid of you," said he, smilingly.

``Pray let me hear what you have to accuse him of," cried Colonel Fitzwilliam. ``I should like to know how he behaves among strangers."

``You shall hear then, but prepare yourself for something very dreadful. The first time of my ever seeing him in Hertfordshire, you must know, was at a ball in Meryton and at this ball, what do you think he did? He danced only four dances! I am sorry to pain you, but so it was. He danced only four dances, though gentlemen were scarce; and, to my certain knowledge, more than one young lady was sitting down in want of a partner. Mr. Darcy, you cannot deny the fact."

``I had not at that time the honour of knowing any lady in the assembly beyond my own party."

``True; and nobody can ever be introduced in a ball room. Well, Colonel Fitzwilliam, what do I play next? My fingers wait your orders."

``Perhaps," said Darcy, ``I should have judged better, had I sought an introduction, but I am ill qualified to recommend myself to strangers."

``Shall we ask your cousin the reason of this?" said Elizabeth, still addressing Colonel Fitzwilliam. ``Shall we ask him why a man of sense and education, and who has lived in the world, is ill qualified to recommend himself to strangers?"

``I can answer your question," said Fitzwilliam, ``without applying to him. It is because he will not give himself the trouble."

``I certainly have not the talent which some people possess," said Darcy, ``of conversing easily with those I have never seen before. I cannot catch their tone of conversation, or appear interested in their concerns, as I often see done."

``My fingers," said Elizabeth, ``do not move over this instrument in the masterly manner which I see so many women's do. They have not the same force or rapidity, and do not produce the same expression. But then I have always supposed it to be my own fault, because I would not take the trouble of practicing. It is not that I do not believe *my* fingers as capable as any other woman's of superior execution."

Darcy smiled, and said, ``You are perfectly right. You have employed your time much better. No one admitted to the privilege of hearing you, can think any thing wanting. We neither of us perform to strangers."

Here they were interrupted by Lady Catherine, who called out to know what they were talking of. Elizabeth immediately began playing again. Lady Catherine approached, and, after listening for a few minutes, commented to Darcy on Miss Bennet's skill.

The entire party was then forced to listen as Lady Catherine expounded upon the musical talents her daughter Anne would exhibit if only her health had allowed the opportunity for musical instruction. Both Darcy and Fitzwilliam gave a small collected sigh as she droned on about musical characteristics that were not only excellent, but imaginary; Miss Bennet was the only one in the room with a view to witness both sighs and she smiled as she continued to play.

Late into the evening she played and the carriage was eventually made ready to return the visiting party to the parsonage. Manners provided the gentlemen an excuse to walk the party to the drive and Colonel Fitzwilliam expounded on the wonders of the evening and suggested it be done again. Mr. Collins graciously accepted the report of an evening well spent and Elizabeth held back as the Colonel then attempted to aid a clumsy and awkward Mr. Collins into the carriage.

"You are fairly quiet, Mr. Darcy," said Elizabeth. "I am sure your cousin is quite sufficient to see us safely upon the road and I would not wish to inconvenience you with social etiquette you do not care for. Nor do I wish to inflict upon you the sight of Mr. Collins attempting to enter a carriage." she said with an odd expression as she watched the colonel untangling Mr. Collins foot from the step.

"I will admit, Miss Bennet, at times it is difficult to decide whether you jest with me or display honest concern."

"Perhaps it is both. As I mentioned in past conversation I prefer complex personalities to simple ones; they are vastly more interesting. I do not believe I could hold such a belief and maintain a simple personality. Your confusion of my intent will be taken as a compliment to my complexity; from a gentleman as complex as yourself, the compliment is to be deemed of high rank."

Mr. Darcy nodded politely and guided her to the carriage door which was now clear of the clumsy Mr. Collins. Colonel Fitzwilliam and Mr. Darcy both bade the party a good evening and watched as the carriage retreated.

Chapter 27

Early the next day, Darcy took it upon himself to visit the parsonage. To his dismay the Collinses were in the village and he was greeted, welcomed, and shortly sitting alone with Miss Elizabeth. The dismay Darcy felt was not for the specific absence of the Collins but in the idea he must now solely converse with Elizabeth; and she with him.

He found the conversation awkward and stilted, and himself, wishing for another person to alleviate the tension of his playing center stage. Attempting to make a go of it, he inquired into her family, views on travel, lodging, and a few other odd topics. Miss Bennet was her usual civil self and answered his inquiries; adding her viewpoints where necessary. From time to time she would look quizzically at Darcy in her attempt to discern his motives and feelings of unease. This did nothing to help Darcy; instead it drove him to further distraction.

Eventually the Collinses returned from the village and after sitting quietly for a few minutes more, he made his excuses, wished everyone a pleasant day, and left. Heading back to Rosings Darcy shook his head and reminded himself that his current feelings of dread and embarrassment were exactly why he did not recommend himself to strangers.

The following day Darcy was content to walk the park of Rosings. He was finished with his daily letters and had just concluded arrangements for himself and his cousin to return to town on the morrow. He had mixed feelings on returning to

London. Business needed to be attended to, even though he could manage from here. He was inclined to stay-on for the society of Miss Bennet, but his fiasco the day before taught him that he still had much to learn about conversation. His discomforts now lead him to re-focus and retreat into the safety of the world of business; this was a world he found much more comfortable.

As he walked, he suddenly found himself confronted with Miss Bennet, who appeared to have turned from another direction and was now upon his position.

"Oh! Mr. Darcy, I did not expect to see you there."

"No, I should imagine not, I do not frequently walk the park." For a moment both of them stared in silence until Miss Bennet broke the peace.

"I often walk this path to gather my thoughts. I hope it is not an imposition."

"None at all, I have just concluded my daily letters to London and decided to explore the park."

"Well, it appears we are headed in the same direction and I can conjure a measure of civility and allow you to accompany me." she said with a wry smile as she studied Mr. Darcy.

Mr. Darcy nodded and fell into step beside Elizabeth. After a minute of awkward silence, in which Darcy attempted to think of something to converse about, Elizabeth came to his rescue and forwarded one of her observations.

"You appeared very ill at ease yesterday when you called upon the parsonage. I attempted to discover the nature of the uneasiness and could only conjecture your prior admittance to social awkwardness must be the key. Did you not feel well at ease for conversation?"

Darcy found the forthright statement and question initially offensive, but Elizabeth's kind countenance calmed his nerves and allowed him to collect his thoughts.

"I freely admit that in matters of business, politics, and other subjects of importance I am more at ease. I prefer conversation of serious topics than the trivial ones with which most social engagements are comprised."

"Well then let us talk only of serious matters and dispense with the triviality of ordinary subjects."

"If it were so easy I should find the balls, and evenings spent entertaining strangers, to be more enjoyable."

"I imagine you would, but here, on the walk, with nature amongst us, and the sun shining, we may think of such trivialities and how they can be amusing. What do you think of the Napoleonic Code?"

Darcy was shocked by such a question and the sudden change in direction of conversation did not allow his mind a quick recovery. It was a few seconds before he could gather his resources and respond.

"I believe the code to have merit by way of opportunity; where before there was little."

"Merit and opportunity; how dreadful to say. Napoleon, with one simple writ, allows for equality amongst men and forgets the women that aided him his position."

"The Napoleonic code appears to be an interesting set of laws designed to allow the French citizenry more freedom from aristocratic despotism from which they suffered. I might agree more enthusiastically with the code if the English were to suffer under the aristocracy as the French certainly have."

"You mention nothing of the codes abuses toward women. Do you profess such a belief as to make women subservient to men in all matters? I can imagine the wife of your house; always obedient and attentive to your needs."

"I now perceive you to jest with me."

"Ah, do you now begin to understand the complexity of my nature? If it is so, then I must change tactics to prevent my entire persona from exposure."

"I believe you to be cunning enough to vex me on many subjects; but tactical changes can often be countered."

"Yes they can, but I shall merely stop the advance and retreat to conversations of flowers, and Ball gowns, and many other various trivialities," Elizabeth said as she returned to her face a wry smile.

"Fear not Mr. Darcy, I will spare you the displeasure of a feigned retreat. I do notice you have less movement in your left arm than in your right. Is this an old war wound?"

"I was never in the war, but it is an old wound, and well spotted." Darcy was amazed at Miss Bennet's prowess and presence of mind as he told her of his injury and recovery.

The walk continued for several more minutes and it was not until well after they parted ways when he realized how skillfully Miss Elizabeth had put him at ease. Her regard for his uneasiness touched Mr. Darcy and he found himself quite comfortable talking with her.

Entering the house, oblivious to most of his surroundings, Darcy headed to his office. Colonel Fitzwilliam accosted him on the way and asked if Darcy knew the whereabouts of his favorite cufflinks. He could not find them and was not leaving the park on the morrow if they were not safely packed.

"We are not leaving tomorrow."

Not waiting for a reply, Darcy continued deeper into the house, leaving a confused and speechless cousin.

Chapter 28

The next day Darcy was walking the park but was disappointed in not encountering Miss Bennet. Returning to Rosings he answered letters and studied his current schemes. He would need to leave for town soon and deal with Ackerby's organization with more direct methods. Subtlety was working well, but Darcy could see the need to strike more direct blows. Papers were strewn about the office with a methodology few would understand, but Darcy moved about the room with ease, consulting one report and then another. He found his mind wandering to distraction more often than he pleased. Sighing slightly he left the office to make arrangements for his return to town.

The next morning after breakfast Darcy left Rosings and walked the park. This day he did happen upon Miss Bennet, who appeared all surprised to see him once again upon the path.

"Mr. Darcy, another fine day to you."

"To you as well Miss Bennet, it appears the fates wish to subject us to a mutual experience of the park."

"Fates?" she asked as he turned in step with her. "Which fates did you have in mind? I find I prefer the Greek versions to the Roman; the names are more to my liking."

"Each with power over the gods; it is said even Zeus must obey the will of the fates. Yes I can see how that would please you endlessly."

Elizabeth took the jest in good humour and responded in kind.

"Mr. Darcy you offend my honour once again, and if you do not cease I shall be forced to retaliate as I have in the past. The colonel is not here to bear witness, but I will be sure to inform him of the retaliation; I imagine he will be happy to listen."

"You spend a great deal of time with my cousin do you?"

"I would not classify the time we enjoy as a great amount. He is a pleasing man, well mannered, with an ease of conversation I imagine you envy. It is easy to see the education and bearing in him. Should he have been a first born son he would at this moment be a fine Earl, one for which his father would be proud. We have conversed on the few occasions his walks took him to the parsonage. Mrs. Collins and I find him very gentlemanly and cannot fathom a reason for his not taking a wife."

"My cousin has an interesting military career which keeps him away much of the time. For this reason he has not seen fit to marry."

Darcy looked about the park and returned his eyes suddenly to Miss Bennet. For a second he caught a look of annoyance, which was rapidly replaced with a smile when she noticed his quizzical stare.

"Well, I believe when the colonel sets his mind to the serious contemplation of marriage, his rank in life and bearing will find the matter settled quickly. Those qualities will compensate for his lack of money and title."

"Do you spend a great deal of time on the contemplation of marriage?"

"My own personal marriage I do not, but I have been known to contemplate the marriage of others. I can see the marriage of Miss De Bourgh to be advantageous to many men, even men of great stature. Anne is a pleasant enough girl; I imagine she will make a fitting and obedient wife to whomever chooses to marry her. For years I have imagined my dear friend Charlotte to be married. I did not suppose she would marry my cousin, and so soon after he proposed to me."

This news startled Darcy and he begged her to explain. Elizabeth then informed Mr. Darcy that the trip which precipitated the first meeting of himself and Mr. Collins was intended as a visit to repair family relations. Mr. Collins then used the opportunity to offer marriage to her. The offer was refused and shortly Mr. Collins found himself engaged, and then married to, Elizabeth's friend, Charlotte. The speed of the entire affair was astonishing to most people.

"It is odd that he did not offer marriage to the eldest daughter."

Elizabeth appeared irritated by this remark and only commented.

"Mr. Collins believed her feelings did not lend themselves to him, but he was mistaken in the assumption that mine did."

"In many marriages, affections become of little consideration. Still it was lucky of Mr. Collins to find a wife in the immediate vicinity as Hertfordshire so that his needs were met. That particular countryside does not offer the diversity of the town."

Elizabeth took exception to this remark but let little show, other than to make a reply of her own.

"I imagine the countryside has a great deal to offer any gentleman who chooses to overcome the pride of claiming high society."

Darcy answered calmly. "I did not intend to offend; only to comment on the level of population, not its quality of gentry."

Miss Bennet replied with an observation on the population of London and compared it to other cities of high population; to which Mr. Darcy asked if Miss Bennet had ever visited the cities of which she spoke. The two continued along the path and, as with the previous walk, separated at Rosings. Darcy entered the house and as he passed the drawing room the Colonel looked up from his papers.

"Ah, there you are cousin. You will be happy to know I am packed and ready to be off tomorrow as planned."

"We are not departing yet," replied Darcy, leaving Fitzwilliam confused and bewildered once again.

Chapter 29

Letters strewn throughout the room and a confused Mr. Darcy would have been a vision accosting anyone entering his office. He had spent the previous evening compiling notes when a letter arrived from town. It was from Miss Dache and related a new development in London to which she asked for his personal attention. Mr. Darcy at first believed Miss Dache might be attempting to lure him back to town, but reading the letter further and reminding himself of Miss Dache's character disproved the notion.

Mr. Fitzwilliam Darcy,

It has been some days since you have written and I can only imagine you are quite enthralled with your current visit. I do hope you plan to return to town quickly; I should so much like to see you again. Our mutual friend, never wanting for a dire predicament, has taken it upon himself to act in a most rash way. I fear his current actions may lead to social and financial injuries for which you and I will both be required to repair. His current manners are most peculiar and irrational and I find myself at odds with how to deal with him. I rest easy in the knowledge that your insight and guidance will prevail in taming our friend's deeds. I am attaching proper correspondence with this letter; perhaps you can make sense of them as such business and social matters confuse me.

Marianne Dache

The packet of information accompanying the letter told a very odd story to Mr. Darcy. In all appearances Colonel Ackerby appeared to be failing in his enterprise. This was to be expected eventually, but the peculiarity of the failure puzzled Darcy. Odd transactions from banks, miscellaneous slayings, and reports of the Colonel rearranging his ranks were all well detailed and confirmed. He was seen in public without his usual retinue; and on one occasion determined to be drunk.

A few letters, intermixed with the reports, were from men of respect, urging a very sudden move upon Ackerby. One bold man suggested a constant mark on the colonel so he may be dispatched should he be found in public unawares. Darcy took his usual dislike to the idea of wanton killing.

It was the next morning while Darcy glanced at the financials when he realized the wild nature of the Colonel's speculation. Ackerby was indeed becoming desperate and had poorly hidden his tracks. Financial losses had piled up and Ackerby, like a poor gambler, was betting high on more outlandish business and criminal enterprises. The money transfers, slayings, political involvement all pointed to a scheme regarding government expenditures for upcoming war contracts. If Ackerby could be pushed the right direction he would be forced to overextend. When his information eventually proved false his finances would crash. This could be a fatal blow to his organization.

Darcy, excited to see an unbelievable opportunity, analyzed the data and began to formulate a plan. Ackerby still needed two more pieces of information and those could only be found in high level offices. With the right team and connections Darcy could plant misleading information. Once the information was stolen, Ackerby would speculate incorrectly and he would begin to fall. It would take four days to arrange matters and Darcy believed the situation would allow the time. The contractual departments would not have the final reports regarding the deals for a few days, which is what currently prevented Ackerby from moving forward. Pulling out paper, Darcy began to address a letter and unfolded his plan. Glancing at a clock he suddenly became aware of the time. Realizing the situation permitted, he grabbed his coat and headed out to the park for a constitutional.

The weather was pleasant for this time of year and as Darcy ambled about he tried to fix the details of his plan. His eyes kept looking on the path, ever searching for Miss Bennet.

Coming to mental attention he arrested his sights and focused on the situation in London. Again his eyes wondered the parks paths and again he reined them in. Sighing in frustration he grew angry with himself and his inability to focus.

"You seem very deep in thought Mr. Darcy," Elizabeth said as she approached from a side path.

Gazing in her direction Darcy was confronted with a mixture of emotion; happiness to see her and anger at himself for the confusion she caused. Miss Bennet for her part seemed determined and slightly annoyed for which Mr. Darcy attributed the incline of the path she was upon.

"I am attempting to conclude a business matter in London and the details elude me," Darcy replied to Elizabeth as she fell into step with him. For all his lack of focus, Darcy had not misjudged Miss Bennet's probable approach and direction. As the Fates, and Mr. Darcy, once more directed, the two walked together.

"I am pleased to hear it. We shall be forced to immediately engage in conversation regarding serious topics. This will appease any discomfort you may feel at the idea of trivial matters."

Mr. Darcy politely declined the invitation to discuss matters of business citing the boring nature of the enterprise and various obscure details which would prove less than entertaining to Miss Bennet.

Arching her eyebrow and donning her teasing smile Elizabeth replied. "All right, it shall be trivial matters then. Our recent conversations have been much too serious and as you know, I am prone to discussions of frivolity. Perhaps we will spot a deer or a rabbit on our walk which will provide us with an enjoyable conversation topic."

It was Mr. Darcy's turn to arch an eyebrow. Miss Bennet did not seem in any hurry to continue talking and looked at him as if to say she had all day to await a reply. Mr. Darcy thought for a moment and decided to relate the current situation with Ackerby. He disregarded the names and was general in the details for which he claimed secrecy of the business deal required it.

"This business opponent you mention; he appears to have many qualities of a complex character."

"I should say so; I found him many times to be competent, intelligent, and cunning."

"If he is as complex as you, then I imagine the two of you make an interesting evening at a ball. I sense you are uneasy on the business matter. Do you not wish to enter into an enterprise which may cost him so dearly?"

"While I rarely wish anyone harm, this particular deal is a matter of business. We shall each of us do our best, but the stakes are high and a miscalculation could cost dearly. This of course is often the case with business. My concern is not over his calculations but his apparent loss of sense. I have not been in his presence, but my intellect and prejudices have concluded him to be a competent individual. I find his current actions to be at odds with that assessment of him; but business is often won or lost on such matters and I shall perform my duties as I must. If his character is flawed to the point of allowing such wild speculation then perhaps it is better for nature to take its course, and for me to act quickly upon the opportunity provided."

"Whenever one observes an enemy committing a gross error, one should assume that there is a trick beneath it."

Darcy stared at Miss Bennet, who having finished her quote from Machievelli's Discourse on war, continued to walk at a very casual gait.

"Tell me Mr. Darcy, what is the cost if you miscalculate?"

The whole scheme came into focus and Darcy was hit with the sheer genius it. Ackerby must by now realize the nature of his attacks and was creating a situation to draw out his unknown opponents. Darcy would need to return to his office to study reports and verify, but he was certain the insight given by Miss Bennet would explain his nagging doubts. Recovering his senses Mr. Darcy addressed his companion.

"My costs could be noticeable but nothing for which I am unaccustomed. I do take care to perform due diligence and I am sure as I analyze the enterprise I will find my opponent recently widowered or taken ill. Those facts will easily explain his lack of judgment."

Elizabeth agreed it would likely be so.

Darcy now had his mind set on the matters in London which distracted him, and attempts to attend to his companion led to a more stilted conversation. He inquired to the happiness of the Collins, and then Miss Bennet's opinions on the parsonage and her lodgings. Topics varied from Colonel Fitzwilliam to many insignificant subjects. Miss Bennet sensing the odd mood of her companion performed civilly and wondered to the nature of these odd topics. Seizing upon the triviality she led Mr. Darcy down a metaphorical journey into mundane social issues as their feet carried them along the literal path. In a matter of minutes Darcy was once again focused on his companion.

Arriving at Rosings he found himself less inclined to return to his letters and more inclined to continue the walk with Miss Bennet. The choice was not his to make however, as she veered off the path and headed to the parsonage with a firm, but civil, wish for a good day.

Darcy watched her leave for a minute then headed back into the house and directly to his office. Letter after letter was written asking for more details and direct observations on key individuals. If Ackerby was to set a trap, then Darcy would be ready to avoid it.

Chapter 30

The following evening the household of Rosings made ready to receive the Collinses and Miss Bennet for evening tea. Darcy was much unaware of the activity as he had spent the entirety of the day in his office coordinating his plans. He was upset at the thought of missing a possible walk with Miss Bennet, but he consoled these feelings with the thought that Miss Bennet was not inclined to walk the park daily and a chance encounter would be just that; chance.

Darcy's aunt soon took it upon herself to call on her nephew and demand his presence for the arrival of her guests. Darcy sighed with resignation and, as his business was concluded, accompanied her to the drawing room. While waiting for their guests, conversation centered on topics of interest to Lady Catherine, as they typically did. Eventually Darcy and his cousin were relieved by the announcement of the Collins.

"And where is Miss Bennet this evening? Is she not aware the invitation was for the entirety of the rectory?" asked Lady Catherine in her commanding voice.

"Indeed she was my Lady and I must apologize profusely for her absence, but Miss Bennet has taken ill with a very serious headache."

Colonel Fitzwilliam appeared shocked by the news Mr. Collins delivered.

"Oh dear I do wish she will be well. I only just left her these last few hours. We encountered each other in the park and engaged in lively conversation. She appeared well at the time."

"Indeed she must have been Colonel, but since that time she has taken quite ill with a headache and I could not convince her to attend. I assure you my Lady I did impress upon her the importance of invitations to Rosings and begged her to suffer the pain so that she may be able to attend this evenings tea. I could not convince her and the headache seemed to only worsen."

Lady Catherine began to expound on the nature of headaches and how to deal with them. She then offered comments suggesting they should be tolerated a great deal, so one may attend to social engagements.

Darcy stood from his chair and made an excuse of forgotten business he needed to attend to. His aunt tried to convince him to stay but Darcy ended the matter abruptly by leaving the room.

A few minutes later Darcy was standing on the doorstep of the parsonage and ringing the bell. It was answered by a servant and Mr. Darcy was allowed entry into the front parlor where he saw Miss Bennet who appeared to be regarding several letters strewn across the furniture. She appeared completely amazed to see him. Taking a seat he informed her that his visit was to inquire into her health and wish her a speedy recovery.

Elizabeth stared coldly at Mr. Darcy and spoke very plainly.

"I shall be well," was the only reply she made.

Darcy sat for a moment longer and when he realized no more information would be forthcoming he attempted to think of something to say. Even a trivial matter would be welcomed but he could think of nothing. He stood and walked about the room looking at various objects. Figurines and paintings seemed much too trivial to discuss as his mind tried to find something, and the only thought that came readily to mind was how difficult a task it was to converse with this woman in contrast to the difficulty of his actions in London. Miss Bennet watched him pace the room and offered no help as she stared at him with an expressionless face. Finally Darcy snapped his mind to attention and decided he could take no more of the duality of his thoughts and feelings.

``In vain have I struggled. It will not do. My feelings will not be repressed. You must allow me to tell you how ardently I admire and love you."

Elizabeth's astonishment was beyond expression. She stared, coloured, doubted, and was silent. This he considered sufficient encouragement, and the avowal of all that he felt and had long felt for her immediately followed. He spoke well, but there were feelings besides those of the heart to be detailed, and he was not more eloquent on the subject of tenderness than of pride. His sense of her inferiority, of its being a degradation, of the family obstacles which judgment had always opposed to inclination, were dwelt on with a warmth which seemed due to the consequence he was wounding, but was very unlikely to recommend his suit.

Elizabeth grew red as Darcy commented on the nature of her inferior familial connections and attributes of members of her family. At the mention of a suit between them she became more rigid and her pride was injured with Darcy's admission the union would be a degradation to his family. With keen and cold eyes she replied to Mr. Darcy.

``In such cases as this, it is, I believe, the established mode to express a sense of obligation for the sentiments avowed, however unequally they may be returned. It is natural that obligation should be felt, and if I could *feel* gratitude, I would now thank you. But I cannot. I have never desired your good opinion, and you have certainly bestowed it most unwillingly. I am sorry to have occasioned pain to any one. It has been most unconsciously done, however, and I hope will be of short duration. The feelings which, you tell me, have long prevented the acknowledgment of your regard, can have little difficulty in overcoming it after this explanation."

Mr. Darcy, who was leaning against the mantle-piece with his eyes fixed on her face, seemed to catch her words with no less resentment than surprise. His complexion became pale with anger, and the disturbance of his mind was visible in every feature. He was struggling for the appearance of composure, and would not open his lips, till he believed himself to have attained it. The pause was to Elizabeth's feelings dreadful. He turned to the mantelpiece to avoid her gaze and gain his composure. At length, in a voice of forced calmness, he turned back and said,

``And this is all the reply which I am to have the honour of expecting…."

The turn he was completing became a dodge as his arm raised to defend against the dagger now heading toward him. With little thinking, and a great deal of training, his body moved backward and away from the attack. The motions of the two individuals in the room took only a few seconds and now Mr. Darcy stood on one side of the room, opposite the door, with a determined Miss Bennet standing in way of his escape. She appeared calm but resilient in her current endeavor, and she addressed Mr. Darcy calmly as she arched her eyebrows.

"Had not my own feelings decided against you, had they been indifferent, or had they even been favourable, do you think that any consideration would tempt me to accept the man, who has been the means of ruining, perhaps for ever, the happiness of a most beloved sister?" The last of the sentence was said with a seething manner and mean eyes.

Mr. Darcy changed colour; but the emotion was short, and he listened without attempting to interrupt her or to move in any way which might provoke a direct attack. He thought about quitting the room rapidly, but her manner, her skill, and her eyes kept him in check. He found himself emotionally stalled and could do little but listen as she continued.

``I have every reason in the world to think ill of you!" she claimed derisively. "No motive can excuse the unjust and ungenerous part you acted *there*. You dare not, you cannot deny that you have been the principal, if not the only means of dividing them from each other."

She paused, and saw, with no slight indignation, that he was listening with an air which proved him wholly unmoved by any feeling of remorse. He even looked at her with a smile of affected incredulity.

Mr. Darcy, for his part, began calculating an exit, while wondering how Miss Bennet came upon the facts of his involvement in separating her sister from his friend.

``Can you deny that you have done it?" she repeated coldly.

With assumed tranquility he then replied, ``I have no wish of denying that I did every thing in my power to separate my friend from your sister, or that I rejoice in my success. Towards *him* I have been kinder than towards myself."

Elizabeth's eyes flared and she disdained the appearance of his civility. His reference to self kindness was an insult that only angered here further. She moved in a menacing way as if to feign and attack, and Darcy watched her carefully.

"Arum Maculatum," she said as she maneuvered to keep Darcy confined with no escape. The words jarred Darcy, and Elizabeth noticed his reaction. Up to this point she had surmised Darcy's role in poisoning her sister and allowed him absolution only after determining to her convictions that the incident was accidental. "I am also aware of the poisoning of my sister by your tea! Do not think me as incompetent as our local apothecary."

``But it is not merely these affairs," she continued, ``on which my dislike is founded. Long before my sister left for London, my opinion of you was decided. Your character was unfolded in the recital which I received many months ago from Mr. Wickham. On this subject, what can you have to say? In what imaginary act of friendship can you here defend yourself? or under what misrepresentation, can you here impose upon others?"

``You take an eager interest in that gentleman's concerns," said Darcy in a less tranquil tone, and with a heightened colour. He moved slowly watching the blade and judging Elizabeth's skill.

Several months prior to this evening Elizabeth had become quite fond of Mr. Wickham and listened eagerly to the tales the charismatic young man told of the man whom she suspected of poisoning her sister. She felt sorry for Wickham's misfortunes laid upon him by the conceited Mr. Darcy, and, as she held that conceited man at bay, she made it clear her thoughts were so.

``Who that knows what his misfortunes have been, can help feeling an interest in him?"

``His misfortunes!" repeated Darcy contemptuously; ``yes, his misfortunes have been great indeed." It was now Darcy's turn to become angry and the tension began to mount.

``And of your infliction," cried Elizabeth with energy. ``You have reduced him to his present state of poverty, comparative poverty. You have withheld the advantages, which you must know to have been designed for him. You have deprived the best years of his life, of that independence which was no less his due than his desert. You have done all this! and yet you can treat the mention of his misfortunes with contempt and ridicule."

``And this," cried Darcy, ``is your opinion of me! This is the estimation in which you hold me! I thank you for explaining it so fully. My faults, according to this calculation, are heavy indeed! But perhaps, these offences might have been overlooked, had not your pride been hurt by my honest confession of the scruples that had long prevented my forming any serious design. These bitter accusations might have been suppressed, had I with greater policy concealed my struggles, and flattered you into the belief of my being impelled by unqualified, unalloyed inclination -- by reason, by reflection, by every thing. But disguise of every sort is my abhorrence, and unfortunately sometimes a burden I only bear when I must." He said this last line in a trailing and contemplative tone. Coming to his senses he stated loudly and with a sense of pride "Nor am I ashamed of the feelings I related. They were natural and just. Could you expect me to rejoice in the inferiority of your connections? To congratulate myself on the hope of relations, whose condition in life is so decidedly beneath my own?"

Elizabeth felt herself growing angrier every moment; yet she tried to the utmost to speak with composure when she said,

``You are mistaken, Mr. Darcy, if you suppose that the mode of your declaration affected me in any other way. It has only spared me the guilt which I might have felt in refusing you, had you behaved in a more gentleman-like manner."

She saw him start at this, but he said nothing, and she continued,

``You could not have made me the offer of your hand in any possible way that would have tempted me to accept it."

Again his astonishment was obvious; and he looked at her with an expression of mingled incredulity and mortification. She went on.

``From the very beginning, from the first moment I may almost say, of my acquaintance with you, your manners, impressing me with the fullest belief of your arrogance, your conceit, and your selfish disdain of the feelings of others, were such as to form that ground-work of disapprobation, on which succeeding events have built so immoveable a dislike; and I had not known you a month before I felt that you were the last man in the world whom I could ever be prevailed on to marry."

``You have said quite enough, madam. I perfectly comprehend your feelings, and have now only to be ashamed of what my own have been. Forgive me for having taken up so much of your time, and accept my best wishes for your health and happiness."

With these words he moved to her, feigned his direction, bypassed her untrained blade, and hastily left the room. Elizabeth heard him the next moment open the front door and quit the house.

Taking a deep breath, Elizabeth placed the blade calmly on the table near the letters she had been reading. She headed to the window and watched as Mr. Darcy left the parsonage, on his way to Rosings. He did not run, but it could certainly be said that he did not amble. The gait of his retreat pleased her immensely and she smiled with eyes brightening as her anger vanished to be replaced with wicked amusement.

"Run little man," she said to him, "and if you should choose to inflict your sentimentalities of love upon me again, I will not withhold my blade, as I have chosen to do today."

Turning back to her letters she began to gather them up and sort them by date. It was only a few hours since her walk in the park with Colonel Fitzwilliam where he, with a little encouragement, informed Elizabeth about Darcy's role in separating Mr. Bingley from Jane. It did not take much convincing because the Colonel believed he was regaling Miss Bennet with a heroic tale of Mr. Darcy's amazing feats; had he been aware he was informing the sister of the intended feat he would surely have shown more discretion.

At first Elizabeth was incredulous, but as the Colonel completed the tale Elizabeth knew it to be true. She was angered at the idea that the man who betrayed her friend, Mr. Wickham, had also destroyed the happiness of her sister, who so dearly cared for Charles Bingley. Leaving the Colonel at the park, she had returned here to the Parsonage to analyze all of her sister's letters from London. She arranged them and collated them. When she encountered remarks of sadness with regards to Jane's inability to see Charles, she grew angry. It was then that Mr. Darcy chose to enter the room and profess feelings of love.

Elizabeth was now calm as she considered the letters, her sister, and the infuriating Mr. Darcy. She truly did not wish harm to anyone, and her dislike of Mr. Darcy to this point was kept in check by civility and social graces. The anger she felt at his recent sins was now subsiding, and she had to admit the attack on him was uncharacteristic. Indeed she could not believe what had come over her and a feeling of shame crept in, only to be mixed with anger. She thought to herself that she should feel no shame of actions when dealing with the likes of this man; but she could not deny that her actions saddened her.

Sitting in a chair, with Jane's letters in one hand, she placed her elbow on the arm rest and her chin into her palm. She glanced at her letters and the thought of her sister, alone in London, saddened her more. She wished she could do more to help her, and she dearly wished for her sister's happiness; but how could this be achieved when the powers of a man like Mr. Darcy could prevent it. At a loss for ideas, and with the weight of emotions upon her heart, she dropped the letters and began to cry.

Chapter 31

"You damnable fool." Darcy muttered to himself as he entered his office at Rosings. The walk from the parsonage had been quick and focused; leaving little time to think on the situation with any attention to meaning.

Locking the door of his office he headed over to his desk and withdrew a small box from a drawer. Within lay a dagger and Darcy took hold of it with mean force. Pulling it from its sheath he marveled at the blade as it shone in the light. The glint from the blade cast an eerie reflection of himself and the shadowy image appeared to reveal more of his mood than his countenance. Only now did he take a moment to collect his thoughts.

With the dagger still in hand he headed to a chair and as he sat deep into the recesses of the wingback, his mind sank deep into thought. Questions came quickly to mind.

"How did she know about the poisoning? How did she know about her sister Jane?"

Wickham had no doubt prejudiced Mr. Darcy in Miss Bennet's mind with regards to the relations between the two gentlemen. Darcy's mind seethed with anger at the thought of that charismatic charmer, with a smile upon his face, deceiving Miss Bennet.

His mind began to recount the meetings between Elizabeth and himself. For the first time, he took a clinical look at her and viewed her as an adversary rather than a simple country lady.

Assumptions built with deductions led to inferences and the mind of Darcy soon saw a hazy image of the young lady come into focus. Her walk through the mud to Netherfield showed a constitution of determination as well as physical fitness; this combined, with her ability in dance, confirmed his idea of her being very physically capable.

The answers came quickly to Darcy now that he was looking for pieces of a puzzle he was heretofore unaware needed assembly.

Miss Bennet's book the night she attended Jane was the one he left in the drawing room. The one she seemed interested in reading and his mind now concluded must have been his book on local flora; marked and noted on sections of Arum Maculatum.

He could recall Elizabeth's inquiries into the nature of her sister's illness. He further recalled the amount of time Elizabeth spent with Jane, which Darcy originally assumed showed affection, and was now seen as both affection and guardianship against an unknown foe.

Elizabeth's charming nature had led Darcy to reveal much and he now reminded himself of just how much private information she had garnered from him. His old wounds, his business in London, relationships with Charles and Fitzwilliam; the latter individual he now assumed was her source of information regarding her sister in London. He could hold no animosity towards his cousin as he knew Fitzwilliam would not knowing put Darcy in an awkward situation. No, concluded Darcy. Miss Bennet had very skillfully drawn the information from the Colonel.

“Clever lady!” Darcy marveled aloud to the room.

Deciding what to do next was Darcy’s current dilemma. He glanced at the blade still in his hand and stared. Taking a deep breath he thought on Miss Bennet and the content of her character. The affection towards her sister, the generosity in her spirit, and kindness when engaged in argumentation, all were attributes for which Darcy was sure he had not misjudged. While he might fault Elizabeth for her erroneous conclusions he could not bring himself to condemn her for shallowness of the soul.

Standing up, Darcy put the dagger on the desk and walked to the bookcase where tripping a few hidden catches revealed a compartment. Darcy pulled paper and ink along with a quill, closed the compartment, and headed back to the desk. Initial reticence of action receded and as he wrote his mind focused on the task. As one might expect in many endeavors, the simple engagement of actions can convince the person of the correctness of the solution.

Mr. Darcy, already skilled with words, found the letter to flow exceedingly easy for him; and when done, the pages reflected articulate sentences combined with personal feelings. Feelings Darcy was unaware he could so eloquently express in words.

Chapter 32

Elizabeth awoke the next morning to find herself in much better spirits. The emotions of the night, having taken their toll, had moved on and left her surprisingly refreshed. She readied herself for the day and then ate her breakfast thoughtfully, after which she decided upon a stroll.

Nearing the park, she avoided her usual route in favor of walking the lane. She made no excuses for her direction as the choice was an obvious attempt to avoid an encounter with Mr. Darcy, should he choose to walk the park.

On her return she moved to the edge of the park and enjoyed the beauty of the trees. Every day the view changed with spring flowers blooming and trees becoming more full. About to depart, she caught sight of a gentleman within a grove bordering the park. Fearful it might be Mr. Darcy she attempted to move off, but a call of her name arrested her movements and she turned to face the caller. It was indeed Mr. Darcy and Elizabeth's heart pounded with dread, as one does in uncertain and tense situations.

Mr. Darcy approached Elizabeth slowly and with controlled movement. His hands were freely visible and he displayed no signs of being armed. Instead, in one hand, he held a letter, and as he approached he slowly raised the letter as a display of innocence. Still several feet away he stopped and addressed her formally and in a tone Elizabeth found to be a little too haughty.

"Miss Bennet, I have been walking the grove for some time in hopes of encountering you. I wonder if you would do me the honour of reading this letter."

Mr. Darcy moved to put the letter on a nearby log in what Elizabeth could only assume was an attempt to be non-threatening. Elizabeth arched her eyes and affected a wry smile as if to say "Are you so afraid of me?" She did not mouth a single word of her thought but Mr. Darcy appeared to surmise the meaning of her look. He stood to attention and slowly walked towards her. His perceived haughtiness was now in check and Elizabeth was amused. She gauged his approach and tensed herself should he move suddenly, but he did not, nor did he do anything other than to extend the letter which she took automatically. Darcy Bowed slightly with civility then backed away several feet, quickly turned, and left. Elizabeth watched all of this keenly and when Darcy was well and gone she returned to the lane and headed away from the parsonage.

Amusement and curiosity took hold as she opened the letter. Within the outer envelope were pages of material in neat, closely written script. It was marked from Rosings and dated that day.

Be not alarmed, Madam, on receiving this letter, by the apprehension of its containing any repetition of those sentiments, or renewal of those offers, which were last night so disgusting to you. I write without any intention of paining you, or humbling myself, by dwelling on wishes, which, for the happiness of both, cannot be too soon forgotten; and the effort which the formation and the perusal of this letter must occasion should have been spared, had not my character required it to be written and read. You must, therefore, pardon the freedom with which I demand your attention; your feelings, I know, will bestow it unwillingly, but I demand it of your justice.

I would also beg you to read this letter quickly and to commit any parts wished for reference to memory. The letter you hold within your hand is written in such a method as to make the ink delible, and within a short period of time the words will begin to fade and become quite unreadable. I will trust to your nature that the contents of this letter will not be shared before the qualities of the ink are allowed to fulfill their purpose and eradicate the sensitive information which is about to be revealed to you.

As you are no doubt aware, the events of the last hundred years have shown remarkable changes to the Nobility. The loss of the Americas, the fight for freedoms and equality, and the rise of wealth of many a common man, have affected the ranks and moralities of royalty and gentry the world over. I would surmise, and I believe you would agree, that the likes of Napoleon would not have risen to power should the Nobility and the Gentry of France acted in a more honourable manner.

Fearing these changes and observing less honourable acts from the aristocracy, the Highest Order of the previous century decided to form an organization with the intent of upholding honour and justice for all England's people. I daresay, the idea of separation of powers the Americas use, was garnered from individuals within our influence.

While the former colonies now use many of these ideas openly we use them more discretely. It is our objective to ensure the Gentry and Nobility do not stray into serious offences and when they do we will insure they are not able to use their influence to continue such endeavors. When the laws of nature, such as deception, corruption, and intimidation are used to allow people of influence to a avoid justice then we move to safeguard the laws of men; all men.

I will reveal very few details, but of my lineage I will tell you that in the past my ancestors proved their courage and ability with regards to subtle and clever solutions to problems, which if left unchecked, would expand to greater proportions of villainy. It was at this time that my ancestors were approached by the Highest Order. The Darcy family was respected, wealthy, and with close ties to Nobility, without having an official claim to the throne. My family has accepted the requested duties and requisite responsibilities. The methods of the duties are much in line with my cousin Colonel Fitzwilliam, whose family might well have our duties if not for the fact they possess the title of Earl. However, the methods we share may be similar in training and mental requirements, where they differ is in the execution; Fitzwilliam on a battlefield and myself within the shadows. It is with pride that my ancestors acceded to the requests of past nobles and it is with pride that I now continue those duties. These duties are to ensure the Gentry and Nobility remember our code and adhere to it.

We are Honourable. We are Accountable. We are the Gentry.

As to specific offences of which you claim against me, I offer you an explanation of my actions and revelations of facts I do not believe you possess.

Concerning your sister, you are quite right in your deduction of her former illness; it was my tea which caused her illness. I have found the brew of that particular tea useful to temporarily disable an individual without affecting great harm. The tea was left foolishly unsecured and was administered to your sister by a mishap of the ladies attending to her. I do not believe the ladies intended any malice and, if not for the dire state of your sister, haste would not have been necessary and the tea would not have been mistakenly offered. The details of this accounting I believe you may already be aware. Once I learned of the mistake, I took great pains to examine your sister and see to her welfare. I will assure you as a gentleman, if her health had been in great jeopardy I would have spared no expense to remedy the situation.

As to the matter of Charles I will state clearly that the accusation you lay against me is indeed true. I do agree with the charge, although not the animosity for which you delivered it. I will try to explain as best I can.

We were not long in Hertfordshire before I suspected Charles to be partial to your sister. His easy and trusting nature allow him to be blind the fallacies of others, and with concern for his well being I took it upon myself to acquaint myself with your sister. Her look and manners were open, cheerful, and engaging as ever, but without any symptom of peculiar regard, and I remained convinced from scrutiny, that though she received his attentions with pleasure, she did not invite them by any participation of sentiment. -- If *you* have not been mistaken here, *I* must have been in an error. Your superior knowledge of your sister must make the latter probable. -- If it be so, if I have been misled by such error, to inflict pain on her, your resentment has not been unreasonable. But I shall not scruple to assert that the serenity of your sister's countenance and air was such as might have given the most acute observer a conviction that, however amiable her temper, her heart was not likely to be easily touched.

That I was desirous of believing her indifferent is certain, but I will venture to say that my investigations and decisions are not usually influenced by my hopes or fears. I did not believe her to be indifferent because I wished it; I believed it on impartial conviction, as truly as I wished it in reason.

My objections to the marriage were not merely those which I last night acknowledged to have required the utmost force of passion to put aside in my own case; the want of connection could not be so great an evil to my friend as to me. But there were other causes of repugnance; causes which, though still existing, and existing to an equal degree in both instances, I had myself endeavored to forget, because they were not immediately before me. These causes must be stated, though briefly.

The situation of your mother's family, though objectionable, was nothing in comparison of that total want of propriety so frequently, so almost uniformly, betrayed by herself, by your three younger sisters, and occasionally even by your father. Pardon me. It pains me to offend you. But amidst your concern for the defects of your nearest relations, and your displeasure at this representation of them, let it give you consolation to consider that to have conducted yourselves so as to avoid any share of the like censure is praise no less generally bestowed on you and your eldest sister, than it is honourable to the sense and disposition of both. I will only say farther that, from what passed, my opinion of all parties was confirmed, and every inducement heightened, which could have led me before to preserve my friend from what I esteemed a most unhappy connection. He left Netherfield for London, as you, I am certain, remember, with the design of soon returning.

I took the opportunity of the London trip to assail my friend of the shortcomings of you sister and reminded him of the responsibilities for which he must attend. I will freely admit my attempts were met with more resistance than expected and I can only deduce Charles feelings for your sister were stronger than initially believed. This proved to be less important as my business concerns in London turned dark. The nature of those affairs I cannot detail, but I will inform you that Buckingham itself is aware.

I took it upon myself to assist with the matters in London, as my family swore to do. It was not long before the situation degraded into a less manageable ordeal and one which was more dangerous. The recent arrival of my sister, Georgiana, was of immediate concern and for her protection I installed Charles into my house as an almost permanent guest. They are as of yet unaware of my concerns or the true nature of Charles visitations. It was at this time your sister arrived in London.

Not wishing to disrupt my household or my security precautions I allowed Miss Bingley to handle the affairs of you sister. In one regard Caroline and I found ourselves mutually agreed; that it would be in Charles better interests to not marry your sister. I used this agreement of opinion to deceive her as to all my motives and the matter was settled.

There is but one part of my conduct in the whole affair, on which I do not reflect with satisfaction; it is that I condescended to adopt the measures of art so far as to conceal from Charles your sister's being in town. I knew it myself, as it was known to Miss Bingley, but her brother is even yet ignorant of it. My angst over this concealment might vex you now that you have a tacit understanding of my business, but I find when innocents are involved one should defer to open means. The tense situation of which I found myself engaged allowed only moments to consider strategy, and those tended to be of a more cruel nature towards your sister and Charles.

That they might have met without ill consequence is, perhaps, probable; but his regard did not appear to me enough extinguished for him to see her without some danger. Perhaps this concealment, this disguise, was beneath me. It is done, however, and it was done for the best. On this subject I have nothing more to say, no other apology to offer. If I have wounded your sister's feelings, it was unknowingly done; and though the motives which governed me may to you very naturally appear insufficient, I have not yet learned to condemn them.

With respect to that other, more weighty accusation, of having injured Mr. Wickham, I can only refute it by laying before you the whole of his connection with my family. Of what he has *particularly* accused me, I am ignorant; but of the truth of what I shall relate, I can summon more than one witness of undoubted veracity.

Mr. Wickham is the son of a very respectable man, who had for many years the management of all the Pemberley estates; and whose good conduct in the discharge of his trust naturally inclined my father to be of service to him; and on George Wickham, who was his god-son, his kindness was therefore liberally bestowed. My father supported him at school, and afterwards at Cambridge; most important assistance, as his own father, always poor from the extravagance of his wife, would have been unable to give him a gentleman's education.

My father was not only fond of this young man's society, whose manners were always engaging; he had also the highest opinion of him, and hoping the church would be his profession, intended to provide for him in it. It was the closeness of Georges' father, and my own father's feelings toward the young man, which allowed

George access to much of the information, pertaining to my family, you now possess.

As for myself, it is many, many years since I first began to think of him in a very different manner. The vicious propensities, the want of principle, which he was careful to guard from the knowledge of his best friend, could not escape the observation of a young man of nearly the same age with himself, and who had opportunities of seeing him in unguarded moments, which Mr. Darcy, my father, could not have. Here again I shall give you pain, to what degree you only can tell. But whatever may be the sentiments which Mr. Wickham has created, a suspicion of their nature shall not prevent me from unfolding his real character. It adds even another motive.

My excellent father died about five years ago; and his attachment to Mr. Wickham was to the last so steady, that in his will he particularly recommended it to me to promote his advancement in the best manner that his profession might allow, and, if he took orders, desired that a valuable family living might be his as soon as it became vacant. There was also a legacy of one thousand pounds. His own father did not long survive mine, and within half a year from these events Mr. Wickham wrote to inform me that, having finally resolved against taking orders, he hoped I should not think it unreasonable for him to expect some more immediate pecuniary advantage, in lieu of the preferment by which he could not be benefited. He had some intention, he added, of studying the law, and I must be aware that the interest of one thousand pounds would be a very insufficient support therein. I rather wished than believed him to be sincere; but, at any rate, was perfectly ready to accede to his proposal. I knew that Mr. Wickham ought not to be a clergyman. The business was therefore soon settled. He resigned all claim to assistance in the church, were it possible that he could ever be in a situation to receive it, and accepted in return three thousand pounds. All connection between us seemed now dissolved. I thought too ill of him to invite him to Pemberley, or admit his society in town.

In town, I believe, he chiefly lived, but his studying the law was a mere pretence, and being now free from all restraint, his life was a life of idleness and dissipation. For about three years I heard little of him; but on the decease of the incumbent of the living which had been designed for him, he applied to me again by letter for the presentation. His circumstances, he assured me, were exceedingly bad.

He had found the law a most unprofitable study, and was now absolutely resolved on being ordained and asked if I would present him to the living in question. You will hardly blame me for refusing to comply with this entreaty, or for resisting every repetition of it. His resentment was in proportion to the distress of his circumstances -- and he was doubtless as violent in his abuse of me to others, as in his reproaches to myself.

After this period, every appearance of acquaintance was dropped. How he lived I know not. But last summer he was again most painfully obtruded on my notice. I must now mention a circumstance which I would wish to forget myself, and which no obligation less than the present should induce me to unfold to any human being. Having said thus much, I feel no doubt of your secrecy.

My sister, who is more than ten years my junior, was left to the guardianship of my mother's nephew, Colonel Fitzwilliam, and myself. About a year ago, she was taken from school, and an establishment formed for her in London; and last summer she went with the lady, Mrs. Younge, who presided over it, to Ramsgate; and thither also went Mr. Wickham, undoubtedly by design; for there proved to have been a prior acquaintance between him and Mrs. Younge, in whose character we were most unhappily deceived; and by her connivance and aid he so far recommended himself to Georgiana, whose affectionate heart retained a strong impression of his kindness to her as a child, that she was persuaded to believe herself in love, and to consent to an elopement. She was then but fifteen, which must be her excuse.

I joined them unexpectedly a day or two before the intended elopement; and then Georgiana, unable to support the idea of grieving and offending a brother whom she almost looked up to as a father, acknowledged the whole to me. You may imagine what I felt and how I acted. Regard for my sister's credit and feelings prevented any public exposure, but I wrote to Mr. Wickham, who left the place immediately, and Mrs. Younge was of course removed from her charge. Mr. Wickham's chief object was unquestionably my sister's fortune, which is thirty thousand pounds; but I cannot help supposing that the hope of revenging himself on me was a strong inducement. His revenge would have been complete indeed.

The revenge he would bear upon me contained for him a double meaning; one of finance, the other of honour. His love of spending and my denial of money lent to him the idea of my part in his financial ruins. He also reproached my family's duty and honour amongst the Gentry. I have no doubt Mr. Wickham would have derived great pleasure by acquiring my sisters inheritance and offending my honour. He was of the correct belief that he would be able to manipulate these circumstances and avoid censure by me, as my responsibilities are only for the gravest trespasses of honour. You might believe his actions to be of the gravest nature, however, the scandalous actions of a cad and a fifteen year old woman are not actions which draw our attention; I do hope you are never witness to the disgraces of honour to which I allude.

This, madam, is a faithful narrative of every event in which we have been concerned together; and if you do not absolutely reject it as false, you will, I hope, acquit me henceforth of cruelty towards Mr. Wickham. I know not in what manner, under what form of falsehood, he has imposed on you; but his failings in life are his own.

You may possibly wonder why all this was not told you last night. But I was not then master enough of myself to know what could or ought to be revealed; and the tense arrangements in which we found ourselves did not lend to the ease of conversation.

For the truth of every thing here related, I can appeal more particularly to the testimony of Colonel Fitzwilliam, who from our near relationship and constant intimacy, and still more as one of the executors of my father's will, has been unavoidably acquainted with every particular of these transactions. His affiliation with my family has been hinted and I will inform you the bond is tight and his family obligations, while different than my own, our sworn to the same oath. If your abhorrence of *me* should make *my* assertions valueless, you cannot be prevented by the same cause from confiding in my cousin; and that there may be the possibility of consulting him, I shall endeavor to find some opportunity of putting this letter in your hands in the course of the morning for I fear we must depart rapidly; the business in London grows serious, and I have already tarried to long at Rosings.

I would ask of your honour, and I do not believe I have misjudged you in that respect, for your discretion in regards to the contents of this letter. Of the individuals involved in our mutual acquaintance very few are privy to my family's duties; those being Mr. Wickham, Colonel Fitzwilliam, and I hesitantly add my Aunt, Lady Catherine De Bourgh. I trust to your discretion and I will only add, God bless you.

Chapter 33

Elizabeth could hardly believe the tales which assailed her emotions as she read the letter. Her initial state upon opening the letter was of disbelief; not thinking the letter might contain an apology. The revelation of his family's obligation left her incredulous and she could not decide to what extent they could be believed. Her disbelief that an apology was offered was found to be grounded; and with a haughty air she read the tale of her sister's sickness. It was as she expected, and the tale confirmed her deductions of the evidence. She would readily give Mr. Darcy marks of commendation if his account, claiming concern for Jane, were to be believed; but his continued tale of the separation of her sister from Charles removed any such ideas of positive qualities.

Those passages were exceedingly difficult for her to read. The criticisms on her family angered her and would have generated a more deep disdain for the letter writer if she did not also feel a cutting shame with the realization of the truth in the sentences. The truth about her family was nothing for which she was unaware, but to have those faults stated so clearly by another individual was most hurtful.

Elizabeth had paused in her reading as emotions swept over her; she realized part of her sanity lay in the false belief that her family's failings, while noticeable to her, would go unnoticed by others, or at least deemed to be not as dire as Elizabeth believed them. But, here was evidence to the contrary, written succinctly, in a tone which suggested a calmness of emotion by the writer. The words could have been a scathing indictment, delivered by a member of the clergy, and they would have had no more affect.

The account of the London affair had a similar effect of her emotions. At first she was not sure whether to believe much of it but she could believe the intentional separation of Charles and Jane and this stirred her ire. If his declaration regarding his family duties was to be believed then the motivations of his actions would lend leniency, but Elizabeth was too prejudiced against Darcy to allow that idea to linger.

It was not until she read the account of Mr. Wickham that Elizabeth allowed the idea of goodness to be associated with Mr. Darcy. The accounts written corresponded very well with the accounts for which the charming Mr. Wickham had himself already related.

Elizabeth paused and remembered her few encounters with Mr. Wickham; he was charming and very handsome, with graceful habits which quickly endeared him to people. She now recounted stories of how the young boys trained in youth, and even a proud tale of the nobility bestowing honour on the Darcy's, for which Mr. Wickham attempted the acquisition of status by association.

Only when she read the details of the gentlemen's disagreement did the accounts begin to vary. Elizabeth, greatly prejudiced against Darcy, had a difficult time believing the accounting she was reading; and she could not readily believe herself to be deceived by charm and wit so easily as to have this grossly overestimated the character of Mr. Wickham.

The charges against Mr. Wickham were serious and, if correct, must lead to a reexamination of character; both Wickham's and Darcy's. It was with a mixture of emotions that Elizabeth returned the letter to the envelope and vowed not to read it again, or give it any more notice.

The avowal did not last the return to the parsonage and she soon found herself sitting on a fallen tree engrossed with the details. The accounting of the poisoning matched hers, and she had already concluded the accidental nature of the incident while in conversation with Miss Bingley. The reason a gentleman could possess such a tea was explained well in this letter, and served to allay her disdain for anyone to posses such a concoction; but the validity of his claim would be difficult to prove and perhaps should not be attempted, if it were true. To the truthfulness of the claims, Elizabeth could only employ methods of anecdote.

Each encounter with Mr. Darcy was, to this point, tolerable, but tainted by his air of haughtiness. This conceit led her to ignore the multitude of comments declaring his worthiness as a gentleman; comments of which she now took the time to remember. The breeding of the family was easily confirmed and kindness of the Darcy family was also verified by Elizabeth's own Aunt Mrs. Gardiner, to whom she trusted implicitly. Mrs. Gardiner had spent her childhood near to Pemberley, the home estate of the Darcy family, and had imparted to Elizabeth information detailing the kindness and respect the former Mr. Darcy enjoyed. She had further informed Elizabeth of the high esteem of which much of the Gentry and Nobility held the Darcy family. Elizabeth, upon hearing those tales, attributed those qualities only to the elder Mr. Darcy as she could not bring herself to believe the son capable of fulfilling the role his father left him; at the time she pitied the family, believing the son to be failing in his duties. Introspection allowed her to conclude the honour of the family, and references to esteem by nobility, could support the claims of responsibilities to the nobility.

Elizabeth now turned her attention to Mr. Darcy himself and could recount several reports in which he was favorably recommended; if not in personality then indeed in honour and actions. To Mr. Wickham she could not lay such claims. She had found herself amused by him, and his pleasing nature had soon prejudiced her against any failings, of which there was little hint. Caroline Bingley and Mr. Darcy offered small warnings against the man, but these warnings were suspect by Elizabeth's perception of the individuals purporting them. Now, as she assessed Mr. Wickham, she could find no support of his character, nor claims of honour to which he had a right. His life before Meryton and Elizabeth's acquaintance was unknown and therefore his character unverified.

Elizabeth's knowledge of the Gentry, its associations and its rules of conduct, was well grounded. Her appetite for reading and learning served her well as she thought about the necessity for the Gentry rules. It was not a whimsical set of standards but carefully considered guidelines to assist the English with character analysis. Elizabeth agreed with one sentiment of his letter to a great degree, and, as she stood and continued her journey to the parsonage, she thought long on the concept. Recent changes in the world were assailing themselves upon the ideas of honour and nobility. If Mr. Wickham possessed the character Mr. Darcy claimed then he did so in a society which only recently allowed such behavior. In times past, such an individual would not have been allowed into society without recommendation. These new faults of society needed to be addressed, and the honour of the Gentry needed to be upheld.

Elizabeth was not so easy to relinquish her prejudices against either man and decided for the moment to re-address the issues as they presented; the first re-dress arrived with her return to the parsonage after hours of thought on the letter.

Entering the parsonage she was immediately told of the visitation by both gentlemen. Mr. Darcy stayed only a few moments but the Colonel appeared anxious to meet with her and waited nearly an hour. He at last excused himself and departed. Both men did offer their wishes for health and apologies, for they must take leave of Rosings.

Elizabeth thought for a moment on the Colonel; she would miss his charm and well meaning personality. Thoughts of this kind were short lived as she decided his long wait at the parsonage must have been to verify any details she would ask of him; and she could easily envision the good natured man taking the time to honestly answer any concern she may possess. Her mind then turned to her letter, and, clutching it to her breast, she headed to her room.

Chapter 34

The ride to London passed swiftly while Darcy and Fitzwilliam conversed. The two gentlemen spent much time in consideration of Miss Bennet's criticisms and analysis of her character. Colonel Fitzwilliam concurred with his cousin's assessment and believed Elizabeth would keep the confidentiality of the entrusted information. He further believed, once fully aware of the facts, she would re-assess his cousin's character and exonerate him of some of the charges. She may not fully raise him to honourable status in her estimation, but she would not keep his character wallowing in the dredges. Mr. Darcy found this idea pleasing in one respect and annoying in another, although he could not say why the good opinion of Elizabeth concerned him to such a degree. To Colonel Fitzwilliam, the concern of Miss Bennet's opinion had very obvious roots.

In the course of conversation the subject of Elizabeth's attack was broached; Colonel Fitzwilliam found this topic of interest.

"While I find Miss Bennet charming and of sharp wit, I would not have guessed she could summon the anger to attack you, or anyone, with a blade. It must speak to a darker aspect of her character to which only you can attest. I imagine your training served you well in the throes of an angry woman determined to inflict harm. My experience has taught me the dangers of such women: unpredictable, rash, and as much a danger to themselves as the intended target."

"Your experience would have been quite useless in this situation. While I found Miss Bennet's actions to be precipitated by anger, her movements and tactical positioning showed raw talent and some skill. The dagger she sported was held well and always at the ready. Never once during our heated debate did the blade waiver. I am sure if she had more formal training I would not have escaped unscathed, unless the lady desired it to be so. I am not convinced the latter option was not the case."

"Really!" cried Colonel Fitzwilliam sitting upright. "I had initially assumed Miss Bennet had taken leave of her senses and displayed a mean temper heretofore unknown. This development certainly lends new light to her character; perhaps she is more devious than we thought."

"I have considered the option but readily rejected the notion. Miss Bennet has had ample time to do me harm if she was so desirous, and I believe the attack was precipitated by the anger she felt at that particular moment, when confronted with the man whom she blamed for her sister's misery. I can well attest to the desire to harm an individual in such a situation."

Fitzwilliam did not need to be told that his cousin was referring to George Wickham and his atrocious behavior as regarded young Miss Darcy.

"I apologize for my role in this debacle. If I had but kept your confidence, and not disclosed the information to Miss Bennet, then this entire affair could have been avoided."

Darcy smiled at his cousin and lightened the mood. "I appreciate your concern, but it is perhaps best it was done as it was. We shall, all of us, move on, and perhaps the actions of these last few weeks will fade into memory and become our last acquaintance of Miss Bennet."

Colonel Fitzwilliam watched his cousin turn to the window and gaze out. Darcy was quite right, and the two gentlemen may never see Miss Bennet again, but the Colonel did not believe his cousin wished it to be so.

London was arrived at by dinner time, and the gentlemen had an enjoyable time of greeting the household, eating dinner, and stretching from the journey. After dinner, Fitzwilliam took his leave, as he was anxious to return to his London residence and sleep in his own bed. The cousins gave each other fond farewells and bade good health to one another.

Before bed, Darcy took to his office and read correspondence in an effort to keep abreast of the Ackerby situation. Things had not progressed rapidly, but there was a report regarding Ackerby's latest moves. Mr. Darcy's insight into the situation proved to be correct; Ackerby, as it was learned, was not the fool he pretended. Darcy sighed as he thought about the affair; deciding the situation could wait until morning, he headed to bed.

Chapter 35

Spring advanced and Darcy kept to his duties. It had been two weeks since Rosings and, although he had been away from London for that same amount of time, nothing seemed to have been missed by his absence. He found most of his orders had been followed fairly well and the debacle regarding arms contracts had been avoided. He was upset to learn about the assassination of a well to do merchant, no doubt entangled in the affair in some facet or another; but the tactical situation seemed to be well in hand.

On this particular evening Darcy was pleased to entertain the Bingleys, whom he had a difficult time visiting since his return to town. The festivities began simply as they always did, which was a preference for Mr. Darcy due to his abhorrence of gaudy show.

"I do wish for the company of Miss Darcy. She could make these evenings ever more entertaining. Is she doing well in school?" Caroline asked after they had retired to the drawing room.

"Quite well, if her letter is to be believed," replied Darcy.

"That is splendid to hear!" announced Charles.

"It will not be long before her education is complete. Do you have your sights on any particular matches for her hand? I would think you to be very involved in her choice of husband."

Darcy could not respond to Miss Bingley's inquiry as the arrival of Miss Dache was announced. Darcy nodded his permission and presently Miss Dache was amongst the crowd; much to the dismay of Miss Bingley.

"Ah, Miss Dache, how nice it is to see you again. I was just asking Mr. Darcy whether he had designs for his sister's marriage. Mr. Darcy himself seems determined to stay a bachelor, but he cannot object to his sister's happiness by becoming married. Perhaps you can provide a ladies viewpoint and we may tease the information out of him."

Miss Dache took a chair and responded to Caroline's mocking tone with civility and calm.

"My impression of Mr. Darcy does not lead me to believe he wishes to be a consummate bachelor, rather that he is particular about his possible choice of spouse. I imagine he will take the same care, if and when, he chooses to be involved with his sister's marital plans; however, I find the notion of achieving happiness by marriage to be fallacious. Miss Darcy may well be content by never marrying."

"Never marrying!" cried Caroline with mock astonishment. "Mr. Darcy, please tell me you do not wish for your sister to spend her adult years alone and without the blessing of children?"

Darcy rolled his eyes at the topic of conversation and replied that he did desire happiness and marriage for Georgiana. Caroline, perceiving a victory over Miss Dache, continued with her bullheaded tactics of social criticism and false flattery. Miss Dache responded well to each slight and then counterattacked with cold intelligence.

Several minutes and topics passed until Miss Dache was forced to end the banter.

"Mr. Darcy, I did not call on you this evening for social interactions but to request your presence. My father is attending to business this evening and requests your personal guidance. I do have a letter for you."

She handed the letter to Darcy, who opened it and read it quickly. The letter described an interesting engagement this very evening between their mutual friend and an employee of the crown. Lord Dache was asking for a personal view of the engagement to be followed by Mr. Darcy's opinion on the matter.

Darcy thought for a moment after reading the letter and then addressed his friends.

"I fear I must leave you to your own devices this evening and accompany Miss Dache. I hope to conclude business quickly but do not wish to keep you should I not return until late."

Caroline fussed about this and cast an evil eye to Miss Dache, who at that moment took an opportune time to look at Caroline. Miss Bingley could not disguise her look fast enough and Miss Dache returned a look of her own. Miss Bingley was well aware the look Miss Dache threw, it was one she had attempted more than once but could never quite accomplish. It was the look of a superior, whether they be of employment or society. It simply said one thing very angrily. "Remember your place!" Caroline turned away, took a moment to collect herself, then began to converse with her brother.

In the carriage, and out on the streets of London, Darcy and Marianne sped away. Miss Dache took a few moments to fill in the details for Mr. Darcy, who listened earnestly and asked questions when needed. Once the details were concluded, Miss Dache took the time to lighten the mood. Her attempts were not successful.

"Miss Bingley seems very interested in your thoughts on marriage; I cannot say she is alone in that interest. Do you ever consider it Mr. Darcy?"

"I would think this topic of conversation is not apt at this point in time."

"It could have more bearing than one might think. Can you imagine Miss Bingley in this carriage tonight, about to engage in the activities that you and I are about to engage? I would think her cutting tongue would not prove sufficient in the dark arena of social evils."

Darcy only stared at Miss Dache and did not reply.

"Still, I imagine she would make a suitable wife if you were to implement her in restricted social endeavors. Of course there are other options for marriage that may be more suited to you."

Darcy knew Miss Dache was referring to herself, but his mind momentarily wandered to Elizabeth and his face betrayed his thoughts. It was the keen eye of Miss Dache that caught it.

"Ah, a look of contemplation upon your face," Marianne paused for a moment and then looked at Darcy quizzically, "but not, I should think, for me. Who is this mystery lady? I assume she must be a mystery, otherwise my inquiries into your life have left something to be desired."

Darcy jumped slightly at this comment and Marianne smiled with amusement.

"Did you think you were the only one with access to spies and delicate information? I took the initiative to garner much about you, Mr. Darcy, but a serious attachment to any lady was not in the information of my reports. Fear not though, I am sure she will be found eventually."

"You take much interest in trivial affairs then?"

"I take an interest in competition. Of Miss Bingley I see none; if she held any serious hope of your hand I would be astonished. Your affinity towards her is that of a friend, but if you wished it to go further you would have done so by now."

"You understand me very well in your own opinion; I should not put too much faith in it though."

Rather than responding to the advice Miss Dache smiled and returned the topic to an area of her control."

"This lady, of whom you are contemplating, can you envision her in this carriage this evening?"

Darcy had never thought of Elizabeth's role in his life if he were to marry her; but the sight of her, with an unwavering dagger in hand, put a smile on his face as he contemplated Miss Dache's question. To his chagrin the ever watchful lady caught his thoughts again and before she uttered a word he swore to himself and refocused his mind.

"So there is potential to this lady," she said with a smile.

Taking a deep breath, Marianne continued.

"I will need to double my efforts on information gathering. I give you compliments on the concealment of this lady, my resources may not be as formidable as yours but they are adequate. I suppose it speaks to your skill that she has eluded any mention in my reports. If you choose not to tell me her name I am sure I will learn it in short order, and perhaps I will test her fortitude in person."

Darcy's eyes glared and his face grew stern.

"If you choose to meddle in any of my social affairs then you and I will have more than an uncivil conversation. I would suggest you attend to yourself and your own weaknesses before deciding to test others."

Miss Dache merely nodded her understanding and glanced away for a moment.

"I apologize if I gave offense. My comments, often meant in jest, can sometimes be misconstrued. You and I are on the same mission to protect honour, not disavow it."

Darcy accepted this apology and turned his own attention to the outside. Marianne watched him briefly and then turned her thoughts inward. "He cares for this one," she thought,"this could be trouble."

The carriage stopped and the two occupants exited. It was now dark and Darcy and Miss Dache strolled along the street as if on their way somewhere. Miss Dache took the opportunity to slip her arm into Mr. Darcy's and whispered that the act would give the appearance of propriety. Glancing around, Darcy realized something was wrong. The report he was given did not match the street they were on, nor the positioning they were now taking; he made his concerns know to Marianne.

"You are correct, Mr. Darcy; I have brought you here under slightly false pretenses. Do you see the gentlemen just there?"

She pointed with a nod of her head rather than the use of an arm or hand. Darcy rotated as if glancing at buildings and saw the two gentlemen leaning against a set of stairs. They were smoking and laughing and appearing to have a good time, although they did not appear to fit with the citizenry of this area. Their clothes were too worn and everything about them spoke of the lower classes. Darcy could even hear an odd curse from time to time.

"Those two gentlemen, if that word is applicable, are here to assassinate the government worker I informed you of. It seems the employee of the crown is to be carrying some documents this evening in an attempt to disclose them for the purpose of impressing a lady. These two men are to intercept him, relieve him of the documents, and kill him. Although I imagine the order of events may vary. I believe the end result is to obtain the documents without anyone being the wiser. If the man is dead, he cannot inform anyone of the stolen papers."

"And you chose to tell me this now rather than at my office. This is a matter for which other means can be used. We could have removed the documents or the employee. Why is it you wish to be here tonight and to bring me with you?"

"Mr. Darcy you amaze me. With your skill I would imagine you would like the thrill a little more, but look; now it begins."

The two men stood to attention as a man exited a building several doors down. Darcy could easily assess their intent, even if he could not see their weapons.

"Mr. Darcy, would you be so kind as to protect a lady if she should need it?"

Taking her arm back, Miss Dache headed to the man leaving the building. She waived to him and called out as a friend. Meeting him at the bottom of the stairs she spoke with him briefly. The conversation could not be heard, but the effect was apparent when the man tipped his hat and re-entered the building.

Miss Dache seemed content and headed back down the street, but she did not walk directly towards Darcy and it took only a moment for him to realize her intentions. Darcy wanted to head her off, but he knew she would reach the men before he would.

As she passed, the men could not help but make an inappropriate comment and waived to her in a manner equally rude. Marianne took the arm of the closest man and screamed. The appearance, to anyone turning, was of a woman being attacked.

The men were greatly surprised and the first man was more so as Marianne took out a bosom dagger and plunged it into his throat. The second man quickly recovered and grabbed for his blade, but his hand did not reach it. Instead it was bent back by the now arriving Mr. Darcy.

Darcy bent the arm farther, leaned the man forward, throwing him off balance; then a quick sweep of the leg and Darcy guided the man down head first into the ground. A solid thud was heard and the man did not move.

"Mr. Darcy, you do care!" said Miss Dache with wide excited eyes and a devilish grin upon her face.

"That was reckless and unnecessary," replied Darcy as he looked about to see if anyone had witnessed the display. As it happened, a man was directing a constable to their position.

"Do not worry, Mr. Darcy, the constable is ours and as expected. Although a live assassin was not to be expected," she commented as she looked at the man Mr. Darcy had subdued. Moving to his position she extended her hands to his head and stopped only when Darcy grabbed her.

"This wanton killing will not happen while I am here. The constable is almost upon us and I suggest you affix your story, not break this man's neck."

"Should he regain consciousness and remember these events it may not play well; better he not be able to tell any tale." She stared at Darcy who did not move in his resolve. No words were spoken, but Miss Dache eventually nodded and backed away from the man on the ground.

The constable was soon amongst them along with a curious bystander or two. The facts were obvious to everyone. A lady had separated briefly from her gentleman companion only to be assaulted by these two men. The lady, fearing for her life, grabbed for her dagger out of sheer terror and blindly stabbed, causing the death of one of her attackers. The other attacker was tripped from behind and luckily hit his head and passed out. Everyone agreed it was an unfortunate situation with a fortunate ending, and as more constables arrived and the situation taken in hand, Darcy and Miss Dache were politely escorted away from prying eyes.

The carriage ride home was done in more silence than the one which had brought them deeper in to town. Miss Dache was thrilled with the evening's events, but Darcy was more solemn and spent the ride in contemplation. Attempts at conversation were not met with much success, and it was only on one topic he showed any interest.

"You handle yourself very well, Mr. Darcy, and I do appreciate you assisting me; even if the assistance was chosen by your nature as a gentleman rather than done out of freedom of options. I will confess my motivations for this evening were more to witness your abilities and to ascertain if we will work well for future engagements."

"You conceive of many such evenings as this do you?"

"Not at all, but do not fool yourself Mr. Darcy; the events of this evening would have been dealt with by us, either by direct or indirect means. I simply chose to be involved directly rather than send off a letter to less than scrupulous individuals. The involvement, I believe, worked very well. We were able to foil the assassination attempt, witness each other's skill set, and involve the local authorities with positive effect. I would say it was more productive than overrunning the streets of London with assassins attacking assassins."

Darcy only nodded his understanding to Marianne while thinking the evenings events had done all of what she claimed, but the lady's real motivation was to demonstrate her abilities to him. Miss Dache was still excited about the evening and could hardly keep from smiling as she rode with her companion. She was impressed with Mr. Darcy, and, had she known his thoughts about her evening's motivations, she would have readily agreed and then added that the evening was an interview of his abilities as well. An interview that she was excited he passed.

Chapter 36

Into June Darcy applied his intellect monitoring Ackerby and interfering where he could. He could foresee the battle was to drag out longer than he had hoped. Still, Mr. Darcy and his associates had only been working for a few months, and many of the Gentry were pleased with the work against the Colonel and the financial gains reaped by interfering in his plans.

On occasion Miss Dache would arrive to deliver intelligence or retrieve dispatches. Her meetings were short and polite and no doubt an attempt to develop the relationship with Mr. Darcy. Whenever Caroline was present the two would engage in a verbal sparring match for which Miss Bingley was always the loser; but her obstinacy would not allow her to quit; this trait might have been more admirable if she were not the instigator of the sparring matches.

As the weather warmed, Darcy's spirits lifted. His sister would be arriving within the month, and the two would head to Derbyshire and their home of Pemberley. It was a family custom to summer in Derbyshire, and Darcy looked forward to it. London was very eventful, but he longed for the openness of his estate and a break from the serious events he was now embroiled; he only wished he could conclude his dealings with Ackerby. The Colonel seemed very determined to continue his affairs, and many of his recent operations proved his ability to adjust and adapt. Financial matters were more difficult to interfere with, and Darcy could sense the application of much more intelligence; to which he attributed the Colonel hiring a more able minded financial advisor. All attempts to penetrate Ackerby's organization to determine the identity of the individual had been unsuccessful, and Darcy was growing frustrated with the slow progress.

Evening often found Darcy in his office looking at notes and issuing directives as he saw fit. One particular evening he sat and read only one report while he drank a glass of wine. It regarded a recent commission of an officer, and Mr. Darcy was not amused. He tried to focus but could find little solace in his thoughts which circled around the new appointment of George Wickham. Not only was this man granted the commission, but it was granted to the regiment stationed in Meryton.

Darcy mulled the report and could not help thinking of Elizabeth. It was for her concern that he had used his resources to determine the current state of Wickham, but at this point in time he could only hope Miss Bennet had believed his words and now held Mr. Wickham in a more realistic opinion.

Tossing the letter aside, Darcy headed over to the window and looked out at the waning sun. A few minutes later he was back for the letter and, as he reached for it, his mind arrested his hand. There, next to the letter, was a report of a suspected attack. Along with the report was a coded message from someone in the Ackerby organization. Very little could be made of the message, and the attempts he had made to ferret out the sources and meaning of the messages were not met with success, but Darcy was now struck with an idea.

He took to his desk and set about writing dispatches to several key individuals.

The next night was another grand event at White's and the room was filled much like the previous visitation. There were a few additions; the most notable to Darcy was Lord Dache. The other members were new admirers of the man addressing the group. Darcy mused and decided that, if they should all have daughters, then the next year's social calendar would be very full.

"Gentleman, I appreciate you attending this evening on short notice, I shall respect your time and get straight to business."

"As you know, Colonel Ackerby has proven most cunning and difficult. We have made great headway and interrupted many of his plans, but I fear his organization is still too large to simply remove him from it without leaving the organization still functional."

The military men in the room understood and, with the reports they were privy to, many agreed. The matter was not left to much debate as Darcy continued.

"Up to this point we have deployed subtlety and it has worked well. I wish to continue with this method but begin an all out attack. I shall not go into the details at present. If this is to work then we shall need an organization such as we do not currently possess. Our current system is becoming antiquated. Our reports are slow; they must be collated, and then clarified, and re-collated. If we are to continue, we need a more organized intelligence force; runners, analyzers, spies, supplies, and a central location from which to work. I have a location in mind which is suitable. I have also assembled a list of names of people I need. Many of these individuals work within your influence. I would ask you to have them report to this location as soon as possible."

"What exactly is your plan, Mr. Darcy?"

Darcy looked about the room and answered to no one in particular.

"The colonel runs much of his organization like a military spy network. Communication is run directly from him outward, but in many situations his only means of reciprocal information is in completed tasks. His lower ranks do not necessarily report all information back to him. This may work effectively with well disciplined troops, but with the amateurs of the London streets it could prove a problem. Recent movement on his financial front suggests new management in the area of fiscal responsibilities. This, combined with Ackerby's use of confusing tactics, has led to unusual orders for his men; his men have become accustomed to such orders and seem to carry them out; if the pay is there. If our reports are to be believed, this pay is being changed as we speak, to reflect the new financer's style. My intention, gentleman, is to use the Colonel's own codes against him. To dispatch messages of our own and, rather than attacking him from the outside in, we will take him from the inside out. His men are ill equipped to deal with counter espionage techniques. We shall plant false orders, leave the men pay of our own, and declare the acts as utmost secret. If all goes well we will be able to carry out acts of theft or other illegal ventures. When we have destabilized his known network we will strike."

"You mean we will kill him! It is about time, I should have liked to see this scoundrel hanged by now."

"We may or may not kill him, but I can assure you the choice will be his to make."

Darcy then took a few minutes to explain several scenarios for the end of Ackerby, and as the men listened, they nodded solemnly. The details Darcy laid out were organized and accompanied with contingencies for his contingencies. The previous meeting in this room had ended with skepticism, but there was not a single gentleman who now doubted Mr. Darcy's competence. A few doubted the plan and voiced concern, but not a single one lacked conviction in the man attempting to carry it out.

"Before we adjourn I must address a concern in regards to your social life, Mr. Darcy."

Darcy turned to Lord Dache and raised an eyebrow.

"My social life, Lord Dache?"

"Yes, while I admit you have done a remarkable job, you are about to undertake something which is very sensitive. I am worried about your social life and the engagements a single man of your position are required to attend."

Darcy instantly saw the direction of this conversation.

"You would prefer I get married and settle down my extravagant lifestyle?" Darcy said this as a jest, and it was not lost on the crowd.

"Not I alone. Many of us would prefer you well married and settled. The knowledge you possess and the power you are about to wield is reason enough for us to be wary. The uncertainty of your social life is not something we wish to concern ourselves with, but more than one good man has been lost to an ill conceived marriage."

"I was not aware that I appeared so irrational in my social life as to affect an opinion of wanton disregard for secrecy and honour."

Frustrated, Lord Dache raised his voice.

"My God, look about you, Mr. Darcy. Do you see a single man in this room who is not titled? Your own namesake, Fitzwilliam, represents an Earl, and he sits just there."

Darcy was not unaware of Colonel Fitzwilliam's older brother, the Earl, sitting in the room; but as the relation made no difference to this meeting they had only exchanged nods upon initially seeing each other.

Darcy was accustomed to social situations in which ladies tried to press themselves and their availability on him. He was even familiar in dealing with fathers who also wished for their daughters union. It did not take much skill for Darcy to end the current situation since it did not require concern for the emotional state of a young lady or the honour of her father. This situation only took an admission of respect and simple deferment.

"I see you point my Lord. I had not considered this as a matter of concern and thusly have not contemplated the issue much. I shall endeavor to correct this oversight."

Darcy nodded slightly at the lord who, in finding his viewpoint validated and politely dismissed, was left with nothing but a quick reply of agreement. The gentlemen took their leave and Darcy himself headed home. The carriage ride was grueling, and his mind was stirred with anger. He could not help think that he had more important things to do than contemplate marriage; but for some reason, in the middle of White's, in the middle of an attack on English Gentry, and with a rogue Colonel determined to gain power, the men of London politics and finance saw fit to play matchmaker.

"Do these people not have more important matters of which to attend?" he muttered to himself.

Chapter 37

Within a few days of organization, the intelligence group Darcy was working with showed tremendous results. They were now housed in a business district with ease of access to transport, banks, runners, and many other useful resources. To the people on the street it appeared to be business as usual, but within the small offices on the second floor, Mr. Darcy commanded a small team of perhaps a dozen.

Three gentlemen alone were tasked with analyzing the various letters which had been intercepted. It was their task to break the code, and it had not taken long. His cousin, Colonel Fitzwilliam, was among one of the men constantly heading in and out, and his keen eye was useful to point out the similarities between Ackerby's codes and those used by spies on the mainland. The analyzers took up this idea and requested information to be retrieved by other men in the office. Colonel Fitzwilliam himself aided in one such operation by personally relieving an old military acquaintance of one of his diaries, which contained clues to this particular brand of spy code.

Other men mapped London and marked each operation and known activity of Ackerby's organization. And still others worked with pure finance, marking suspected payouts and bank accounts. The office flowed well and Darcy kept each man on task and the occasional woman as Miss Dache made a point to inject herself into the operations; to say she was impressed was an understatement.

Darcy would look up from time to time, as he darted about the room or conferred with a gentleman, only to see Miss Dache observing. His initial assumption was that Miss Dache was watching the flow of information so she might add insight; but he soon concluded that, while she had the capability to assist, she took more joy in watching him work.

The code was eventually broken and the very day Darcy felt confident in its validity they put it to use. The code itself was not terribly difficult and its function was also easy to replicate. Most of the messages were simple commands as Darcy expected, with little flow of information back to Ackerby. Any information required by Ackerby seemed to be learned either by reading the obituaries, or on occasion by anonymous drops at odd locations.

Within this system Darcy now used rogue runners to deliver messages directly to Ackerby's men. The distance and redundancy Ackerby used to shield himself now worked to his disadvantage. Darcy created false burglaries and offered payment up front; the flash of gold and a coded message quickly calmed the suspicions of anyone on seeing a new delivery agent.

Darcy wisely chose his agents and selected those men with the rugged features born from the streets and fine tuned by battle with Napoleon. Any suspicious stares given these men were countered with a glare of evil and an attitude that told the recipient to take the gold and move on.

Miss Dache appeared to have the time of her life and a permanent smile was on her face, except when she was on a mission. Darcy attempted to dissuade her of this choice, but she would not brook any opposition and insisted on being directly involved on more than one instance.

The rapidity of the attack called for swift action on all fronts. Darcy knew he could not affect Ackerby for long before the ruse was realized and countered in some manner. The odd messages which Darcy started as a trickle began to pick up speed and take on life of their own. Some messages asked for new recruits and, on rare occasions, elimination of particular unstable men who already existed among the ranks. This tactic allowed Darcy to weed out the more dangerous men and to introduce some of his very own. While Ackerby's network was not completely known, the maps and group analysis allowed for them to disrupt much and create enough false cells that Ackerby would soon be hard pressed to tell his real troops from the false. Darcy did not care for this brand of deceit, but he believed Ackerby would appreciate the concept of donning your enemy's uniform.

Each coded messages soon bore an interesting symbol of Darcy's design. Most of Ackerby's coded messages were left wanting a signature or some form of identification; to that end, Darcy added a simple symbol to identify a possible new officer in Ackerby's ranks. The symbol began to be shown slowly and on the most profitable burglaries or any job paid up front in gold. It did not take long before the symbol was recognized and desired.

It was not two weeks before Colonel Ackerby realized the trouble he was in and began to marshal his core men. Darcy's attack by its nature had to be done on the outer most layers of the organization, but with new men and trusted loyalty of those ranks, Darcy was able to move upward, closer to Ackerby. The Colonel eventually learned of this, and local eyes swiftly brought information to Darcy of odd meetings.

Darcy smiled to himself as more than one runner brought news of movement and of various men calling to Ackerby's location; the identity of anyone meeting with the Colonel would be learned, as it had been these past several months. Darcy bowed his head and thanked the Spies of Sussex and the London solicitor branches for their roles. Miss Dache's family had also played a role and he commended her for their input.

"You seem pleased with yourself, Mr. Darcy, but I cannot understand why. Surely the colonel will begin to take control of his organization," Miss Dache commented as he stared out the window.

Darcy turned slowly and gave a knowing stare at Miss Dache.

"He is too late."

He handed her a paper and, taking it, she read it quizzically. It was a daily for London dated that very day. On the main page was an interesting article in regards to a glorious naval battle between Napoleon forces and the British. In reality it was not much, nothing like Trafalgar, but to the British any skirmish involving the French was news worthy. The article went on to commend, with great abundance of words, the courage and actions of Colonel Ackerby. Apparently, years before this battle, the Colonel was engaged in military affairs which led to certain important information to be learned about the French and any possible naval maneuvers. The papers could not say exactly what the details were, but they were profuse in their praise.

"Is any of this true?"

"The general message is true. There was a minor skirmish between a British naval vessel and a French frigate with the result being our victory. The captain happens to be within our influence and will gladly abide our story of Ackerby's involvement. I should imagine the sudden exposure to the British public will hinder his movements and allow us to sow more dissent into the ranks. If you will read on you may learn of a rumour regarding Colonel Ackerby's return to active duty. It happens to be quoted very ingeniously from a well reputed Admiral."

"And when this proves false?" Miss Dache asked.

"I am sure the confusion in his ranks will continue and he will be hard pressed to convince his troops otherwise; especially when the military minds of England say it is to be so. The next batches of coded messages will be delivered confirming a change in Ackerby's leadership."

"Lord Ackerby may have the skill to pull everything together and rebuild."

Darcy sighed solemnly and returned to the window.

"Perhaps, but while his organization is in disarray, and with no clear command, I fear the Colonel may be martyred while England praises his past courage."

"You will do this yourself I assume."

Darcy did not reply; he simply looked out the window to the passersby's below.

Chapter 38

"Dear brother, you look much more at ease than the last time I saw you."

Darcy looked up from his reading to his sister who had just entered the room. Smiling, he put down his reports and greeted Georgiana.

"I am much happier thank you. My work of the last few months is still not concluded, but I have every hope the matters shall be resolved within a few months and all for the best. I am pleased to see you; pray tell me, how was your schooling?"

"It was very pleasant and challenging as I am sure you hoped for. But tell me, if you will, do you know Lord Ackerby personally?"

"Why would you inquire into that particular gentleman?" asked Darcy with a sense of shock.

"His name is amongst the daily news reports. There have been pictures and tales of his heroism making him quite fashionable conversation. I thought you might be able to introduce me to him at a ball or dinner engagement should such an event occur."

"And why would you think I know the gentleman?"

"Oh, am I incorrect in my assumption? I seem to recall hearing his name the last time I visited."

Darcy's mind calmed and made an intuitive leap to a ready answer.

"You may have, but I must admit I do not know the gentleman personally. He might have come across my path in a matter of business; but much to my amazement his new found popularity is met by him with great enthusiasm."

"Do I sense a criticism of the Lords' personality?" Georgiana asked of her brother while smiling and offering a teasing look.

"Not at all, dear sister, I am merely commenting, more to myself, on the interesting paths life and events choose to take. The Lords' warm reception to his sudden fame has taken hold of his attention in a way that is proving very beneficial to his character and simultaneously making my life easier. Many a man under the view of the public become dishonourable. I am pleased these events appear to have the opposite effect."

"It is always pleasing to hear when someone can stand up and be honourable." Georgiana made this statement with a voice that trailed off and a gaze that wandered out the window. Sensing the intrusion of George Wickham into his sister's mind, Darcy felt her pain and turned the topic.

"I do not believe we have any upcoming events offering the opportunity to meet the Lord, but if I do encounter him I will give you a report."

Turning back to her brother, Georgiana smiled widely again and seemed to become enthused.

"I should much rather hear a report on Miss Elizabeth Bennet."

If the inquiry into Ackerby was shocking, the present inquiry would have to be classified as pure amazement to Darcy. He could not control his facial features at hearing his sister's remarks.

"How are you aware of that young lady and to what do I owe this sudden interest?"

"Oh, you do have a lady of interest!" cried Georgiana after seeing the surprise on her brother's face; to which she attributed great care for Miss Bennet.

"I would not conjecture as far as you have on the matter. It is safe to say I am familiar with Miss. Bennet and find her to be an accomplished young lady; but you have not answered my question regarding your inquiry."

"Dear brother, I may not be as wise to the world as you, but I can assemble a puzzle when laid before me. My inquiry is simple enough to explain. I had occasion in the last month to be visited by Miss Dache; she was in the vicinity of my school and was ever so kind to visit and inquire into my studies. We spoke at length and she mentioned a familiarity with your social circles, such as the Bingleys and our cousins the Fitzwilliams. She mentioned another young lady who appeared to catch your eye, but Miss Dache could not recall her name. I was not able to help her remember the name as I was unaware of any lady you might have an affinity towards. After Miss Dache departed, my curiosity led me to your letters of these last few months, and I came across an interesting comment in a piece of correspondence from Rosings. You mention Miss Bennet by name and praise her abilities at the piano. The mention of any lady in a letter from you must have significance when accompanied by your praise. I then recalled, although you may not, Caroline mentioning Miss Bennet many months ago. I also recall your off hand comments regarding Miss Bennet's intelligence. These small facts led to my suspecting her as the recipient of your affections; your countenance a moment ago, upon hearing her name, confirms my suspicions."

Darcy could easily understand Miss Dache's inquiries to his sister and the situation disturbed him. He did not believe Marianne would be hurtful or even truly deceitful, but he did respect the wiles of women and the subtleties they could employ to ensure the success of their goals. In Darcy's mind, Miss Dache was instilled with the artful skills of many ladies, made more dangerous by an underlying coldness as to their deployment. His main calming thought was his belief Miss Dache meant no harm to his sister; Georgiana was just a means of information.

"Miss Bennet is indeed a handsome lady. Your cousin and I were able to enjoy her company on many occasions at Rosings; however, I first met her in Hertfordshire at an assembly in Meryton as you may recall; since then she has impressed me with her accomplishments."

"I should like to meet the lady that so impresses my brother. I can only imagine she must be a very worthy lady to be held so highly in your esteem."

"I believe a meeting with Lord Ackerby may be more statistically likely. Miss Bennet resides in the county of Hertfordshire and we have no immediate plans to visit the area. I will additionally admit to you that Miss Bennet and I did not leave each other's company on the best of terms. I fear her estimation of me is less than mine of her."

Georgiana looked downcast as it was now her turn to feel sorrow for a sibling.

"That is truly upsetting. I should have liked to meet the lady of your admiration; but I must be honest, dear brother, as I care for you so deeply. You do not present a façade that allows for ease of relationships. Perhaps she mistakes your shyness for pride of character."

"You wish to speak to me of shyness; I do not profess that particular attribute to myself. I simply find the boorishness of the trivial to be arduous and I am ill equipped to hide the fact."

"Well, perhaps my shyness and your implacable attitude shall see us grow old together and end up at Pemberley alone and unmarried."

With a smile and a nod Darcy concurred, "I could think of no finer company."

"Brother, would you do me a favor?" she asked in a sincere and solemn tone.

"You know you must only ask," was his reply.

"Will you promise me to try to be more concerned with the trivialities? I know from our close relationship your capabilities for depth of emotion, but you conceal it behind a wall of stone. This may be what disinclined Miss Bennet from you and perhaps many other accomplished ladies." Georgiana paused for a moment before continuing. "When I see you standing in a room filled with people, alone in your thoughts and alone in your soul, I am saddened. It reminds me too much of myself, and I believe one of us should be free of this torture. You are the strongest and it would give me pleasure to see you happy."

Darcy thought back to his conversations with Miss Bennet; particularly the ones along the paths at Rosings. She had made an attempt to dismiss the trivialities and put him at ease. He now suspected the cleverness of conversation and skill which she employed to put him at ease. Her motives may have been suspect but the willingness and skill had not been. He could not fault her on the motives; he realized with the information at her disposal she was following her heart much as he had done with his beliefs regarding her sister, Jane. Elizabeth had on more than one occasion made an effort to accommodate his character, even defending him to her own mother on a point of argument. Her penchant for generosity in conversation to himself, and others, led to further admiration of her character. Darcy nodded to his sister and decided he would follow the lead of Miss Bennet and attempt to soften his hard exterior.

The following weeks Darcy, his sister, and the Bingleys, made arrangements to summer at Pemberley in Derbyshire. Darcy was happy with the fortunate turn of events in London. At his most recent meeting at White's he was praised for his work and commended on the apparent redemption he affected on one of their own. Darcy was not convinced Ackerby would use his new found fame for continued good use, but he could not argue that the Colonel appeared to preferred the benefits of positive social interaction over the negative. The Barons criminal endeavors were all but subsided and Darcy, along with the men in the room at White's room, need only perform a cleanup.

The cleanup needed constant supervision, but this did not require the specific use of Darcy's talents and was passed on to Lord Dache. Darcy was also pleased to learn Mr. Knightly of the emissary branch would work with the wayward baron and reacclimatize him into the Gentry. Mr. Knightly's skills were formidable and his manners pleasing; he would make the options clear to Ackerby and dissuade him from future transgressions. The final result of the meeting at White's was a mutual respect for the abilities and responsibilities of many families; and an overall high esteem for Mr. Darcy. It was with well wishes and many congratulations that the gentlemen sent Darcy away; and all begged him to enjoy his summer with his family, as the warm weather and quiet of the countryside were well deserved by his recent efforts.

Chapter 39

Riding across the countryside, away from the lane, proved a more enjoyable journey for Darcy as he guided his horse onto the grounds of Pemberley. He chose to arrive a full day ahead of his sister and guests in order to put the house to order. Mrs. Reynolds, his house keeper, was notified of the party's arrival and, being the fastidious woman she was, had most likely finished the preparations. He knew she would scold him for arriving a day early, but his offenses would soon be forgotten due to the warmth of spirit she possessed for Darcy and his sister.

The sun shone warmly and he made no hurry to arrive. It had been many months since his last visit, and he enjoyed the view of trees and vast farmlands that stretched away from his property. The house itself came into view and Darcy smiled. It was amazing how such a place can fill someone with peace. He believed material collections could not, nor should not, replace the peace of mind brought by a solid constitution of character; but that ideology met with resistance when his mind found peace at the sight of Pemberley.

He brought his horse to the stables and left it with an attendant. There was a brief moment of salutations and a welcome home to which Darcy kindly thanked. Walking around the lane from the stables, he was deep in thought when he suddenly took to surprise. There on his grounds, not 20 yards away, was Miss Elizabeth Bennet who, in appearance, was casually walking the lane. His initial surprise was matched by the obvious look of surprise on her face. Not sure what to do or how to respond to this situation, Darcy examined the area and could see an elderly couple walking the grounds several yards away. The image brought to mind thoughts of a small family outing. Elizabeth turned towards the couple and began to walk their direction, but Darcy called out to her in a move that honestly startled both of them.

Walking calmly towards Elizabeth he made no sudden moves but was soon of the belief he was in no danger as he had been on their last encounter. Miss Bennet seemed to be held in check by embarrassment and uncertainty, emotions which Mr. Darcy was inexperienced with in regards to the lady.

"Miss Bennet, I was not aware you were in the country."

"I do not believe it to be common knowledge," she replied while unable to meet his gaze. "My aunt and uncle brought me here just yesterday to tour the local villages. We are staying at the Inn in Lampton and the easy distance to Pemberley allowed us an opportunity visit. I can assure you my intentions for being here are of innocent curiosity for this magnificent estate and nothing else."

Darcy caught the subtext of her meaning and knew she did not mean for a repetition of their disagreement involving heated words and a dagger.

"I trust the journey was well and you have rested since arrival?"

Elizabeth sensed his unease but could not bring herself to help him; this lack of assistance sprouted from her extreme embarrassment at being caught touring his estate. Truthfully, she was visiting the countryside and, had she any inclination he was about, she would have avoided the area but fate would seem to play her for amusement.

The two continued with the conversation in a very stilted and awkward manner.

"And how is your family?" he asked, as he could think of nothing else to say.

"They are quite well. Jane is now home at Longbourn and each member is well."

"Each of them well? That is good to hear. And your father, I imagine him to be fine."

"Yes, fine indeed. He is dealing with summer projects."

"Ah, that is good to hear, and are all your sisters are enjoying the summer and keeping well?" The absurdity of the questions he was asking did not escape Mr. Darcy and his embarrassment seemed to be in competition with Elizabeth's; his only enjoyable thought was that their last meeting of anger and weaponry was to be treated as if it had not occurred.

"Yes, my sisters are enjoying the summer. My youngest sister Lydia is away to Brighton for the summer to visit with the Militia and Colonel Forsters wife, but the rest of us are enjoying the summer activities."

A moment's pause in the conversation turned into two and then three. Darcy could think of nothing else to say and Elizabeth could do little to make eye contact. It was with civility that Darcy broke the silence.

"If you will excuse me, I have had a long ride and need to refresh myself." he bowed politely. Elizabeth returned the gesture and they parted company.

Darcy headed into the house and up to his chambers. He was vexed and could not believe his inability to think clearly when engaged in conversation with this lady. As he cleaned up at the washbasin he wondered what she must be thinking of him at this moment. He had thoroughly embarrassed himself, and his inept attempts to converse had embarrassed Elizabeth as well. He was now determined to have a glass of water, change his clothes, and hide in his room attending to letters. This is exactly what he did do for a few minutes.

Sitting at a small desk in his bedroom, Darcy felt refreshed. He had changed clothes and eaten a small amount of cheeses and breads brought to him. His mind was still difficult to bring to task and when he was struck with the insanity of his actions he grabbed his current work and headed to his office on the main floor.

Settling into the room, he opened his drawers, took out fresh paper, readied ink, and then opened a window for fresh air. He could see that out on the grounds walked Miss Bennet and her companions, along with his gardener,. They were arriving back to the main grounds from the higher levels of his estate. He was surprised to see them still on his property. Watching them talking and viewing his estate he thought about Miss Bennet. She could not see him from her vantage point and Darcy was treated to a heartwarming view of the lady he had so ardently and recently expressed affection.

She smiled as she conversed with his gardener. In the small amount of time she was acquainted with his staff she appeared to have a more intimate relationship than he. Elizabeth stooped to examine a flower and, plucking a petal, showed it to the other lady of the party. They then examined the foliage together as the gardener chatted with the gentleman. Darcy found he liked the view very well and, deciding against the awkwardness of the situation, headed to meet with them.

His approach could not be hidden and the distance to them gave him time to think. He saw Elizabeth start when she spied him, but he could not help this and his determination was steeled with the idea that, once being seen, he was committed to the meeting.

Elizabeth watched his approach and thought Mr. Darcy might turn off the main path, avoiding them and turning onto a side path. Her mind was mixed with emotions of embarrassment and nervousness. She could not guess Mr. Darcy's feelings, but she also could not believe he held her in much esteem after their last encounter. That encounter had left her with an initial conviction of action, but his letter, and her contemplation of its truth, had since robbed her of the conviction and cruelly replaced it with shame. The robbery of that conviction was tortuously done a little each day as she watched the ink slowly fade from her letter.

As he neared, she might have been amused to learn that his determined approach was born from his inability to quit after being seen. For his part, he would have been amused that Miss Bennet saw the obvious retreat ,while his mind would not have seen it even if the side path were marked with waving banners.

Again they met and the two engaged in conversation. This time Mr. Darcy was very civil and his initial surprise from the previous meeting seemed to have vanished. He talked at ease about his estate, the buildings, and the grounds, and the attendants of which he was very fond. Elizabeth commented on the pleasantness of the staff, including Mrs. Reynolds, the housekeeper, whom they had already met and found to be very pleasant. Darcy smiled at the compliment and then surprised Elizabeth by asking for introductions to her companions.

Elizabeth was taken aback but composed herself and with some pride turned to her companions. She introduced them as the Gardiners who were also her Aunt and Uncle. Mr. Gardiner was a well respected merchant from London and Elizabeth took more joy in introducing them than she believed she would. The respectability of her relations gave her a sense that not all of her family needed for propriety. She half expected Mr. Darcy to find some fault with the Gardiners and she watched his face for the telltale sign of his pride and judgment for which he was known. She was curious when she did not see it, and more astounded when he heartily greeted the couple and began talking about the local countryside.

The four of them headed down the path at a leisurely pace, while the estate gardener took his leave and left the group. Elizabeth was quite left out of the conversation while her aunt and Darcy found a common ground of conversation regarding the local area. While they had never met, both of them owed their childhood to this part of England. Elizabeth stayed perplexed and then her eyes widened with a sudden realization; Mr. Darcy was trying. To what ends she could only guess, and the difficulty of the task was known only to her; for her aunt and uncle were happily engaged in conversation, and their first impression of this man must certainly be different than hers.

After a few turns of the path, the Gardiners found topics which interested only the two of them and separated from Elizabeth and Darcy who continued on the path for a minute or two before either spoke.

"I trust you are well Miss Bennet and that my letter was not of such a personal or shocking nature as to insult you in any way."

"It was not. I was uncertain to its truthfulness, but a re-examination of events, along with more than one encounter with Mr. Wickham upon my return to Hertfordshire, convinced me of its veracity."

"You were not offended by an explanation of my family's duties?"

"Confused would be a more apt description. We all have duties in the Gentry and many of them are of a military nature. I imagine the rise of Napoleon has something to do with this. I have made inquiries of my own and have learned that, whatever the exact duties may be, the Darcy family is held in high regard amongst the nobility. I believe even Mr. Wickham holds the duties in high regard, if not a personal belief in their underlying tenets. I am amazed you did so little upon his first dishonouring your sister, but I understand the need for restraint in matters of social dishonour."

Darcy blanched and Elizabeth immediately felt sorry for the remark. She attempted to think of a way to recover, but Darcy nodded and continued his walk.

"Your aunt and uncle are very respectable people. I believe him well suited as a merchant."

Taking the conversation cue Elizabeth followed him.

"Yes, I would agree. Thank you for making the effort to talk with them. I know how difficult it can be for you and how much you may not like the activity."

Darcy looked at Elizabeth trying to determine if she were sincere; he detected no trace of deception.

"It has been brought to my attention that my current social skills could use some practice."

"Any comments on my part were not meant as an insult."

"I was not necessarily referring to you, although I believe you are also a proponent of my practicing. I was instead referring to my sister, Georgiana. She will arrive on the morrow with the Bingleys, and she is particularly interested in meeting you. I wonder if you would allow the opportunity for her to make your acquaintance."

Elizabeth was once again surprised by Mr. Darcy, and she readily acceded to his request, although if she were pressed she could not say she was very aware of how she acceded; her mind was too caught up with thoughts of astonishment. If his sister was inclined to meet her then she must have heard favorable information from someone; the idea of Mr. Darcy being that individual allowed her to further conjecture he must still hold her in some regard. While she did not hope for his feelings, she found the idea of his approval to be affirming.

The walk ended several minutes later and the master of Pemberley saw to the carriage arrangements of the guests. Bidding them farewell, the carriage drove off and Darcy headed into his home.

Within the carriage Mrs. Gardiner smiled and commented on the pleasant nature of Mr. Darcy.

"He was not exactly as I envisioned him from your description Lizzy."

"Indeed not, had I but met him this day I would be hard pressed to believe my own description. Perhaps limited exposure has not allowed a full imprint of his character or perhaps Mr. Darcy's nature is more sociable while at home on his estate."

Conversation continued as they journeyed back to the Inn and Elizabeth was able to better focus than earlier in the day. Her mind did wander occasionally to events of the last hour, but she could not come to a satisfactory understanding of them.

Chapter 40

It was the next day When Mr. Darcy and his sister came to call on Miss Bennet, and the Gardiners, at the Inn. Elizabeth was once again surprised by the actions of her former adversary but not so far as to refuse the honour of the visit. After a few minutes of banter, Elizabeth realized she liked Miss Darcy quite a bit. Where her brother appeared proud, she appeared shy and quiet spoken. This appeased Elizabeth's concerns which had been slightly formed by the local villagers. Of Mr. Darcy they talked of kindness and honour; of Miss Darcy they spoke of quietness and pride; of Wickham they spoke of debts and curses which should not be stated in front of ladies. Elizabeth quickly learned the pride of Georgiana was no more than misconstrued shyness.

Darcy pleased himself by watching his sister and Miss Bennet converse and after a few minutes remembered himself. Charles Bingley was also among the group and would like to meet with Elizabeth; Darcy then asked permission for his entry. Miss Bennet readily agreed.

Charles entered and Elizabeth was greeted by his usual jovial self. He eagerly questioned her about her health and family. More than once did he ask about her sisters to which she stated all were well. Elizabeth could not discern, but she chose to believe that Charles interest was still for her sister Jane. With a gentle smile Elizabeth chose to test her idea.

"My youngest sister is in Brighton enjoying the summer. You remember Lydia do you not?"

"Yes, I believe I do. She is your youngest sister if memory serves."

Elizabeth nodded agreement.

"My other sisters Mary and Kitty are happily spending the summer helping my father with matters of the estate."

Turning to Georgiana, Elizabeth smiled and asked if the young lady's tea needed to be refreshed. After Miss Darcy replied it did not, Charles reapplied himself to the conversation.

"Excuse Miss Bennet, but I believe you also have another sister, do you not?" The eagerness in his voice was obvious to everyone including the young and naïve Georgiana who looked at Miss Bennet and then to Charles confusedly. Darcy caught Elizabeth's eyes as she turned back to Mr. Bingley and his look told her he was not amused. She smiled at Darcy who merely nodded and altered his look to present a demeanor that could not have been clearer than if he had stated it. *Very clever, you may proceed.*

"Yes, I forgot to mention my elder sister Jane. She is quite well and the summer seems to be lifting her mood. I imagine the sun is very healthy for her."

"Her mood? Has she been ill?!" he cried and asked with genuine concern.

"Not so much as I can assert, but the recent winter was heavy on her spirit. I cannot claim to know all the details, but I believe the weather caused her to be less than her usual cheerful self. You remember how cheerful she can be I am sure."

"Indeed I do, her smile was the most enchanting. It pains me to think of her in ill spirits."

"Well, your pain should not linger, as I have said, she is recovering."

Mr. Bingley welcomed this bit of news and then turned to his own thoughts. Elizabeth returned her attentions to Georgiana who still presented a façade of shyness. After a few attempts to coax her into conversation she turned to Mr. Darcy for assistance.

"Mr. Darcy, your sister appears to be well on her way to being accomplished. Do you have a particular recommendation of her abilities?"

"I believe she is becoming adept at the harp and the piano forte. Her skills rival your own on the latter instrument."

Both ladies turned to each other and then simultaneous gave mock expressions of displeasure. Georgiana commented that her brother grossly overestimated her ability, whereas Miss Bennet replied in much the same manner. They both agreed Mr. Darcy must be giving undue praise to themselves, but a polite disagreement entailed in which the two ladies both admitted Mr. Darcy must be correct in regards to the other lady.

"My brother is overly fond of me and I fear his affection is clouding his opinion of my abilities."

"I cannot claim to know all of his motives, but I fear he may not have enough experience of my playing to have formed a wise opinion; however, of your playing he must have the requisite experience and therefore a correct opinion."

"Oh no, that cannot be so. My brother is quite clever with his ear, and his honour keeps him from false praise except where I am concerned."

The two ladies fell into very agreeable conversation, and when it faltered Elizabeth turned to Darcy and the couple was able to successfully entice Georgiana to more dialogue. As Miss Darcy and Miss Elizabeth talked in ever more detail, Darcy and Bingley also became engaged. From time to time Darcy would glance at Miss Bennet and remind himself of an important fact; he had not been wrong in his opinion of her character. He also realized his feelings had not abated even in light of the recent tension between Miss Bennet and himself. He did not know if she would forgive him his sins or if she could accept his role in British society, but, as he watched Elizabeth in conversation with Georgiana, he came to realize the simple act of kindness to his sibling was endearing her more to him.

With an open invitation to dinner at Pemberley offered to Miss Bennet and the Gardiners, the visiting party left. Mrs. Gardiner and Elizabeth commented to one another on how gracious the visit was and that the manners of Mr. Darcy surely were as polite and pleasing as the day before; the villagers must be correct in their praise of him. Mr. Gardiner himself left to ready his fishing gear in anticipation of accepting an invitation the gentlemen had extended to him; heading out, he left the women to conversation.

Leaving the Inn, Darcy set his sister in the carriage and was about to enter himself when his eye was caught by a striking figure not too far off.

His mind almost could not grasp the vision but it eventually made sense of what he was seeing. Pretending a change of heart, Darcy begged Bingley to see Georgiana home; he would attend to business in the village and return later. He then unhooked one of the horses and walked the animal away from the Inn.

Not heading anywhere in particular, Darcy made a circuitous route and ended up spending several minutes talking to merchants. Each person was pleased to see him and many offered free samples of bread, or cheese, or other various wares. Many thanked him kindly for settling Mr. Wickham's debts as if they were his own, to which Darcy always nodded and replied it was his honour to assist them as he was also their greatest servant. The merchants always smiled at this comment and could not wish for a more kind master.

It was almost an hour before Darcy made his way down the lane and onto a side path from the village.

"The weather appears to be holding well."

Darcy turned to his new companion.

"Miss Dache, I trust you had a pleasant trip from London. To what do I owe this sudden visit?"

"Business I fear. London affairs are progressing well, but news has reached me regarding a possible breach of security. I am afraid our involvement may be known to unsavory individuals."

"The Colonel?" asked Darcy.

Miss Dache joined Darcy in walking down the path and nodded her head slowly and thoughtfully.

“It is possible but I cannot be certain. I do know there was an odd bounty offered for information and perhaps even an assassination. The format and meaning led me to believe it might be for you and I.”

“So you thought of reaching me personally.”

“I believed the matter concerned both of us, which required a more direct…….” She trailed off as they both realized they were not alone on the path. A figure was returning to the village along their path and shortly Mr. Darcy was confronted with Miss Bennet.

Starting abruptly, Miss Bennet stopped her advance.

“Mr. Darcy, I am surprised to see you so soon again. I was under the impression you had returned to Pemberley.”

Darcy looked a little uneasy and then replied.

“Yes, it was my intention to return, however, I decided to deal with business in the village.” He then fumbled amongst his pockets for a pair of small earrings he had procured for Georgina as if to add proof to his statement. “A gift for my sister,” he said.

“Oh Georgiana will surely love those.” commented Miss Dache.

Darcy took hold of his senses and then introduced the ladies.

“Miss Bennet, please allow me to introduce Miss Marianne Dache. Miss Dache, this is Miss Elizabeth Bennet, she is visiting the area with her aunt and uncle.”

“A pleasure to meet you.”

"And you as well. I did not mean to interrupt your conversation with Mr. Darcy. I felt I needed fresh air and this path is a very easy walk."

"Not at all, Miss Bennet," replied Darcy directly to Elizabeth. "Miss Dache and I were just talking of business in London. She is up from town and was gracious enough, upon spying me in the village, to inform me of current happenings."

Marianne watched the two interact and was momentarily confused by Darcy's reply to a comment directed at her. Her confusion was made clear upon the realization of an intimate relation between the two. She shrewdly watched Darcy's face as he addressed Miss Bennet and suspected this young lady might strongly hold his affections.

"Well, I should not wish to intrude upon business and I am just returning; so, I shall take my leave."

Marianne's eye took notice of Miss Bennet just as much as it had taken notice of Darcy. She could sense a possible return of affection, but with a confidence of character which was immediate cause for concern by Miss Dache. Elizabeth, upon encountering Mr. Darcy in the woods with another woman, showed no signs of jealousy. Either Miss Bennet was very confident in Darcy's affections or very confident in hers. Marianne suspected the former and was fearful of the latter.

"Miss Bennet, Mr. Darcy and I can talk business on many occasions. Please feel free to join us. I am not familiar with all of his acquaintances and would enjoy learning more about them."

Elizabeth politely declined and reiterated her intention of returning to the Inn. She wished the two of them well and continued up the path after everyone performed courteous bows.

Darcy watched her for a few steps and, seeing Miss Dache watching him, he turned to her and the two continued their walk. He did not relish the idea of Miss Dache being cognizant of his feelings for Elizabeth, but he knew her skills would tease out his affections.

"I would suggest the gentleman and lady turn around!" a loud male voice cried, which then arrested the attention of Miss Dache and Mr. Darcy. The two of them turned around to view Miss Bennet 10 yards up the path, held firmly, and with the point of a blade under her chin.

Mr. Darcy readied himself to move, but Miss Dache placed her hand on his arm and held him in check. It was a tense few seconds before the man spoke again.

"I trust a gentleman of your nature might think to protect yourself if this blade was at yer own throat. But it tis not, tis it? This lovely lady ere is much more appealing ta me, and I hope yourself can be more obliging to me demands."

"What is it you want?" asked Darcy coldly.

Elizabeth herself was amazed at how calm she felt. The blade beneath her chin was a matter of concern, but she seemed to deal with current events as if she were a spectator and not a participant. At first the actions of the man grabbing her did not arouse any feelings; he had moved so rapidly from the woods and she was turned around and had the blade to her throat so quickly that there was little time to do anything, even think or feel. Now that she fully realized her situation, she was more at ease and interested in Mr. Darcy's reaction. His questioning of her assailant revealed his calm and calculating side which she found reassuring.

"I want the gentleman's ring if you do not mind."

Darcy looked down at his ring and could guess as to the meaning of this predicament. Miss Dache would undoubtedly realize it as well. The ring held the crest of Darcy's family, was of solid gold, and to those in the know, the confirmation of his role decreed by the nobility. Darcy surmised this man was under orders to retrieve the ring to ascertain this information, which meant whoever hired this man suspected Darcy's role but did not know for certain. Darcy thought for a second, then removed his ring and headed for the assailant.

"Just a minute there sir; if you please. Give it to the lady there and ave er bring it to me. I do not wish for any man to be a 'ero, we wouldn't want to see this young thing get urt now would we?"

"How am I to know the lady will be left unharmed once you have the ring?"

"Oi, that is right insulting that is, I give you me word, how about that; and seeing as I ave a blade to your friends throat I guess you will ave to take me at me word."

Darcy handed the ring to Miss Dache who accepted it and slowly headed toward Miss Bennet. Marianne looked at Elizabeth and saw no fear; instead she saw a determined resistance which she suspected was a character trait of Elizabeth. Looking for a possible opening, she happened to notice the stance of the attacker. As she approached, Elizabeth moved her right foot along the ground till it came into contact with her assailants boot. The adjustment of weight was small as her left leg straightened to ready for support; Marianne registered it, even if the assailant did not.

As Marianne returned her gaze to Elizabeth eyes, Elizabeth met the look and quickly glanced at Miss Dache's waist; indicating immediately to Marianne her knowledge of the Push Dagger concealed within. Miss Dache had to hold in a smile. This attacker was oblivious to concealment of weapons on women, but Miss Bennet was not and had picked up on the fact of Miss Dache's blade. The ladies eyes met again as Marianne closed the gap and a perfect understanding was now between them.

Not too close to arouse his suspicion; Marianne stopped and slowly offered the ring to the left arm holding Elizabeth. As he tried to reach for it, while maintaining his blade position, Elizabeth raised her foot and came down hard on the man's toes. His foot, being only protected by light leather boots, took the brunt of Miss Bennet's heel, and he automatically recoiled in pain. Miss Dache wasted no time as Elizabeth moved one step forward out of the path. The two ladies passed each other as if dancers allowing each other the proper exchange of position.

Marianne stepped into the bent over man, swept his left leg, which was now supporting his weight, drew her blade and had it at the ready. Kicking his blade away into the foliage, she bent down to him, looked him in his now fearful eyes, and attempted to plunge her dagger into his chest.

A strong hand grabbed her wrist on the back swing and she angrily turned to face Mr. Darcy.

Her anger at being denied the kill was now turned to surprise as she glared, not at Mr. Darcy, but at Miss Bennet. No words were spoken as the meaning was as clear to Miss Dache as it had been those months past when Darcy had prevented her a similar kill.

Darcy himself had wasted no time in closing the distance to them. As Elizabeth and Miss Dache stared at each other, Darcy rapidly turned the man over and secured him with a belt, having removed it on his approach so as to be ready for use.

The ladies separated and Darcy turned his attentions to Elizabeth. Convincing himself she was fine, he then turned back to the assailant and inquired as to his motives.

The attacker was of little use and could provide no information other than a scrap of paper with code on it. He could not read it, but his mates had claimed it was a contract for him to steal Mr. Darcy's ring and return it to London. Darcy and Marianne recognized the code and its meaning. This contract was very clever. If the man failed in his mission, or if it was learned Mr. Darcy was merely a country gentleman, then the entire affair would have the appearance of a robbery. This contract was a concern for Darcy but one which could not be settled at the moment. Instead, he set himself the task of marching the attacker to the village in which resided men of law for whom Darcy had trust.

The ladies followed closely behind and of all things began to converse about the weather and the summer foliage that was now replacing the early spring blooms. After several minutes of this, Darcy stopped and turned to them with a quizzical look. Elizabeth caught his eye and questioning look.

"Is there a problem, Mr. Darcy? I realize you may not enjoy the trivial matters of summer flowers but there are others for which the topic is of interest. If you wish for dialogue of a more serious nature then I suggest you turn to your own companion. I should imagine he has nothing but serious talk within him."

She said this as the ladies passed the gentleman and Mr. Darcy could not help but see the teasing smile on Elizabeth's face. Darcy looked at his bound companion who in turned looked back at him with just as confused an expression. Fortunately for the situation, Darcy recovered quicker than the former assailant; for in the moment of mutual confusion he might have easily made an attempt to escape.

Chapter 41

On the following morning Elizabeth and the Gardiners arrived at Pemberley in order to return the kindness the Darcy's visit bestowed on them the previous day. The journey was pleasant, and primarily consisted of Mr. Gardiner's excitement to be fishing with the gentlemen, and Elizabeth thinking on the events of the past 24 hours.

She had found Miss Dache to be pleasant enough and skilled in conversation, as well as physical feats. Their time together was mostly spent in idle conversation in which each lady attempted to learn about the other. They each parted company with respect for the other, although Elizabeth felt inferior in regards to Miss Dache's level of physical skill and training; a training which was not a haphazard installation.

Now at Pemberley, they were met by Mrs. Reynolds who begged a minute for the ladies as she showed Mr. Gardiner the way to the gentleman who were already at the river fishing. Waiting in the entryway, Elizabeth walked around and entered one of the side rooms. Her visit a few days before had acquainted her with the general layout, and she believed she would be forgiven a minor transgression of viewing the lovely portraits and artwork once again. A noise in the next room caught her attention, and peeking through the open door she spied Mr. Darcy heading through. He saw her through the door as well and stopped short.

"Miss Bennet, I was not aware you were here."

She entered the room and looked about. This was the formal sparring hall and along the walls hung weapons of various degree.

"I have only just arrived with my aunt and uncle. Mrs. Reynolds is showing Mr. Gardiner to the river where she believed you to be."

"I was, up until this moment; I decided to fetch a different lure, and I am heading back to join the gentlemen. You are here to visit Georgiana?"

Elizabeth nodded as she headed over to the weapons rack and looked at the swords therein. Taking hold of one of them she admired its sheen and weight. It felt comfortable in her hand.

"Miss Dache seems fairly accomplished; I would surmise she has a vast amount of skills which make her business dealings effective for you."

"I should not like to comment on her business dealings. Her family has duties similar to my own but with varied responsibilities."

Darcy approached Elizabeth and, resting his hand upon hers, he corrected her grip; then, standing behind her, he guided her hand in a quick thrust and swing. Elizabeth felt a rush to her cheeks at his touch and tried to concentrate on the swing rather than his proximity. He backed away and she swung a few more times. Turning and bringing the sword about, she was surprised as a clear tone rang across the room when her blade made contact with a blade in the hand of Mr. Darcy.

The two opponents stared at each other for a moment until Elizabeth, feeling no fear, made another swing. Darcy easy blocked the blow and made no attempt to counter.

"Speed is more important than the wide swings, Miss Bennet. It is much like a dance and the intricate moves are more effective than the grandiose."

"Do you wish to dance then, Mr. Darcy, for I know how much the activity is disliked by you?"

She then moved to her left using footing from her dancing experience. Darcy countered with footing of his own.

"I do not believe I thanked you properly for your assistance yesterday. The gentleman in question is held securely?" She swung again and Darcy parried. He found her determined and untrained but not without raw talent.

"He is detained but not of much use for information. I do apologize for your being introduced to that side of my business. I am pleased you presented yourself with such composure; it displays strength of character."

Another ring of steel was heard throughout the room as the two carefully brought their weapons to bear.

"I believe you were already familiar with my strength of character. I was unsure if you meant for more harm to my attacker. I was pleased you did not kill him."

"I do attempt to avoid loss of life when possible. I also find it difficult to bring my skills and family duties to bear on minor matters of dishonour."

"Minor matters? The man was threatening to kill!" she cried as she made another lighthearted attack.

"Yes, and he is now in custody and will face the law. His choice of career is his own, his attack also was an act of choice, but once thwarted, I was happy to allow the local authorities to handle the affair. I do not set myself up to be judge and jury for all men. On the contrary, the duties entrusted to me and my family are ever present in my mind, and I reserve the use of our resources for only the most heinous of events. It is not for me to correct, or interfere with, the minor acts of individuals with questionable scruples."

A last ring of steel rang out and Darcy lifted his sword as a sign of submission. Elizabeth looked at her sword and the glint of sun from its blade. She brought the blade down to a ready position and addressed her opponent.

"My last attack upon you was with a dagger, and it was dealt with most efficiently. I am curious to know how you deal with a sword."

The world spun and Elizabeth's breath caught in her throat; a throat that now had a dagger close upon it. How the dagger appeared she could not say but its appearance was surprising. She stood straight, with Mr. Darcy behind her, her sword still in her hand but pulled firmly to her bodice by his left hand upon her wrist. The dagger to her chin and throat pulled her head up and away from her body while his breath was hot against her nape. She was not afraid, and the two of them stood silently for the briefest moment, until the tip was removed from her chin and Mr. Darcy rotated around to face her as he had been only moments before. He was polite, raised his blade, and apologized; it was only now that he realized how insensitive his actions could be considering her experience of just the day before.

Nodding to Mr. Darcy, she returned the blade to its rack. Darcy commended her on her talent and offered to instruct her further if she so desired. Elizabeth found herself accepting the invitation before she was fully aware of what she was saying.

Excusing himself, Darcy bowed and left the room to return to his fishing partners. Elizabeth watched him leave and admired him; once again thinking on the man she now believed him to be, as opposed to the one she originally entailed with a coldness of heart and a pride of spirit. She sighed calmly and thought to herself before speaking aloud.

"I was sorely prejudiced against you, and for that, I do apologize." The now empty room accepted her apology with neither approval nor condemnation.

Back in the entryway, Mrs. Reynolds was just returning and proceeded to show the ladies through to the saloon where Miss Darcy sat along with Charles' sisters, Caroline and Louisa. Conversation was fairly stilted with Georgiana showing her shy spirit and embarrassment at Caroline's attempts to tease Miss Bennet. Mrs. Gardiner caught on to the disingenuous nature of Caroline and took an immediate dislike to the lady.

Lunch was served and cleared away, and in due time the gentleman entered after having completed their fishing expedition. With the arrival of Mr. Darcy, Georgiana appeared to open up; Elizabeth and Darcy resumed their gentle coaxing from the day before to which Georgiana responded well. Caroline did not care for the apparent connection between those locked in conversation and guided the topic over to the militia stationed in Meryton. When Elizabeth mentioned the militia's move to Brighton Caroline expressed insincere sympathy.

"I should imagine the removal of many such handsome men to be intolerable to the ladies in your family; especially of a certain handsome man recently commissioned. I would imagine many fitting engagements well suited to your family's station could be found among the ranks."

While Caroline was coy enough to suggest Wickham she dared not mention his name in front of Darcy, who at the understanding of the reference sat rigid. Elizabeth glanced at Georgiana and could see confusion turn to understanding and then embarrassment. Elizabeth suspected Caroline was unaware of Wickham's disreputable treatment of Georgiana and, while she held Caroline in little regard, she did believe her capable of this amount of cruelty if the facts were fully known. Her cruel comment cemented her belief of Caroline's ignorance of the facts. Partially ignoring the comment, Elizabeth addressed Georgiana.

"The thought of handsome men reminds me I need to address you regarding your brother. He is wearing a fetching jacket today do you not think so?"

"Oh, yes! I was with him at its purchase and helped him select this jacket."

Darcy relaxed as the two ladies commented on his clothing. In his glances to Elizabeth he silently sent a thank you to which her eyes replied a heartfelt welcome.

The party was winding down and the guests were readying to leave when the arrival of Miss Dache was announced. She was shown in and politely greeted. She did not intend to stay long and only wished to give regards to Mr. Darcy and inform him she would be heading directly to London. Caroline and Georgiana were surprised to see Miss Dache and admonished Darcy for not informing them of her proximity to Pemberley.

"It is a shame that you must be heading off to London so soon. The countryside is very pleasant this time of year and we have many means of entertainment. We were just discussing ideas with Miss Bennet here. I do not believe you have met her; her family owns a smallish parcel in Hertfordshire, not to your standards I am sure you will agree, but adequate enough that she may attract a suitable husband of minor stature."

Miss Dache's calculating mood took command and, while Elizabeth and Miss Gardiner exchanged glances at the eloquently stated insult, Marianne raised an eyebrow and replied.

"I have met Miss Bennet. We had a small matter of business to attend to to which I was very impressed. If her financial status in life is inadequate to attract a man of significant means then I imagine her capabilities will."

Elizabeth appreciated the comment and gave Miss Dache a quick nod, to which Marianne replied with a nod of her own. Caroline sat dumbfounded and, while she was thinking of something else to criticize, Elizabeth took the opportunity to change the topic. She wished Miss Dache a pleasant journey and encouraged the young Miss Darcy to offer well wishes. Darcy stood to see Miss Dache out, and Caroline could be seen in an envious state; Elizabeth understood the nature of business between the two departing the room and gladly gave them the privacy of a farewell.

Heading out, Miss Dache turned to the room.

"Gentleman, to you I wish good appetite, to the ladies I wish for happy stories, to the others I wish goodbye."

The 'others' of her comment was meant as a polite goodbye to the attendants of the household, but the subtext of her meaning did not escape many as Miss Dache was looking in Caroline's direction when she uttered that particular remark. Elizabeth hid her smile under a napkin and quickly took a bite of a small biscuit.

Darcy walked out with Miss Dache and spoke to her briefly.

"The gentleman from yesterday is still detained?"

"Yes, Mr. Darcy. He is already on his way to London, but I cannot claim any more knowledge about him. He appears to be a minor player and ignorant in his role. I dispatched to London last night, as I am sure you did as well, my replies have not met with much luck. Were yours?"

"They were not, but I have received only one rapid reply which arrived early this morning by carrier pigeon. The general belief being that this man is of little importance and, if he is involved with Ackerby, it is in a minor role or perhaps he is still attached to the small amount of re-organization well underway. I am inclined to believe this last hypothesis. The man's confusion and nature of attack suggests uncertainty on the part of his employer, whoever that may be."

"Agreed, I will head back to London, and if I learn of more serious attacks I will send word immediately. Please take care of yourself and your sister."

Darcy replied he would honour her wishes and, as she rode away, Miss Dache wondered if she was mistaken in leaving him to his current social environment. She found Miss Bennet charming and capable but also knew that the longer he was in her influence the more likely he would fall prey to her charms. Those charms being natural, and of a beneficial intent, could lead many men astray; as opposed to Caroline's insincerity that she was certain Mr. Darcy held in little regard.

Miss Dache considered her choice of kindness towards Miss Bennet and decided she was correct in her actions; she did not wish harm to Elizabeth, but neither did she wish for her happiness if that happiness involved a relationship with Darcy. Marianne considered these ideas and believed she would keep to her current plans by keeping her enemy close.

In the halls of Pemberley the remaining guests finished their preparations for leaving. The carriage was called for and many wishes for a repeat of the day's activities were expressed. Plans were made for dinner the next day and Elizabeth hugged Georgiana goodbye as if they were the best of friends departing each other's company for an indeterminate amount of time. To Darcy she gave only a very warm look as he closed the carriage door and was pleased to have it returned in kind.

Chapter 42

Elizabeth had been a good deal disappointed in not finding a letter from Jane on their first arrival at Lambton; and this disappointment had been renewed on each of the mornings that had now been spent there; but on the third, her repining was over, and her sister justified, by the receipt of two letters from her at once, on one of which was marked that it had been missent elsewhere. Elizabeth was not surprised at it, as Jane had written the direction remarkably ill.

They had just been preparing to walk as the letters came in; and her uncle and aunt, leaving her to enjoy them in quiet, set off by themselves. The one missent must be first attended to; it had been written five days ago. The beginning contained an account of all their little parties and engagements, with such news as the country afforded; but the latter half, which was dated a day later, and written in evident agitation, gave more important intelligence.

It was in an obvious state of distress in which Darcy found Elizabeth an hour later as a servant presented him. Darcy quickly gauged her condition and called for water which the servant hurriedly departed to retrieve.

Elizabeth attempted to eschew the water and her ill feelings by stating she must locate her aunt and uncle.

``Good God! What is the matter?" cried he, with more feeling than politeness; then recollecting himself, ``I will not detain you a minute, but let me, or let the servant, go after Mr. and Mrs.

Gardiner. You are not well enough; you cannot go yourself."

Elizabeth hesitated, but her knees trembled under her, and she felt how little would be gained by her attempting to pursue them. Calling back the servant, therefore, she commissioned him, though in so breathless an accent as made her almost unintelligible, to fetch his master and mistress home instantly.

On his quitting the room, she sat down, unable to support herself, and looking so miserably ill that it was impossible for Darcy to leave her, or to refrain from saying, in a tone of gentleness and commiseration, ``Let me call your maid. Is there nothing you could take, to give you present relief? A glass of wine; shall I get you one? You are very ill."

``No, I thank you;" she replied, endeavouring to recover herself. ``There is nothing the matter with me. I am quite well. I am only distressed by some dreadful news which I have just received from Longbourn."

She burst into tears as she alluded to it, and for a few minutes could not speak another word. Darcy, in wretched suspense, could only say something indistinctly of his concern, and observe her in compassionate silence. At length, she spoke again. ``I have just had a letter from Jane, with such dreadful news. It cannot be concealed from any one. My youngest sister has left all her friends, has eloped; has thrown herself into the power of Mr. Wickham. They are gone off together from Brighton. *You* know him too well to doubt the rest.

She has no money, no connections, nothing that can tempt him. she is lost forever."

Darcy was fixed in astonishment. ``When I consider," she added, in a yet more agitated voice, ``that *I* might have prevented it! *I* who knew what he was. Had I but explained some part of it, only some part of what I learnt, to my own family! Had his character been known, this could not have happened. But it is all, all too late now."

``I am grieved, indeed," cried Darcy; ``grieved, shocked. But is it certain, absolutely certain?"

``Oh yes! They left Brighton together on Sunday night, and were traced almost to London, but not beyond; they are certainly not gone to Scotland."

``And what has been done, what has been attempted, to recover her?"

``My father is gone to London, and Jane has written to beg my uncle's immediate assistance, and we shall be off, I hope, in half an hour. But nothing can be done; I know very well that nothing can be done. How is such a man to be worked on? How are they even to be discovered? I have not the smallest hope. It is every way horrible!"

Darcy shook his head in silent acquiescence.

``When *my* eyes were opened to his real character. Oh! had I known what I ought, what I dared, to do! But I knew not, I was afraid of doing too much. Wretched, wretched, mistake!"

Darcy made no answer. He seemed scarcely to hear her, and was walking up and down the room in earnest meditation; his brow contracted, his air gloomy. Elizabeth soon observed and instantly understood it. Her power was sinking; every thing *must* sink under such a proof of family weakness, such an assurance of the deepest disgrace. She watched Darcy pace the room, love for him, if it were ever possible, was now a vain thought. She found sadness in this idea; sadness which revealed her feelings for Darcy to be stronger than formerly believed, and sadness compounding upon itself with the hopelessness of possible future affection from him.

But Elizabeth realized she could not think only of herself. Lydia, the humiliation, the misery, she was bringing on them all, soon swallowed up every private care; and covering her face with her handkerchief, Elizabeth was soon lost to everything else.

After a pause of several minutes she was recalled to a sense of her situation by the voice of her companion, who spoke with restraint.

``I am afraid you have been long desiring my absence, nor have I anything to plead in excuse of my stay but concern. Would to heaven that anything could be either said or done on my part, that might offer consolation to such distress! But I will not torment you with vain wishes, which may seem purposely to ask for your thanks. This unfortunate affair will, I fear, prevent my sister's having the pleasure of seeing you at Pemberley today."

``Oh, yes. Be so kind as to apologize for us to Miss Darcy. Say that urgent business calls us home immediately. Conceal the unhappy truth as long as it is possible. I know it cannot be long."

He readily assured her of his secrecy, again expressed his sorrow for her distress, wished it a happier conclusion than there was at present reason to hope, and, leaving his compliments for her relations, went away.

As he quitted the room, Elizabeth felt how improbable it was that they should ever see each other again on such terms of cordiality as had marked their several meetings in Derbyshire; and as she threw a retrospective glance over the whole of their acquaintance, so full of contradictions and varieties. She sighed at the perverseness of her feelings which at first were hatred for this man and now were becoming fondness. His comments of just one day prior intruded upon her mind.

"It is not for me to correct, or interfere with the minor acts of individuals with questionable scruples."

Elizabeth realized Darcy could do little to help, other than what he had by calling for her uncle and aunt; furthermore, his family's duties and responsibilities required him to distance himself from her and her family's dishonour. She understood the man and his position. The House of Darcy must be held in high regard, and she would respect that need. Resigned as she was to the idea of his separation, she could not help but grab a small pillow, hang her head, and cry.

Chapter 43

The door swung back with a force that strained the hinges; it was not with strength but speed which caused the door to react in such a manner. Darcy had alighted from the carriage just moments before, and his feet were swift across the street and up the steps to his offices in London. These offices were still in use and many heads turned to him as he entered. It did not take long before he had commandeered several men from non-pressing issues.

Gathered around the table, he threw down a small portrait about the size of a man's pocket watch and addressed the group swiftly and coldly.

"Gentlemen, the man in this image is Mr. George Wickham. Recent reports of the past week have him traveling into London and no farther. He is also believed to be in the company of a young lady. You are to locate Mr. Wickham and report his exact location to me. Do not approach him or make your presence known to him."

Taking up the image, he handed it to one of the office attendants of whose skill Mr. Darcy was well aware.

"Can you make several likenesses and add them to coded messages?"

"I can, and it shall be done immediately." The young man grabbed the image and left to create copies.

"The rest of you will need to study notes I have of Mr. Wickham."

Darcy handed several copies of parchment to the men in the room. His trip from Pemberley was spent wisely in preparation and the planning of actions needed to be performed; not the least of which were his putting to paper pertinent facts of George Wickham.

As the men attended to their various tasks, Darcy drew their attention with a loud hand hitting a table. Turning to him, every man witnessed a cold, calculating, and determined individual.

"Gentleman, it is believed Mr. Wickham intends to dishonour this lady. I cannot attest to what ends or to what means he will employ, but we must find him sooner rather than later. We as families of the Gentry have the backing of the crown itself to protect honour, and we now have the power of a criminal organization built on the ideals of which George Wickham adheres. Let us see what the exercise of this new found power can achieve. Find me this man!"

Each man stood to attention, some of the men that were familiar with military address, stood to formation attention. Darcy nodded firmly and the men scattered to their various tasks. Some immediately departed with their coveted notes in their hands, others were grabbing for London registries, and still others searched through the recent dailies.

It was late into the evening when Miss Dache arrived at the office. She made her presence known to the men and then searched out Mr. Darcy. He was found easily enough, entrenched in a corner office with notes spread about and various reports pinned to the wall. She wasted no time in addressing her concerns.

"Your present operation has come to my attention, and I cannot say I condone it. This Mr. Wickham may present himself as a cad but hardly worth all the effort being expended."

"There are facts and circumstances of which you are unaware and I beg you to leave me to my work," replied Darcy calmly and without looking up.

"Do not play me the fool, Mr. Darcy. I am not a simpleton such as Caroline Bingley. I know well who George Wickham is, his relation to your family, and the living for which your father intended. I am also well aware of his fall from grace. If his current actions have entangled him with a young Miss Bennet then the dishonour is hers and her family's, not yours. You would do better to distance yourself and let the family deal with it."

Darcy could assign her knowledge of Wickham to her detailed analysis of the Darcy family, but her conjecture regarding the youngest Bennet escaped him; he was in little mood to guess as to her intelligence reports or whether she was stating a hypothesis as fact, so that she may judge his reactions. Rather than take a defensive position Darcy preferred to counter attack. The anger in his voice did not escape Marianne.

"Are you also aware of my role in this situation? Can you claim knowledge of the facts which allowed this to happen?"

Marianne appeared confused for a moment and Darcy did not relent on his attack.

"I will deal with this affair, and you will either help or you will stand aside." Moving in close to her, he glared fiercely into her astonished eyes. "It was you who wished to see this side of me; you who claims enjoyment in these types of action. I trust you will not be disappointed by what you will witness."

Miss Dache did not say a word, but the realization of her predicament hit her with full force; she would later understand it to be an epiphany. All of this; this anger, this power, and this determination; for months she strived to see it, and admire it, and now that she had, she was saddened it was not for her.

She turned and headed to the door. Stopping she spoke without turning around. Her voice was calm and quiet.

"Why her?"

Darcy knew she was asking about Elizabeth. He thought for a moment, reflecting on Miss Bennet's smile, her laugh, and her good natured teasing. He almost laughed as he recalled her lighthearted threats to converse about rabbits or deer's.

"I love her," he said with a whisper and solemn tone. He was not sure if Miss Dache heard, but he inferred she must, as she then walked out the door.

It was a few long days later when a first positive sign of Wickham's location was learned. His current state left little in the way of solid social or familial contacts. Any individual with a past association claimed no knowledge of his whereabouts or any desire to learn of them. He was found to be disreputable even amongst the disreputable. Eventually, he was located by repeated application of intelligence and bribery to Mrs. Younge, a former accomplice of Wickham.

That very evening Darcy was on the London streets with a dagger in his possession and determination in his heart. He followed the address to its location and waited patiently. This part of town suited the character of George Wickham with its less than savory citizenry.

After a quarter hour, he saw the light in the suspected residence move about and a face came to the window; it was definitely George Wickham. He appeared distraught and haggard. Darcy made a few hand signals and then headed into the street oblivious to the carriages around him. His actions forced one carriage to stop and the driver yelled at him. This commotion drew the attention of Mr. Wickham who, looking into the street, recognized his former friend. The remaining color drained from his face and he retreated from the window.

A few minutes later the rear door of the seedy establishment opened. George took a quick look around and, seeing the alley empty, he entered and made his way away from the building. His world turned upside down and his head hit the ground sending flashes of light into his brain. After a moments recovery, he attempted to sit up, but a stiletto boot pressed into his throat.

"George Wickham, I presume," Miss Dache stated more than asked.

"You have upset more than one of my very good friends, and, if you should possess any intellect, I would suggest you do not move from the position you currently find yourself."

George smiled and attempted to speak, but Marianne hushed him.

"Shhh, Mr. Wickham. That silver tongue of yours will be quite useless on me; I may even conjecture that its use would bring about more hostility for you than I am currently displaying." She dug her heal into his throat as if to make her point.

A stern voice behind her captured both of their attention. Marianne removed her heel and glared at Wickham before she headed to the hotel to attend to the youngest Miss Bennet. The interactions of the next few minutes were something she desired to see, but an accidental viewing by the youngest Miss Bennet could not be allowed.

Once she was out of site, George propped himself up and attempted to speak to Darcy.

"Fitzy, it is good to see you. You are looking very well. Now, I understand your anger, and for my part I regret my recent actions." As he talked he took to his feet and Darcy closed the distance slowly.

George smiled and appeared very kind and jovial. He attempted to speak again, but Darcy quickly hit him with a closed fist directly over the heart. Wickham wheeled backward and fell to the ground. He tried to regain his balance and his head exploded with light as Darcy hit above the ear. Darcy's skill was well known to George who knew he could not beat his former friend, but thoughts of fighting, or fleeing, left him as fear took hold.

Darcy continued his calm attack, hitting George with well placed blows. Each blow would bruise, of this Darcy was certain, but the bruises would be concealed by clothing, or in the case of the head, by hair; Darcy was very careful to keep his hits within the hairline.

The attack ceased, and when George could make sense of the world he saw that the gentleman had made their way to the end of the alley and almost to the next street. Darcy stood calmly a few feet away and said nothing. He just stood in the alley staring coldly at George, who then took the opportunity to get to his feet.

Wickham took a defensive pose and begged Mr. Darcy to stop and allow an explanation. Darcy did not respond; he only stood in a resolute manner. Wickham found the cold silence more intimidating than the previous attack and realizing the cessation of the assault was an opportunity, he backed away from Darcy; who curiously did not follow.

Careful in movement Wickham reached the street and, observing no movement from Darcy, he turned and headed off. Wickham had not gone 50 feet before a ragged man leaning against a building called out to him.

"Ay now. Is you not that George Wickham characher I is 'earing much about?"

George looked at the man now addressing him. The man was using a dagger to clean his nails which were excessively dirty. The nails, as George took in the whole figure, were perhaps the cleanest part of the individual. His face was dirty and mis-shaven, his clothes a mixture of old and older, and when he smiled, his teeth were either missing or so stained as to appear to be missing. The man laughed at George and gave a bit of warning.

"I should not 'ead down this side of the street. A nice respetabel gent like as you might get 'urt." The man scrunched his nose and contorted his face with a look of disgust as he leaned in to Wickham to speak quietly. "Filled with unsavory types it is. This side of the street."

George's eyes widened and he backed into the street almost to be hit by a man on a horse. The horse reared and nearly took off George's head.

"Whoa now!" yelled the man to his horse as he reigned it into control. The gentleman appeared to be a tradesman by his outfit and, with concern, he addressed Wickham.

"Careful there, George!"

Wickham started at the sound of his name.

"Old Black here almost removed your head; if I had not carefully reigned him in, you would be in terrible shape." Moving on, the gentleman passed George and glared as he did so.

George came to his senses slowly and finished his crossing. Quickening his pace he headed down the walk with a careful eye at passersby's. While he passed a group of several men and ladies he was forced to walk amongst them. They were busy talking amongst themselves about current London affairs. He arrived at the other side of the group in pain as his gut had been firmly assaulted; he could not claim how it happened nor did he see which one of the men or ladies had assaulted him.

Bending over, he took to a step and breathed heavily. After a minute of rest, Wickham was addressed again, and he was relieved to look up at a local constable. George sighed with relief.

"Are you unwell?" asked the constable.

“I am not quite sure,” George responded with his charming smile, now mollified by pain and fear.

“I believe someone may want to do me physical harm. Could you escort me away from here?”

“The constabulary of London has better things to do than to assist an obvious drunk. Now move along before I take you in.”

George was again shocked and only moved from his step when the constable reached for him. Now that Wickham was moving along, the constable only glared, and then went about his business.

The street continued in its affront of horrors to George. He senses were assaulted by an elderly lady, a naval officer, merchants, and prostitutes. There was not a street he could walk nor any path he could trust; and every person he passed became suspect in his eyes. To the innocent he appeared crazy and to the others he appeared despicable. Wickham retreated from each person he encountered and bounced his way across the streets of London as if he were a raindrop making its way down a cedar shingled roof.

Dazed and disoriented, he finally found solace in a back alley where he sat, fearful of the possible approach of anyone. He watched the entryway for signs of an approach; while many passed, none entered. He started at the sound of a cat, which at that moment had jumped onto a pile of refuse. Wickham calmed his nerves for a second as he looked at the animal, but his breathing was still heavy.

"It's just a cat!" he said aloud, as much to declare a fact as to calm his nerves.

"I would not be as certain as you of the cat's innocent intentions."

Wickham heard the voice but could not locate the speaker. He looked about the alley and found more than one darkened area which could hide his addressor. While Wickham could not locate Darcy, it was a certainty it was he who had spoken.

Wickham's eyes did turn to the man as he made his appearance by exiting the shadows. Darcy slowly approached George, and when he reached him he bent his knees to be able to address the sitting man.

"There is no place you can hide, no haven from which you will find safety, no church which will grant you sanctuary, in which I will not be able to find you and deal with you. I can interfere with your life at will and lead you the direction I so choose, even if the direction is towards hell. I have tolerated your abuses against society, and even myself, for the sake of pride; and you have been much too eager to take advantage of that weakness. I can assure you George, I am no longer amused."

The men stared at each other, and Wickham, having learned his first of many new lessons, kept his voice to himself. Darcy coldly stared at George and with little emotion made his declaration of intent known.

"It was my concern for appearances which has led to this disaster; my sense of duty will now correct it."

Chapter 44

Lydia was as unintelligent and rash as Darcy remembered, and he was hard put to believe she was related to either of the other Miss Bennets. After his initial confrontation with George, Darcy insisted on seeing Lydia. The insistence was in the form of a polite request, but one which Wickham knew was tantamount to a more dangerously worded order.

Lydia was pleased to meet Mr. Darcy and asked for news from the world. She was dreadfully bored in this London room but still excited about her prospects of marrying George. Darcy was tactful and artful in his arguments, but no amount of skill, logic, or even emotion, could penetrate the stupidity he encountered. Resigning himself to her obstinate nature, Darcy excused himself and addressed Wickham.

It was commanded that the gentleman and lady were to stay where they were until further arrangements were made. Should Wickham decide to vacate the area, Darcy would be immediately informed and the matter of honour would be settled quietly. This was made clear to Wickham with no room for interpretation.

Darcy returned to his London home and set about designing a plan. His most fond hope was to separate Lydia from George and find a way to repair her reputation or at least limit the damage. Her stubbornness was cause for more trouble than he wished, but he decided her foolishness would become apparent to her in the coming years. If she was so desirous of this man then she shall have him; it was at this point that Mr. Darcy set about arrangements for their marriage.

Debt reports would have to be called in, arrangements made for their settlement, Wickham's commission dealt with, and affairs of Lydia's entitlement. This solution required more complex arrangements than if Lydia were too come to some semblance of sense and return home; the more detailed plan would require the appearance of propriety and honourable intentionality of those involved. In the end, it was an interesting test of the current network Darcy was overseeing.

Wickham was made aware of the plans and his displeasure was as apparent as it was irrelevant. Darcy applied to the scoundrel for a full accounting of his debts which were to be verified by financiers. Discrete runners were sent to villages which were unfortunate to have received Wickham recently, and an accounting of his debts in those locations was also collected.

Arrangements for the release of the commission were completed and the official paperwork was dated and miss-addressed. Apologies were sent to the regiment in Brighton for the confusion in hopes the clarification would allay any fears of misconduct. Official seals on the articles would certainly help with the intended effect.

George was very displeased to learn his former childhood friend intended for him to join the regulars, and this idea shocked him.

"Dear, old friend, the work of the regulars is for the common man. You must have some pity on me and my future bride. Think how she will react to the housing arrangements of the regulars. This is no place for a lady."

This was the first sign of resistance Wickham had shown to anything recently, and Darcy was not about to let it kindle into anything more. His eyes flared and anger tinged his voice.

"Old friend, I would have you in a jail cell if the situation allowed, under constant guard, and every move monitored or controlled; but I cannot, so I will control you through the regulars. Your silly wife will find sleeping on the ground and bringing her husband meals to be very beneficial to her personality development. Your pay will be adequate and its expenditures counted. If you cannot control your vices, then I shall employ the army to do it for you. And might I add, desertion from the regulars is a death sentence; choosing to disobey my edicts will be less pleasant than that." And thus ended any resistance by Wickham.

The time came to inform the Bennet family of the arrangements. Darcy chose to approach Mr. Gardiner rather than Mr. Bennet himself; he believed Mr. Gardiner's disconnection from the affair would allow for calmer consideration of the facts. It took a considerable amount of convincing but Darcy was victorious in the end, at which point he was much more admirable of the Bennets and the Gardiners.

For Mr. Gardiner, he admired his insistence on assisting Mr. Darcy and for shouldering the financial burden. Mr. Gardiner was a well to do merchant and possessed the required finances, if only barely, and the sense of honour to wish to deal with his family's shame, even if it was his niece and not his daughter. Darcy was hard pressed to convince the man that Wickham's actions were a result of pride on his own part and therefore he should shoulder the guilt and the penalty.

Mr. Bennet had impressed Darcy with his resolve, his resources, and his cunning. Elizabeth's father had learned little of Wickham while in London, but that was in part due to Darcy keeping information from him. There had been more than one report of opposing inquiries into the location of Wickham, and Darcy had them traced back to Mr. Bennet. What Darcy found admirable was the skill and methods used for the inquiries; these seemed at odds with the expected skills of a simple country gentleman, but Darcy could spend little time in contemplation of their meaning.

The Gardiners, now with an understanding of the arrangements, were happy to take over the operation and insisted Mr. Darcy should rest. With the subtle and covert arrangements completed, all that remained was for the actual social niceties of the wedding and the proper arrangements between families. Darcy, being impressed with the skill and understanding of the Gardiners, quit London and returned to Pemberley for a relaxing visit with his sister and guests. He did not intend to return until the wedding day was fixed.

The wedding day did eventually arrive, and Darcy stood in the church with Wickham; it was a small affair consisting primarily of the wedding couple, the Gardiners, and Mr. Darcy. As the vows were exchanged Wickham looked about as if searching for an escape. His displeasure was barely noticeable, and his smile ever present; except when his eyes met an individual in the church who returned his gaze with steely determination. Mr. Darcy, being no fool, had placed individuals throughout the church in line of sight of any direction Wickham chose to turn. Over one shoulder he encountered Miss Dache, another direction was a man polishing a crucifix while glaring at the groom, even the altar was occupied by an altar boy who appeared menacing to George.

The wedding concluded and congratulations were given to the bride and groom; the former wishing her family were in attendance and that the affair had not been so small. With a sigh of relief, Darcy then reminded Wickham of the future arrangements. He was to visit his new parents, be polite, enjoy what little time he had, and then report for his assignment within a month. Wickham agreed and then assumed his normal jovial attitude, smiled to his new wife, and proceeded to act as if he were the happiest, luckiest man, in all of England. Darcy shook his head and whispered to himself regarding the brazen display of bravado.

Chapter 45

A few days at Pemberley were enough to produce a restless Darcy, who then took it upon himself to convince his friend Charles, of a needed visit to Netherfield. It did not take much convincing and in short order the plans were set. The whole party, except for Miss Darcy, would leave in a week and visit the grounds of Netherfield, ostensibly so Mr. Bingley and Mr. Darcy could conclude their initial assessment of the area in order that they may determine its feasibility as an estate for the Bingleys. Caroline and Louisa were not excited about this move, but Charles' excitement, and their affinity for him, was too much for them to condemn the idea.

The party was settled at Netherfield only a couple of days before Charles suggested the men explore the countryside and perhaps make a visit to the Longbourn estate. Charles, in his attempt to convince his friend, suggested Miss Elizabeth Bennet might be pleased to see him and would appreciate more recent social updates, as they were forced to curtail their last encounter unexpectedly. Darcy, feeling only slight shame at manipulating his friend this way, readily agreed.

Exploring the countryside was pleasant and very short. Darcy could not help but notice the eagerness that Charles had when he decided to take the lead. He further conjectured the most skilled navigator would have been hard pressed to find a quicker route to Longbourn. Darcy was still concerned for his friend and the entailment of his emotions, but he was also more apt to trust in

Elizabeth's statement of her sister's feelings. He would now make a more concerted effort to watch the eldest Miss Bennet for signs of affinity, and if needs be, he would modify his understanding of her. The rest of the time would be spent gathering subtle and firsthand accounts of Mr. and Mrs. Wickham's recent trip, which had,m only a few days prior, concluded with their departure.

The gentlemen were greeted civilly by the Bennet family and were shown into the drawing room where time was spent in idle conversation. Mr. Darcy, not being in a very conversational mood, spent his time watching the eldest daughter. He was pleased to see Elizabeth and gave her a warm hello. At least to his understanding it was warm, but Elizabeth did not take it as such. She instead found him to be cold and aloof this day.

On more than one occasion did she attempt to engage Mr. Darcy in conversation or to divert the current dialogue onto topics she knew he would be fond; this was to no avail and he appeared to have reverted to his original prideful self. Her current understanding of his character allowed him the benefit of doubt, and she searched for meaning to the visit.

The Bennet family had been informed of the return of the Bingleys and of even the prideful Mr. Darcy; the village was a cauldron of gossip and schemes of all sorts were attributed to the return of the individuals who were all but set on abandoning the local area. The arrival this day of the two gentlemen was not announced nor expected, but Elizabeth was not completely surprised. She did find Mr. Darcy's lack of conversation annoying and, for a moment, surmised he was keeping a distance from a family that so nearly met with social disaster by the foolish actions of the youngest daughter.

Elizabeth fidgeted nervously. She was disappointed in the current rapport with Mr. Darcy, and then she was angry with her disappointment. These feelings did not last long as her Mother talked at length about her new son-in-law. Mrs. Bennet, who only a few weeks before this day was intent on injuring the young man who ran off with her daughter, was now nothing but glowing admiration for him. She found him delightful and ever so clever; not content to spout her own opinions of Mr. Wickham, she prodded the others in the room to agree with her assessment. Elizabeth's prior feelings of anger and doubt were now changed to shame and embarrassment.

She looked to Mr. Darcy hoping he would perhaps change the subject or at least sense her discomfort and offer a nod of understanding. This was not to occur as he was focused on his friend and Jane as they talked. She thought for a moment that his incivility and prideful nature were more entrenched than she recently let herself to believe, and perhaps all was lost between them but an occasional courteous salutation. She could not blame him his opinion of her and her family, but she did wish it were not so, and for a moment she hated that pride of his.

Jane laughed at a comment of Mr. Bingley's and Elizabeth, who had been looking to Darcy, saw his eyes widen and his features focus. Elizabeth turned to her sister Jane and then back to Darcy;

once again did she look between the two. Mr. Darcy did not waiver his look and remained focused on either Mr. Bingley or Jane.

"I know that look," Elizabeth whispered to herself as she came to an understanding; Mr. Darcy was very carefully and meticulous watching her sister. She concluded he must be re-evaluating his original assumption of affection towards Charles. This could only be due to her influence. In fact, she recalled all those months ago that Mr. Darcy commented on the permanence of his opinions. For him to re-visit his decisions was a great compliment indeed. "Oh, you wonderful man." She thought to herself. If Darcy was intent on watching and judging her sister then she would allow for his current incivility towards her. As a whole, she did not encourage judgment of this type, but she now knew Mr. Darcy's motivations were pure and Mr. Bingley, being the recipient of those motivations, albeit unknowingly, had a great friend in Darcy.

The afternoon concluded with an invitation to dinner on the following day. The gentleman agreed to the invitation and returned the next day well before dinner; where the conversation and idle games of the day before continued as if they had not let off. Elizabeth hoped Mr. Darcy would be in a more receptive mood to conversation, but he was as focused as he had been the day before. This is not to imply he was abhorrent in his manners; rather that he was polite but curt. It was this day when Elizabeth understood another nature of his character which was the discomfort he felt amongst strangers, especially those engaged in such frivolous talk. She was logically aware of this and had seen it before; at Rosings amongst the Collinses. But this level of experience was new to her, and she realized the brashness of her mother, and being surrounded by several women, most of whom he knew very little, were not experiences for which he received enjoyment. For the first time she found something in Mr. Darcy that her father also had in common. She smiled for a moment as she thought about her father, who at this very moment was shut in his office; most likely with a good book. She now believed that if Mr. Darcy were not intent on watching for her sister's feelings, he would gladly join Mr. Bennet in his office; and the two of them would spend many hours reading quietly and never speaking a word. This idea pleased Elizabeth.

Darcy, for the previous visit and the current one, was indeed intent on watching Jane Bennet. He found the time well spent and it alleviated his mind from the inane banter of Mrs. Bennet, to whom he found overly opinionated; a vice made more distasteful by the baselessness of the opinions. He did attempt more than once to converse with Elizabeth, but the degree of conversation he wished for was not to be allowed by Mrs. Bennet. Darcy readily saw the embarrassment on Miss Bennet's face and on one particular comment; when Mrs. Bennet had the nerve to subtlety suggest part of Mr. Wickham's troubles were due to the Darcy family, he witnessed Elizabeth turn away with a mixture of shame and discomfort. Not wishing to injure Elizabeth, Darcy focused on his task at hand, which was to assess Miss Jane Bennet, and withdrew himself from the artillery path of Mrs. Bennet's comments.

The dinner party ended and all individuals parted ways on amicable terms. Charles was excited as usual and made grandiose claims of throwing another ball to which everyone was invited. Darcy was hard pressed to pull his friend away and thought at one point Charles hand would fall off from all the waving.

The trips were not in vain for Darcy. He learned the eldest Miss Bennet did have feeling for his friend; to what extent he could not quite determine, but he witnessed enough to settle his mind and allow his friend a blessing on the relationship. He did smirk for a moment as he had an odd thought; he considered the idea of Jane Bennet as a spy. The idea was ludicrous of course, but Darcy could not help but wonder; if she could fool him so easily by her control of apparent affection, how much could she baffle someone attempting to learn information from her?

Of the other matter, that of Wickham, Darcy was happy to consider the matter settled. He was able to confirm his reports of the recently married couples visit, the warm welcome, and the happy departure. His most recent intelligence stated Wickham had reported for duty and was beginning to settle in. Darcy only hoped the settling would be the beginning of a new and much needed habit.

Caroline and Louisa were still up and in the drawing room when the men arrived and greeted them with many questions about the dinner, to which Charles was eager to answer. Being tired, Darcy was more inclined to bed and a good night's sleep; he had to travel to town early the next morning and would not return for nearly a fortnight. Before bed, he determined to allow for some chance in his life and, believing little harm could be done, he informed Charles of his subterfuge regarding Jane Bennet's visit to London. He begged for his friend's forgiveness and added that his motivations of the time were for Charles' benefit.

"Darcy, this is astounding. I would not have thought you capable of such a plan."

"I assure you I am capable of much more, but my intention was never to maliciously deceive you, only to protect you from a lady I deemed possessed no feelings for you. I had just suffered the ordeal of convincing you of my belief when her arrival was made known to me. I did not relish the idea of repeating the ordeal."

"And now, you tell me this now. Why is that? Do you feel a sudden pang of guilt?"

Charles was upset but not so outwardly angry; Darcy did not believe his friend had the capability for that amount of anger.

"It has come to my attention that I was incorrect in my assessment, and the lady does indeed have very strong feelings for you. I was not certain until these last two day, but I do now perceive her feelings and believe she would not discourage yours."

This news brightened Charles immediately and any ill feelings for Darcy were now forgotten as he was now beside himself with joy; as he talked excitedly, he drew Darcy into his ramblings. Charles commented on her hair and her voice, all to which he begged Mr. Darcy to agree with. Darcy could not help but smile at his friend and accede to his begging by agreeing to just about every romantic notion he vocalized. After several minutes, Darcy had to take his leave and headed up to his room for the night. Halfway up the stairs Charles called out to him.

"Darcy, do I have your blessing to marry Miss Bennet?"

Darcy stood still for a minute in shock before he good naturedly asked "Do you require it?"

"No, But I should like to think I have it nevertheless."

"Then you have it, my friend."

They smiled at each other and separated, Darcy to his room and Bingley to an office. Unknown to the men, Caroline had stood in the hallway and listened to the conversation. The topic and resolution was a concern for her. If Darcy approved of the Bennet family enough to allow her brother to marry into it, then he could not be so disinclined to the idea of wedding Elizabeth. Caroline headed to the drawing room and began to think of schemes to prevent such a disaster.

Chapter 46

Doors could be heard slamming and a loud voice permeated the house. Darcy looked up from his report and gazed at Miss Dache who appeared as bewildered as he. The ruckus did raise concern so she stood and made her way closer to the office entryway while reaching for her blade.

"Where is he?" a loud female voice rang throughout the house.

"Do not prevent me from entering this house you stupid servant, and do not touch me. Do you know who I am? I will be shown to my nephew immediately. Immediately, do you hear me?"

Darcy rolled his eyes and signaled to Miss Dache not to worry. Marianne took a more relaxed stance at a bookcase by the door but did make sure to stand in a place that would not be visible to anyone entering. Several more calls loudly rang out and Lady Catherine de Bourgh barged into the room.

"Ah, there you are Nephew. I would speak to you immediately!"

The servant attempted to apologize as he followed her into the room, but Lady de Bourgh began to pelt him with her purse and inform him of her status in life. The poor man was left to defending himself against an aggressive but ultimately harmless attack. After a moment she stopped; Darcy caught the man's attention and signaled with his eyes a sincere apology and motioned for him to leave the room.

"My dear aunt, to what do I owe this visit?"

"Do not play coy with me nephew. I am here to correct a vicious rumour that has come to my attention. I did not wish to confront you directly, but my attempts to settle the ludicrous nature of this rumour have been most insidiously blocked. I will know the truth of the matter and scorn that wretched Elizabeth Bennet."

The door of the office shut and Catherine turned at the noise.

"And who is this? Are you now in the habit of entertaining ladies without proper supervision? Are you now collecting them so they may see to you and your household?"

Darcy sighed and then stood to address his aunt.

"Lady Catherine de Bourgh, may I introduce Miss Marianne Dache. Miss Dache, Lady Catherine de Bourgh."

Marianne bowed slightly in polite respect.

"I do not care to be introduced to anyone at this moment. Dismiss her and let us address this issue."

"I am still unaware of what issue you are referring; and Miss Dache and I were in the middle of important business dealings."

"I do not care for your business dealings nor do I care for women who choose to engage in them; you may conclude your business later and this young lady may return to her own residence and her own family. I only hope they are more respectable than your recent associations."

"Her father is Lord Dache, and her business is of Noble intent," replied Darcy coldly.

This gave Lady Catherine pause as the information began to clear for her. She was not an entirely stupid woman and the position of the Dache family was known. The realization of the nature of the business matters, as well as Marianne's family position, did cause for an interesting reaction in Darcy's aunt. She did recover quickly and still insisted on being heard. Darcy nodded to Miss Dache, who nodded in return and left the room, only to take up position in the hallway with the intent on listening to the conversation. She believed she may not hear Darcy's side, but she had no doubt she would hear his aunts.

"What is it I can do for you?"

"I would have you quell this rumour of marriage to Miss Bennet."

On the outside of the door Marianne almost gave her position away when she gasped. Inside the room, Darcy kept his composure as he responded.

"Marriage? Please enlighten me as to the details of what you have heard."

"You may be aware that your friend Mr. Bingley has just this last week proposed marriage to Jane Bennet."

Darcy admitted that he was aware of the fact; he had only been in London three days when he received the letter from Charles informing him of the matter.

"Well imagine my surprise when my reverend, of all people, should visit me to inform me of his family's good news. He then informed me that Miss Elizabeth Bennet was soon to be engaged to you, and both weddings were to be performed before year end. Well, I cannot tell you how shocked I was at this news, so I called my carriage and left for Longbourn to confront Miss Bennet and learn the truth for myself."

Darcy was back at attention for this bit of information. His aunt was a formidable woman, and although she had little power within the family, she did enjoy the portion she had which extended outside, and for most people that little portion was very intimidating.

"And did you confront Miss Bennet?"

"I did. I found the girl obstinate and proud in her station. I asked her directly if what I heard was to be so. She deferred and refused to answer. I tell you nephew I shall not abide such rude behavior. She even had the nerve to contradict me on a point."

"Was she incorrect on the point?"

Lady Catherine paused for a moment and then continued. "I do not recall all of the conversation and the details, but her refusal to answer directly was intolerable and her contradiction of an elder showed ill breeding. She attempted to hide her true nature of private concerns, but I shall tell you this; any concern of hers which involves my family is no longer private to her, and I shall be made aware. I informed her in no uncertain terms that any union she may wish for was as ill conceived as it was insulting. I finally was able to convince the impertinent girl to admit she was not engaged to you."

Darcy nodded his head as if to agree with the statement, but he also was taking in the tale his aunt was telling. He felt sorry for Elizabeth and believed he would owe her an apology for the intrusion of his aunt who now continued her tale.

"After hearing the truth, I was relieved, but that girl still had me as angry as I have not been in quite some time. I did, however, civilly ask her to abandon any idea of a marriage with you and to quit your sphere of influence. To this she categorically denied to do, and furthermore, she welcomed your company; claiming your affections were free to be given to her or anyone of your choosing."

"I believe she may be correct in this matter. My feelings are my own, my placement of them also my own."

"Darcy, I believe you do not see the wickedness of this girl. She means to charm you and see herself installed in Pemberley. Your mother, bless her soul, had always wished that position for my dear Anne; I fear this girl will connive to interfere in that plan. She as much said so when I mentioned my daughter, and it was then I knew her plan. You must be wary of such vile women."

"I shall do my best to consider Miss Bennet's motivations when I am in her company and to refrain from any undo exposure."

"That may well be too late. As I informed her of our family honour and great lineage she informed me of her knowledge regarding the Darcy responsibilities. I was shocked that she could know this and more shocked to learn you were the one to inform her."

"It was a delicate matter which required a small amount of disclosure; she is not privy to all the details or to the responsibilities of the Fitzwilliams or those of your husband. I trust you did not add to the information."

Lady Catherine fidgeted at this point and looked most uncomfortable to Darcy. He watched her and could see her obvious restlessness. She calmed a bit and continued in a bit of an embarrassed tone.

"I was not able to add any information. Miss Bennet ended the conversation and I left."

Darcy raised his brow in surprise and knew something was missing.

"Miss Bennet ended the conversation? Not you?"

"I had other pressing matters to deal with and that woman was too headstrong to see reason. The conversation would not have proven fruitful in any event."

Darcy was very interested in his aunt's discomfort and asked again. "Just how did Miss Bennet end the conversation?"

Lady Catherine fidgeted again and finally said in a more composed tone.

"She threatened me."

Darcy was now amazed and wanted more information. He asked to the details and his aunt was reluctant to release any. She insisted on condemning Elizabeth and, when it occurred to her, she used the aforementioned threat as evidence of her evil nature.

Well accustomed to dealing with his aunt, Darcy assured her the couple was not engaged nor were there any plans for engagement. He consoled her with assurances of his keeping a watchful eye on Miss Elizabeth, and if it was found his trust in her was misplaced, he would deal with the matter. He then suggested she remain at a distance from Miss Bennet, as her proximity may be taken as proof of the rumour. This comment sent Lady de Bourgh into another tirade as she informed Darcy that Miss Bennet had uttered the same concern. To which Darcy could only inwardly smile and congratulate Elizabeth on her intelligence.

The better part of half an hour was spent calming his aunt. At the end, she took her leave. With her departure came more thoughts of Elizabeth. He was prudent to keep his true feelings from his aunt. If she had known her visit had the opposite effect of the one she intended then she would undoubtedly still be in his house and set on remaining until he was of the same mind as her.

A smile crossed his face as he considered the information related by his aunt. Could Miss Bennet have feelings for him? Certainly if she had no intention of returning his affections she would have informed his aunt. Elizabeth did enjoy teasing but it was always done in a kind hearted way. She was not one to aggravate his aunt, even if it were deserved, merely for the sport.

A knock on the door interrupted his thoughts, and answering it revealed Miss Dache, who was returning to finish business. Marianne entered and could not help but notice the distraction to which Darcy was drawn. His thoughts were unfocused and it was difficult for her to bring him to topic. Eventually they were able to conclude their business and Miss Dache left with a list of her tasks to be completed. She also left with a head full of ideas and concerns for the recent developments. She was surprised at the depth of her feelings but also surprised to the extent she liked Miss Bennet. The ladies had only met a few times, and the first time was certainly an adventure, but Marianne did have an affinity for Elizabeth; enough to wonder how this rumour of marriage was initiated, and more importantly, how it had reached Darcy's aunt. Marianne's first thought was of Caroline Bingley, and she set herself to look into the matter when she had a minute.

After her departure,m Darcy made haste to pack his bags. He decided he would return to Netherfield in the morning and properly congratulate his friend, as well as apologize to Miss Bennet for his aunts behavior.

Chapter 47

Charles and Darcy arrived at Longbourn and visited with the family for only a few minutes before Charles suggested a walk. Much talk was made about who should go and in what direction. In the end Charles, Jane, Darcy, Elizabeth, and one of the sisters, Kitty, ventured out for a walk. It did not take long for Jane and Charles, the newly engaged couple, to fall behind. Shortly thereafter, Kitty went her separate way and was glad for it as Mr. Darcy intimidated her, and she could do little to find her voice in his presence. Darcy and Elizabeth walked for a few minutes in silence, but eventually Miss Bennet spoke.

``Mr. Darcy, I am a very selfish creature; and, for the sake of giving relief to my own feelings, care not how much I may be wounding yours. I can no longer help thanking you for your unexampled kindness to my poor sister. Ever since I have known it, I have been most anxious to acknowledge to you how gratefully I feel it"

``I am sorry, exceedingly sorry," replied Darcy, in a tone of surprise and emotion, ``that you have ever been informed of what may have given you uneasiness. I did not think Mrs. Gardiner was so little to be trusted."

``You must not blame my aunt. Lydia's thoughtlessness first betrayed to me that you had been concerned in the matter; and, of course, I could not rest till I knew the particulars. Let me thank you again and again, in the name of all my family, for that generous compassion which induced you to take so much trouble, and bear so many mortifications, for the sake of discovering them in London."

``If you *will* thank me," he replied, ``let it be for yourself alone. But your *family* owe me nothing. Much as I respect them, I believe I thought only of *you*."

Elizabeth was too much embarrassed to say a word. After a short pause, her companion added, ``You are too generous to trifle with me. If your feelings are still what they were last April, tell me so at once. *My* affections and wishes are unchanged, but one word from you will silence me on this subject forever."

Elizabeth, feeling all the more than common awkwardness and anxiety of his situation, now forced herself to speak; and immediately informed her companion that her feelings were quite different, and she was now quite fond of him. The happiness which this reply produced was such as he had probably never felt before; and he expressed himself on the occasion as sensibly and as warmly as a man violently in love can be supposed to do. Had Elizabeth been able to encounter his eye, she might have seen how well the expression of heartfelt delight, diffused over his face became him; but, though she could not look, she could listen.

They walked on, without knowing in what direction. There was too much to be thought, and felt, and said, for attention to any other objects. She soon learned that they were indebted for their present good understanding to the efforts of his aunt, who *did* call on him on her return through London, and there relate her journey to Longbourn, its motive, and the substance of her conversation with Elizabeth.

``It taught me to hope," said he, ``as I had scarcely ever allowed myself to hope before. I knew enough of your disposition to be certain that, had you been absolutely, irrevocably decided against me, you would have acknowledged it to Lady Catherine, frankly and openly."

Elizabeth coloured and laughed as she replied, ``Yes, you know enough of my *frankness* to believe me capable of *that*. After abusing you so abominably to your face, I could have no scruple in abusing you to all your relations."

They both laughed lightheartedly for a minute. Elizabeth apologized for her original prejudices against the man she was falling in love with, but Darcy would hear very little of it. He declared Miss Bennet to be very intelligent and her initial assassination of his character was deserved, based on his apparent actions. The next few minutes were spent quelling each other's sense of guilt for behavior of the previous year.

Elizabeth then asked Mr. Darcy about his involvement in the engagement of Charles and Jane. Darcy readily admitted Miss Bennet was correct in her assessment; he had been reevaluating Jane and when he was certain she did have feelings for his friend, gave his blessing for the union. While Mr. Darcy was not sure Charles would propose, he was not surprised in the least that the event did occur, and less surprised it was only a few days after leaving Netherfield. Elizabeth laughed when Darcy mentioned he thought the couple would have been engaged before he had properly saddled his horse for the trip to town.

They walked on for a long time and informed each other of their lives over the past year. Darcy was astounded to hear Elizabeth's life, her dealings with Wickham, and her aid to her father as he attempted to locate Lydia in London.

Darcy listened with awe as Elizabeth related to him, with his insistence, how she sent dispatches to her father asking him to search for a Mrs. Younge. Knowing Mr. Wickham had used her before, in his attempt to marry Georgiana, she suspected he may be in touch with her again.

"How could you have possibly remembered that piece of information?" he asked incredulously.

"I committed your letter to memory before the ink faded, and I cross reference any information I could with the individuals involved. Mr. Wickham may be a charming man, but he is loose with his talk. Upon my return home, it was easy enough for me to subtly learn the truth from him. If he were a more intelligent man he might realize how much he let slip."

Darcy smiled as she said this and begged her to continue. Elizabeth obliged and informed Mr. Darcy of how she helped her father direct Bow Street runners and even coordinate with inquiries into the dailies. All of this impressed Darcy as well as explained the concerted effort and intelligence behind the search of Mr. Bennet. Darcy then admitted his role in preventing her father from succeeding and when she frowned with slight disapproval he appeased her by relating

Wickham's ordeal. She smiled by the end and absolved Mr. Darcy of any wrongdoing.

Realizing they had walked quite a distance they decided to return to the comfort on Longbourn. Darcy took this opportunity to apologize for his aunt and vowed he would learn who started the rumour and socially chastise the culprit for gossip of such a nature. Elizabeth pointed out the fact that, if they should continue a relationship, the rumour might be found to be true.

"You are quite right, Miss Bennet. I suppose I may owe a debt to the individual; if my aunt had not made me aware of your conversation I may not be here now. I believe she will be quite upset to learn her revelation had the opposite effect of the one she intended."

"As to the individual, I have already addressed Caroline Bingley and I believe that the lady and I have a new understanding."

Darcy was shocked at this news and Elizabeth smiled with delight when she realized his powers were not absolute. He begged her for the details of how Caroline was discovered and dealt with. As Elizabeth described her thoughts, research, deductions, and final confrontation Darcy could not help but become more amazed. He readily admitted to himself, and then to her, that she must be the most accomplished woman in his acquaintance.

"That is high praise indeed. I seem to recall my doubting you knowing more than six accomplished women."

"I now believe I know only one. I thank you for correcting my thoughts on this matter. Please tell me, now that we are on the subject, how did you threaten my aunt?"

Elizabeth smiled. "She told you about that, did she?"

"Only that you threatened her. She was reticent to discuss the matter."

"I assure you, Mr. Darcy, I did not use a dagger. I was eloquent with my words and forceful with my meaning. I think in the end she chose wisely to believe me; but of the details I will leave that for another story. I am more interested in learning of the man who attacked me and of his fate."

Darcy nodded and acceded to her wishes. He begged her to secrecy and gave the general outline of Colonel Ackerby and how his tale interwove into theirs. Elizabeth understood the dangers and, when he spoke of London, she forgave him once more for his part in keeping Jane from Charles. As he finished his story, or as much as he dared to impart, she asked him his intentions.

"Now that you are aware of my feelings what do you intend to do?"

"I shall return this night with you and ask for your hand in marriage. I shall convince you father of my good nature and decent intentions."

"That is a little presumptuous. Do you not think I should be asked first?"

Darcy turned to her and believed she was amusing herself while displaying a playful smile. She enjoyed teasing him and he found he enjoyed being teased by her.

“Miss Bennet,” he said as he looked her in the eyes and drew close. “Will you do me an honour and consent to be my wife?”

Elizabeth moved in even closer till their faces were only but a hands width apart. “Yes, Mr. Darcy, I believe I will.” They both smiled and kissed, ever so gently and kindly.

As they took to the path again Darcy turned to her.

“The life of the Darcy family may not be an easy one. My mother, much as my aunt, was little involved in our responsibilities. If I gauge you correctly, you will not be so uninvolved. I must warn you, however, Ackerby may not be finished; and even if he were, I am still working on disbanding his organization. The man we encountered at Pemberley may not be the last; and this could still be a very dangerous situation.”

Elizabeth smiled her mischievous smile and turned away from him to walk down the path. She called out to him as he followed to catch up.

“Fear not, Mr. Darcy. I shall protect you!”

Part One Finis

How did Elizabeth Learn of Jane's poisoning?

Why did Elizabeth own a dagger?

What were Elizabeth's real motives for visiting
Rosings?

How did she deal with Wickham?

What was her threat to Lady Catherine?

These answers must be learned by reading
Elizabeth's version of the story.

Pride & Prejudice
& Assassinations
Counterpointe

What becomes of Miss Dache?
How will Elizabeth and Marianne interact?
What will develop with Ackerby?
What kind of woman will Mrs. Fitzwilliam Darcy become?

Pride & Prejudice
& Assassinations
A Dache of Hope

Dear Reader,

Please feel free to visit my site and leave feedback, or suggestions and corrections for the book; whether they are for editing purposes or for the storyline.

http://www.leocharlestaylor.com

And follow along with the short stories which will be offered for free, either by direct download off the site or from many e-book portals.

CPSIA information can be obtained at www.ICGtesting.com
Printed in the USA
BVOW04s1257220913

331831BV00002B/81/P

9 781484 060643